LOVE AND OTHER PERILS

A REGENCY NOVELLA DUET

GRACE BURROWES
EMILY LARKIN

GRACE BURROWES PUBLISHING

Ebook ISBN: 978-1941419861

Print ISBN: 978-1941419878

LIEUTENANT MAYHEW'S CATASTROPHE

By Emily Larkin

CHAPTER ONE

The stagecoach door banged shut and the guard gave a final blast of his horn. Willemina Culpepper only just managed not to wriggle with excitement. It was finally happening. Her journey had begun and in a few short seconds the miles would start to roll away beneath the carriage wheels.

Willie let out a tiny sigh of happiness. She wanted to bounce in her seat and say to her fellow passengers, *Oh, isn't it so marvelous to be traveling again!*

But she was twenty-five years old, and twenty-five-year-old ladies didn't wriggle or bounce or blurt out remarks to utter strangers. And, sadly, none of these strangers appeared to share her enthusiasm for travel. The stout matron alongside her sighed and muttered as she rummaged through her reticule. Dawn wasn't quite yet upon them. The carriage was full of shadows, only the faintest of illumination coming from the lamps outside, but there was enough light to see the matron dab the contents of a small vial onto her handkerchief.

A scent wafted its way to Willie's nose. Lavender. It mingled with the other smells in the narrow confines of the carriage: perspiration old and new, tobacco, ale, and for some reason that Willie couldn't fathom, marmalade.

The stout matron pressed the handkerchief to her nose and closed her eyes. A poor traveler, Willie deduced.

With a loud clatter of iron-shod hooves on cobblestones the stage-coach lurched into motion.

"Late," the other female in the stagecoach muttered. "Two whole minutes late already!" She was as thin as the matron was stout, her mouth pinched shut in a way that gave it wrinkles all the way around.

The stout matron sighed. So did the thin woman. Two different sighs. One long-suffering, one annoyed.

Willie bit back a smile. Not at the stout matron's discomfort or the thin lady's irritation, but a smile of gladness that she was in this carriage with them, that she was *moving* again.

She turned her attention to the final passenger. It was from him that the smells of tobacco and ale came. He wasn't sighing like the matron and the thin woman; he was already asleep, his chin pillowed in the folds of a rather dirty muffler.

The stagecoach navigated the tight corner onto the street, swaying ponderously as it did so. The matron moaned and pressed the scented handkerchief more closely to her nose.

Willie didn't mind the swaying in the slightest. She would have preferred to be up on the roof, where the swaying was at its worst, but respectable young ladies didn't travel on the roofs of stagecoaches, where their faces might become dusty and sunburned and their hair windswept, and where every Tom, Dick, and Harry might gawp up at them.

But even if she couldn't be on the roof, her heart beat as fast as the horses' hooves, a quick tempo of anticipation and happiness. Today, she was in London. Tomorrow, it would be Owslebury. And next month, she was off to the continent again!

Willie couldn't quite prevent a squirm of excitement. Fortunately, no one noticed.

The coach halted at the Bell and Crown, its final stop in London, and three more passengers came aboard: a woman and her young son, and a soldier.

The soldier was wearing the familiar green uniform of the Rifle Brigade, with the epaulettes of a lieutenant.

Willie's breath caught in a moment of pure homesickness. Although, could it be called homesickness when it wasn't a single place she missed, but many? She missed Egypt and South Africa and even the disaster that had been South America, and most of all she missed the people who'd been in those places. Men like her father. Men like the officer now settling himself opposite her. Men who'd worn uniforms. Men who'd trained and fought and endured hard-ship, who'd laughed and joked and lived with enthusiasm because they knew that death might be just around the corner.

Willie released a silent sigh. How she *missed* the army. Missed the people and the purpose, the busyness, the travel and the places, and yes, even the discomfort of being on campaign, the heat and the cold, the mud and the rain.

But not the deaths. She didn't miss those. What she *did* miss was the sense that every minute of every day was to be treasured, even if it contained sleet or choking dust or saddle sores, because today one was alive and tomorrow one might not be.

"*Three* minutes late, now," the thin woman said, as the guard secured the door.

That was another thing she missed: the stoicism of army life—and the jokes that went with that stoicism. Here in England, people complained if it rained, or if their shoes got muddy, or if a stagecoach was three minutes behind schedule. Soldiers didn't complain about the little annoyances of life; they joked about them. A lot.

Willie *did* miss the jokes.

"All aboard the coach to Southampton!" the guard cried, and gave a blast of his horn. Willie's heart lifted, while the stout matron sighed into her handkerchief and the thin woman looked at her timepiece and tutted sourly and the man with the dirty muffler snored faintly in his corner.

The mother was fussing over her young son, settling him carefully on her lap, and the lieutenant was taking almost as much care with the covered basket he was carrying. He held on to it firmly, as if something breakable were inside.

The lieutenant glanced up, caught her gaze, and smiled cheerfully. "Good morning."

"Good morning," Willie said. She wanted to say more, wanted to say, *Tell me how things are with the Rifle Brigade. How's Colonel Barraclough? How's Charles Pugsley? What's it like in France right now?*

She would have asked those questions under other circumstances, but there was enough dawn light now leaking into the carriage to see the obvious appreciation in the lieutenant's gaze, and Willie had learned years ago that when men looked at her like that it was best not to encourage them. It had been true when her father was alive and was doubly true now that he was dead.

She was a female, she was alone, and she was on a public stagecoach, and as much as she wished to talk about the Rifle Brigade with this lieutenant, it was wisest not to.

Willie smiled politely at him as the stagecoach rolled out of the Bell and Crown's yard, springs creaking, wheels rattling, harness jingling jauntily. She turned her attention to the window and the glimpses of London it afforded—brick and stone façades, windows and doors. Dawn was pink above the roof tops. Her heart beat a happy rhythm. *It's started. I'm on my way.*

A tiny, shrill squeaking drew her attention. Not the squeaking of springs or wheels or harnesses, but a squeaking that sounded alive, and not only alive but *inside* the carriage.

A mouse?

Mice didn't scare Willie, but she didn't particularly wish to be in a stagecoach with one. Not once her fellow passengers realized there was a rodent aboard. The thin lady would undoubtedly have the vapors. Probably the stout matron, too.

She cocked her head, trying to determine the location of the sound . . . and realized that it came from directly opposite her. More precisely, from the basket that sat on the lieutenant's lap. The covered basket that he held so firmly and so carefully.

There wasn't something breakable inside, she realized. There was something *alive*.

The sound came again, high-pitched, more mew than squeak.

Willie glanced at the lieutenant. Their eyes met again in the half-light, and he gave her a wide, cheerful smile. He reminded her so much of the young officers who'd been under her father's command that her heart gave another great pang of homesickness.

"Your basket is making noises," the little boy seated on his mother's lap observed.

"So it is," the lieutenant agreed.

"What's in it?"

There was just enough light for Willie to see the lieutenant wink at the boy. "Baby monsters."

There was also enough light to see the little boy's eyes grow wide. "Monsters?"

"Monsters with teeth as sharp as needles," the lieutenant said, with utmost gravity. "And claws that would tear your clothes to shreds."

"Oh," the little boy said.

The lieutenant lowered his voice and said in thrilling accents, "I daren't let them out of the basket for fear of the havoc they would wreak."

The boy's eyes were now as round as saucers.

"Do you want to know what type of monster they are?" the lieutenant asked.

The boy nodded cautiously.

The lieutenant winked at him again and laughed, a merry sound. "They're kittens, my young friend."

The little boy laughed, too, a trill of delight. "Kittens?"

"A kitten apiece for my niece and nephew."

"Can I see them?" the boy asked eagerly.

"When we stop," the lieutenant said. "Kittens and carriages don't mix." He smiled at the boy's mother. "And only if your mother allows."

There was enough light, too, to see the boy's mother blush upon receipt of that smile, as well she might; the lieutenant was a good-looking man, with his fair hair and his easy smile and his green rifle-man's uniform. Quite dashing, in fact. But Willie had grown up following the drum. She had met a great many officers, handsome and otherwise, and she knew better than to judge men by their smiles. The lieutenant certainly *looked* attractive, but she knew nothing of his character.

Except that he was cheerful. And he liked to joke. And he gave kittens as presents to his nephew and niece.

THEY CHANGED horses at Twickenham and again at Chertsey, and stopped for a meal at Bagshot. The lieutenant was first out. He set his basket on the cobblestones, then helped the stout matron, the thin lady, and the mother and her son to descend. When he held up his hand to Willie, she took it, even though she was perfectly capable of climbing down from a stagecoach by herself.

It would have been discourteous not to.

The lieutenant was even more handsome in full daylight than he'd been in the gloom of the coach. His eyes were a warm, laughing brown with flecks of gold.

Those laughing eyes and that charming smile and the smart green uniform made her heart flutter a bit. But only a *very* tiny bit.

"Can I see the kittens now?" the little boy asked. "Please?"

"Certainly," the lieutenant said. "Anyone who wishes may make their acquaintance." His smile included Willie.

Willie decided that she would quite like to see the creatures. Purely because she liked kittens. It had absolutely nothing to do with the lieutenant's eyes or his smile.

CHAPTER TWO

For a sixpence, one of the ostlers was willing to let Mayhew decant the furry monsters in an empty horse stall. He ushered his audience inside: child, mother, and one very pretty governess. At least, he assumed she was a governess. She was clearly well-bred, yet she was traveling on a stagecoach, and in Mayhew's experience respectable young ladies who traveled by stagecoach were usually governesses.

"They're a brother and sister," he told his audience, kneeling on the straw and unfastening the strap that held the basket closed. "Someone I know found them in a creek. Tied up in a sack."

"In a sack?" the little boy echoed, his eyes wide with dismay.

"He saved them all," Mayhew reassured him. "And a lady took them home and looked after them, and now they're big enough to have homes of their own. See?" He lifted the lid.

Two furry monsters blinked up at him and opened their pink mouths and mewed.

"Oh," his audience breathed in unison, drawing closer.

"Come on out, little rascals," Mayhew told the kittens. "Time to stretch your legs." And hopefully they'd pee into the straw while they were at it.

The fluffy black-and-gray female scrambled up the side of the basket with the speed and determination of a foot soldier storming a defensive line, which Mayhew had expected. Her less fluffy gray-striped brother stayed where he was, in the warm nest of the basket, which Mayhew had also expected.

"Come along, my lazy friend," he said, lifting the little tabby out. "You can't sleep *all* day."

"What are their names?" the boy asked eagerly.

"I call this one Mr. Bellyrub," Mayhew said, and then he demonstrated why, cupping the kitten belly-up in his hand and rubbing his fluffy stomach.

Mr. Bellyrub immediately began to purr.

"Oh," his audience breathed again.

"Would you like to hold him?" Mayhew asked the little boy.

"Yes! Yes!"

The boy's hands were too small for Mr. Bellyrub to lie in, but his arms made a perfect cradle. Mayhew carefully transferred the kitten. Mr. Bellyrub didn't mind at all. He kept purring.

They made an adorable pair, child and kitten. The governess must have thought so, too, because she smiled—which made dimples spring to life in her cheeks, making *her* adorable, as well.

Mayhew admired her for a few seconds—the nutbrown ringlets peeping from beneath her bonnet, the straight little nose, the rosy lips. *Very* pretty. It was a shame she wasn't the type to make eyes at soldiers. A little flirtation would have whiled away the journey to Southampton most enjoyably, but he knew women well enough to know when they wanted to flirt and when they didn't, and this governess definitely didn't.

He turned his attention to the basket. The nest of rags was still clean and dry. Excellent. He looked around for Mr. Bellyrub's sister. Predictably, she'd vanished. "Uh-oh."

The governess cocked her head at him.

"The exploring officer is on the loose. Careful where you put your feet."

The governess's dimples made a reappearance. "Exploring officer?"

"She was born to be a reconnaissance scout." Mayhew climbed to his feet. "That's my name for her: Scout. Now, where did she get to . . . ?"

The fluffy kitten was at the back of the horse stall, relieving herself. "Well done," Mayhew told her. "Your timing is perfect."

Scout ignored him, and set out to investigate the rest of the horse stall. Mayhew wondered if she was hungry. "I'll fetch some milk," he told the governess. "Would you mind keeping an eye on her?"

"I shan't let her escape," the governess promised.

One of the inn's kitchen maids gave him two saucers of milk, a bounty that both kittens consumed eagerly, and then it was time to restore the furry monsters to their basket. Scout protested shrilly about her incarceration, but Mr. Bellyrub didn't appear to mind at all. In fact, Mayhew thought he was asleep before the basket lid had even closed.

There wasn't much time left for them to eat. Mayhew managed to secure a half-pint of ale and a slice of ham on bread, then the guard blew his horn and it was time to climb aboard. "We should have left ten minutes ago," the Friday-faced old lady scolded the guard. "Ten minutes!"

Mayhew swallowed the last of his ale, then went to help the young mother and her son to ascend.

The guard blew his horn again, a loud *blat* of sound.

"I shall complain to the company!" Mrs. Friday-Face told the guard.

The guard ignored her. "All aboard!" he cried.

Mayhew handed the governess up into the coach. The last of the roof passengers were scrambling into their places and horses were stamping and snorting, impatient to be off. He held out his hand to Mrs. Friday-Face. She ignored it in favor of berating the guard.

Mayhew shrugged, picked up his basket, and climbed aboard. He settled himself on the narrow seat, bumping knees and elbows with his fellow passengers. One of the kittens mewed.

"Last call for the stage to Southampton!" the guard bellowed.

Mrs. Friday-Face finally climbed aboard, bristling with indignation. "Scandalous," she muttered, as she settled herself. "No attempt to keep to the time-bill at all."

Mayhew bit back a smile, and glanced at the governess. She was trying not to smile, too. He saw a dimple quiver in her cheek and—aha!—a tiny roll of her eyes, and then she realized he was looking at her and the dimple vanished. She averted her gaze.

The stagecoach lurched into motion, sweeping out of the inn yard. Mrs. Friday-Face examined her watch. "Twelve minutes late. *Twelve!*"

CHAPTER THREE

It appeared that the thin lady was going all the way to Southampton. She didn't get off in Frimley Green with the mother and her son, or in Basingstoke, when the man with the dirty muffler left the carriage. The smell in the stagecoach changed with each new passenger. Coffee when the attorney's clerk settled into his seat. Cabbage and sweat when the farmer came aboard.

At every stop the stagecoach fell a little further behind schedule —a fact that the thin lady didn't fail to remark on. Each time she did, Willie had to bite her lip a little bit harder to stop from laughing out loud.

The stout matron left the carriage at North Waltham, taking with her the scent of lavender. Her replacement was a sailor, and he was drunk. Willie knew that fact even before he climbed aboard. His too-loud voice told her, and the way he slurred his consonants.

The only vacant seat was next to Willie.

She drew her shawl more tightly around her shoulders and reminded herself that discomforts were part of travel.

"Move over," the lieutenant said in a low voice, as the sailor fumbled to heave himself into the carriage.

Willie glanced at him, and there was something so authoritative in his face that she obeyed, shifting sideways into the warm spot the matron had left. The lieutenant moved, too, taking the place she'd vacated, and by the time the sailor had negotiated the steps, the empty seat was neither next to Willie nor opposite her.

She breathed a silent sigh of relief and loosened her tight grip on the shawl, while the sailor settled himself clumsily and then belched.

The guard closed the door and blew his horn, the driver cracked his whip, and the stagecoach lumbered into motion again. Beside Willie, the thin lady sniffed. "Seventeen minutes," she muttered.

The carriage had been small and cramped before. With the sailor in it, it was even smaller and more cramped. Or perhaps that was because the lieutenant was alongside her now. He seemed to take up more space on the seat than the stout matron had, although that couldn't actually be possible; the matron had been *very* stout, and the lieutenant was quite lean. But Willie was aware of him in a way she hadn't been aware of the matron, aware of his body pressed against hers—his arm, his thigh—and she was aware, too, of his strength and his heat and his maleness.

Willie felt suddenly self-conscious and awkward. Her cheeks grew a little warm.

To distract herself from the lieutenant, she discreetly observed the sailor. He was unshaven and bleary-eyed. The smell of gin wafted strongly from him. He belched again. His gaze drifted past Willie—and then swung back. He looked her up and down, a blatant leer. "You're a spruce one, you are."

"I suggest you keep your tongue between your teeth while you're aboard," the lieutenant said coldly.

The sailor took note of the rifleman's uniform and sneered. "Oh, you do, do you, swoddy?" Then his gaze rose to the lieutenant's face. The sneer faded so quickly that it was almost comical.

Willie bit her lip to prevent herself laughing.

"I do," the lieutenant said. His voice was hard and flat and dangerous, and Willie wasn't at all surprised that the sailor looked away.

Five minutes later, he was snoring.

"Thank you," Willie told the lieutenant, in a low whisper.

"You're welcome," the lieutenant whispered back. His voice sounded like it had before the sailor had climbed aboard, friendly and cheerful.

He'd be a good officer, Willie thought. The sort of officer that men respected. He knew when to laugh and joke, but he also knew when not to. And he knew how to make people obey him.

The lieutenant was still disconcertingly large and warm alongside her, but Willie no longer felt self-conscious. She felt safe. On the heels of that realization came a decision: at the next halt, she'd ask him about the Rifle Brigade. Yes, the lieutenant liked her looks, but she was no longer worried that he'd leer at her like the sailor had, or try to flirt with her, because he wasn't merely an officer; he was a gentleman.

THEY HALTED for another meal at Abbots Worthy. The lieutenant leapt down lightly, then turned to help the thin lady to descend. Willie gathered up her reticule and descended, too. This time she took the lieutenant's hand without a second thought, and noted again that yes, he did have *very* nice eyes.

She inhaled a deep breath that smelled of horses and horse dung and woodsmoke and roasting meat, while behind her the thin lady told the guard off. "Twenty-three minutes behind schedule! I shall complain to the company, don't you doubt it!"

Willie wasn't particularly hungry, nor did she wish to spend the allotted half hour sitting in a stuffy coffee room. "I'll help you with the kittens," she told the lieutenant.

His face lit up in a smile, and Willie told herself that her heart had *not* fluttered, although she was rather afraid that it had.

The lieutenant spoke to an ostler, a coin changed hands, and half a minute later she, the lieutenant, and the basket were in an empty horse stall. Alone.

For a moment Willie doubted her decision, and then she remembered his behavior in the carriage. The lieutenant was a gentleman and as long as *she* didn't flirt with him, *he* wouldn't flirt with her.

He crouched and opened the basket. Kittens blinked up at them. Willie smiled involuntarily, and crouched, too.

"Come on out, little monsters," the lieutenant said, and the kittens did, one after the other, mewing loudly. "I wager they're hungry. I'll fetch some milk."

"I shan't let Scout escape," Willie promised.

The lieutenant gave her a grateful smile and left the stall, careful to close the door behind him.

"Hello, sweethearts," Willie said softly, once he was gone.

The kittens mewed back at her. Monsters or not, they were darlings, with their round little bellies and bright blue eyes, their tiny pink tongues and sharp white teeth. Scout was quite fluffy, with patches of black and gray, while her sleeker brother had smart gray stripes. Willie laid her reticule to one side, picked Mr. Bellyrub up, turned him over, and rubbed his belly. To her delight, he immediately began to purr.

Willie stroked him, and felt the reverberation of his purr, and watched while his bolder sister staggered across the straw, apparently determined to explore all four corners of the stall.

Mr. Bellyrub closed his eyes and Willie felt him relax in her hand, a soft, warm bundle of contentment. By the time the lieutenant returned with two saucers of milk, the kitten was practically asleep, but he roused and mewed loudly to be let down.

Willie set him on the straw and he attacked the milk with so much enthusiasm that he stepped into the saucer.

Willie laughed, and so did the lieutenant. He had a very nice laugh. Her awareness of him spiked again, and with it, the awkwardness.

Idiot, she scolded herself. The lieutenant *was* very attractive, but she was in this horse stall because of the kittens and because she wanted to talk about the Rifle Brigade, not for any other reason. Accordingly, she said, "When did you join the Rifle Brigade, Lieutenant?"

He glanced at her, and she saw his surprise.

"My father was in the army," Willie told him. "He was invalided out in 1806."

The lieutenant sat back on his heels and looked at her, still with surprise on his face. "That was the year I joined the Rifles."

"You were on the Peninsula, then?"

He nodded.

She named several battles: "Salamanca? Vittoria? Tarbes?"

He nodded again.

Willie bit her lip, and then asked, "Badajoz?"

The lieutenant grimaced faintly. "Yes." He looked down at Mr. Bellyrub, then glanced back at her, hesitated, and said, "You know what happened there, I take it?"

"I do. My father corresponded regularly with Colonel Barraclough. He said—Barraclough, I mean—that the events at Badajoz brought discredit to the entire army."

"They did."

"Barraclough also said that he was proud of his officers, that they did everything they could to halt it."

It. An entirely inadequate word for the violence and rapine that had occurred after Badajoz fell.

"We did," the lieutenant said. "For what it was worth." He grimaced faintly again, then cocked his head and said, "Who is your father? What regiment did he serve in?"

"The Sixty-Ninth," Willie said. "He died last year. His name was Culpepper."

The lieutenant's jaw dropped. "Culpepper? Not . . . Colonel Culpepper?"

It was Willie's turn to be surprised. "Yes."

The lieutenant stared at her for a moment, open-mouthed, and then said, in a disbelieving voice, "You're Colonel Henry Culpepper's daughter?"

Willie nodded again.

The lieutenant finally remembered to close his mouth. He looked down at Mr. Bellyrub lapping his milk, and then back at her. This time his gaze wasn't friendly or appreciative; it was something much more penetrating. He looked at her—truly *looked* at her —a head-to-toe glance that was nothing like the drunken sailor's leer. Then, he shook his head and laughed. "So *you're* Sweet Willie."

Embarrassed heat rose in Willie's cheeks. "Wherever did you hear that name?"

The lieutenant shook his head again, laughed again. "The fellows who were in South America used to talk about you. A *lot*."

"They did not," Willie said, as her cheeks grew hotter.

"They most certainly *did*," the lieutenant said. "It was 'Sweet Willie this' and 'Sweet Willie that' the whole first year I was in the Rifles. Some of 'em are *still* talking about you. Barraclough, for one. Pug Pugsley, for another. And Sergeant Jones, remember him?" Then his expression became serious, solemn. "They're still talking about your father, too. By all accounts, he was a remarkable soldier. My condolences on his death."

Willie's cheeks cooled. "Thank you," she said quietly.

The lieutenant eyed her, a faint frown on his handsome face. "What are you doing on a stagecoach, Miss Culpepper? You're not a governess, are you?"

The disapprobation in his voice made Willie smile. "Not quite. I'll be more of a companion. My charges are sixteen and seventeen."

"But surely . . ." He halted, and looked a little abashed.

Willie answered the question that he clearly felt he couldn't ask. "I don't need a position, Lieutenant; I *want* one."

His frown became tinged with confusion.

Willie tried to explain: "England bores me. I want to travel again, and Sir Walter Pike, who's employing me, is a diplomat. The family is off to Vienna next month."

"Your father became a diplomat, I understand? After his injury."

Willie nodded. Colonels of infantry regiments needed two hands, but members of the Foreign Office didn't. "Yes. We were in Constantinople, then Russia, and lastly Brussels. If Father hadn't died when he did, we'd have been in Brussels during the Battle of Waterloo."

The lieutenant grimaced again, not the faint grimace he'd accorded Badajoz, but something much grimmer that thinned his lips and twisted his mouth. "Be glad you weren't there. Waterloo was . . ." He shook his head and reached for the basket.

"I heard it was bad," Willie said cautiously, as he examined the nest of rags.

"Very bad." The lieutenant looked down at the basket a moment longer, then glanced at her. "Have you ever seen an illustrated version of Dante's *Inferno*, Miss Culpepper?"

Willie nodded.

"Waterloo was like that. Only worse."

He was telling the truth—she could see it clearly on his face: the pinching at the corners of his eyes, the pinching at the corners of his mouth.

Willie acknowledged what he'd said with a nod, for it seemed to her that nothing she could say would be meaningful. The Battle of Waterloo had happened. It had been a terrible slaughter. Those were irrefutable facts, and platitudes and words of condolence wouldn't be in the least bit helpful now, nearly twelve months after that battle.

The pinching at the lieutenant's mouth and eyes faded. He looked down at the basket again and put it aside.

Willie changed the subject. "You're on furlough, I take it? Where are you stationed?"

"France." The lieutenant shook off his grimness and smiled at her. "Two of our battalions are there right now; the third's in Ireland."

They talked about army life while the kittens lapped their milk.

The lieutenant told her some of the stories he'd heard about her and Willie had to confess that they were all true, and then he told her some of *his* misadventures. It was the most enjoyable conversation Willie had had in years. She couldn't remember when she'd last laughed so much. She heard the first warning blast of the guard's horn with something close to disbelief. Had she and the lieutenant been talking for half an hour?

She scrambled to her feet. "Where's Scout?"

The lieutenant stood, too. "She was in that corner, last I saw her. Probably made herself a nest." He scooped up Mr. Bellyrub and placed him in the basket.

Willie began searching in the straw for Scout. "I still don't know your name," she told the lieutenant.

"Mayhew," he said. "William Mayhew."

"William?" Willie said.

He grinned at her. "We share a name. Almost. I'm a Will, not a Willie." He rifled through the straw and called softly, "Here puss, puss, puss."

But Scout didn't poke her head up and mew at them.

The guard's horn sounded again.

Lieutenant Mayhew began to grope through the straw more urgently. "Go, Miss Culpepper."

"Nonsense," Willie said, widening her search. She checked one corner, and another. "Here she is!"

"Thank God." The lieutenant grabbed the basket and held it out to her—and said, "Uh-oh. Where's Bellyrub?"

The guard's horn blasted a third time.

Lieutenant Mayhew took Scout from her. "Go!"

Willie ignored him.

"Miss Culpepper—"

"I see him," Willie cried. She seized hold of the kitten, thrust him into the basket, then snatched up her reticule and ran to the front of the horse stall, drawing back the bolt and flinging the door open.

They burst from the stables, out into the yard, just as the stage-coach disappeared from view.

The clatter of hooves and jingle of harnesses faded from hearing. There was a long moment of silence, and then, "They left without us," the lieutenant said, a note of indignant disbelief in his voice.

CHAPTER FOUR

Miss Culpepper took it exceedingly well, Mayhew thought. But then, the daughter of Colonel Culpepper would. She didn't have hysterics or fly into a temper, she merely said, "Well, *that's* a slight setback," and turned to one of the ostlers and inquired about hiring a gig to take them to the stagecoach's next scheduled stop, which was Winchester.

By the time that Mayhew had fastened the basket lid properly, Miss Culpepper had ascertained that the inn did have a gig, that it was available for hire, and was in negotiations as to the price.

The ostler, no doubt thinking that they were pigeons to be plucked, named an extortionate sum. Mayhew opened his mouth to object, and then listened in admiration as Miss Culpepper proved that she was no pigeon. In fact, he suspected that the price she beat the ostler down to was less than anything he'd have managed.

But when she opened her reticule to pay, he said, "Absolutely not, Miss Culpepper. *I* shall pay for the gig."

Miss Culpepper, proving her intelligence further, didn't argue with him.

Mayhew handed over the coins. "The fastest horse you have," he told the ostler. "And there's a half crown in it for you if we're gone in five minutes."

The ostler headed for the stables at a run.

THE GIG WAS ready in four minutes. Mayhew handed Miss Culpepper up onto the seat, passed her the basket, climbed up himself, and tossed the ostler the half crown he'd promised him.

They left Abbots Worthy at a brisk trot. Mayhew estimated that they were six minutes behind the stagecoach, possibly seven.

"I apologize," he said. "This is my fault."

"It's no one's fault," Miss Culpepper said cheerfully, clutching the basket with one hand and her reticule and shawl with the other. The tassels that fringed her shawl fluttered in the warm summer's breeze, and the ribbons on her bonnet did, too. "We'll catch up before the next stop."

Mayhew knew that they would. One horse pulling a light gig was faster than four horses pulling a heavy stagecoach. The chestnut was young, fresh, and perfectly willing to stretch its legs in a gallop. At every bend in the road, Mayhew expected to see the stagecoach ahead of them—until the horse went lame half a mile past Head-bourne Worthy.

They went from tooth-rattling gallop to hobbling walk in the space of a few seconds.

Uh-oh, he thought.

Mayhew drew the gig to one side of the road, handed the reins to Miss Culpepper, and jumped down to examine the chestnut, hoping it was just a pebble lodged in a shoe.

But no, they weren't so lucky.

"Damnation," he said under his breath, and then, more loudly, "It's cast a shoe."

"At least it hasn't thrown a splint," Miss Culpepper said, which was a much better reaction than he'd expected.

"We'd best turn back to Headbourne Worthy," he said. "I'm sorry, Miss Culpepper."

"Don't look so worried, Lieutenant," she said, with surprising equanimity. "It's not the end of the world."

"But your employer—"

"Sir Walter is meeting me in Twyford tomorrow. As long as I'm at the coaching inn by nightfall, all will be well. And Twyford can't be more than a dozen miles from here. Even if I have to walk, I'll get there before dark."

The prospect of walking a dozen miles didn't seem to perturb her in the slightest, and Mayhew was reminded once again that she *was* a soldier's daughter.

"You won't have to walk that far," he promised her.

They did have to walk the half a mile back to Headbourne Worthy, though, leading the horse and gig. But although they were headed *away* from Winchester, and although it was now impossible that they'd catch up with the stagecoach, Mayhew couldn't regret it. He'd never enjoyed a walk more. He liked Miss Culpepper. He liked looking at her and he liked talking with her, and if they hadn't missed the stagecoach, and if the horse hadn't cast a shoe, then he'd have been wholly delighted to spend his time in her company. As it was, he was partly delighted and partly worried. Miss Culpepper shouldn't be wandering the countryside with him; this was how young ladies lost their reputations.

But no one would ever know, and he *would* get her to Twyford by nightfall.

HEADBOURNE WORTHY WAS VERY SMALL. It didn't have a posting inn, but it did have a blacksmith. They left the horse and gig at the smithy, with instructions that both were to be returned to the inn at Abbots Worthy. Mayhew forked over some coins, retrieved the basket with the kittens, and asked the blacksmith how best to get to Twyford.

The man ruminated on this question, his jaws moving as if he were chewing cud, and then said, "Farm cart."

The blacksmith was a man of few words, but with a great deal of chewing and a great many pauses, he informed them that his aunt's brother-in-law's son would shortly be driving his cart from Headbourne Worthy to Winnall, that Winnall was only a mile from Winchester, and that in Winchester they could easily hire a carriage to take them to Twyford.

"When will the cart be leaving?" Mayhew asked.

"Once it's loaded."

"And you think we'd be able to reach Twyford by nightfall?"

The blacksmith chewed and thought and then gave his considered opinion: "Yes."

"Excellent," Mayhew said. "Where can we find this cart?"

They found the cart in the blacksmith's aunt's farmyard. The young farmer's load wasn't vegetables, as Mayhew had supposed, but pigs. *Uh-oh*, he thought for the second time that afternoon. He glanced at Miss Culpepper.

She interpreted his glance correctly. Dimples sprang to life in her cheeks. "Don't look so worried, Lieutenant. I have no objection to traveling with pigs."

"You don't?"

"No. Now, come along; it's time to haggle for our ride." She flashed him a smile and stepped into the farmyard.

Mayhew watched her pick her way through the mud and the puddles, and had a moment of astonished insight. Miss Culpepper was actually *enjoying* this.

CHAPTER FIVE

If their luck had been out earlier, it was now in. The cart was loaded and the farmer ready to depart. Five minutes later and they'd have missed him. As it was, they left Headbourne Worthy perched on the box seat of a cart carrying pigs. Nine pigs, altogether. Willie had counted. And handsome pigs they were, too. Black, with a white stripe over their shoulders.

The farmer was as garrulous as the blacksmith had been taciturn. He talked about his pigs and his other livestock and his crops and the spring just past and the summer they were having. Willie sat on the wooden seat and simply enjoyed it all: the fresh country air, the trees and the hedgerows, the grassy verges studded with wildflowers, the birdsong, the noises the pigs made, the slow *clop-clop* of the horse, the farmer's conversation, his broad Hampshire accent.

Headbourne Worthy to Winnall wasn't a post road; consequently it was not in good repair. The horse picked its way slowly, walking, not trotting. The cart jolted and lurched over ruts and through potholes and puddles, but Willie didn't mind the slowness, or the jolting, or the pigs. She drank it all in—the sights and sounds and smells. Traveling by farm cart was a thousand times better than sitting in a stagecoach, she decided, and perhaps she ought not to be relishing this unexpected little adventure as much as she was, but it was impossible *not* to relish it, partly because it reminded her of being in the army, and partly because there would be no opportunities to ride in farm carts with lieutenants who were carrying baskets of kittens once she was in Sir Walter's employ.

She liked this lieutenant. More, perhaps, than she ought to. She'd only just met him and yet for some reason Lieutenant Mayhew didn't feel like a stranger; he felt like a friend.

They came to a section of road where the ruts on one side had merged into a deep trough. "Hold tight," the farmer said, and jumped down to guide his horse. Willie braced herself. The cart tilted sideways as the wheels on the left descended into the trough and the wheels on the right didn't. The wooden seat was worn so smooth that Willie almost slid off it.

"Careful, Miss Culpepper!" the lieutenant said, and put his arm around her.

Willie's heart beat a fast *pitter-patter* that had nothing to do with the angle of the cart and everything to do with Lieutenant Mayhew's arm around her waist, strong and warm, and then the cart lurched its way up out of the trough and he released her.

"That's the worst of it," the farmer said, clambering back up into the cart. He'd plucked a stem of grass, which he now set between his teeth.

"How much further to Winnall?" Mayhew asked.

The farmer sucked thoughtfully on his grass stem, and then said, "Mebbe half an hour?"

Willie savored every minute of that half hour. In fact, she wished that the afternoon would never end, that the sun would remain halfway across the sky, and that the rutted, muddy lane would go on and on and on, and she'd sit next to Lieutenant Mayhew on this hard wooden seat forever.

Which was a little alarming. Forever? With a man she barely knew?

Don't lose your head over a uniform and a handsome face, Willie scolded herself, as she climbed down from the cart in the farmer's yard. But she didn't think she'd done that. It wasn't Mayhew's uniform or his face that she liked so much—although his eyes were very nice—it was his character, his cheerfulness, the way he'd protected her from the sailor, changing seats, putting the man in his place with a few words and a look.

The farmer wouldn't take payment for the ride. "I were a-comin' home anyways," he said. They drank cool water from his well and the kittens lapped at a little milk, and then the farmer gave them directions to Winchester. "Quickest way's across ol' John Plum's paddock," he said, and then proceeded to tell them exactly how to find John Plum's paddock.

Two minutes later, they were walking along a country lane. The spires of Winchester were visible across the fields, and Willie knew that Twyford was only a few miles beyond those spires.

She also knew that once they reached Twyford, she and Lieutenant Mayhew would part.

It wasn't in Willie's nature to feel melancholy, but she did feel a little melancholy about reaching Twyford. She almost wanted to sigh. She suppressed the urge and strode briskly along the rough little lane and told herself that she was *excited* about reaching Twyford. Excited about starting her position. Excited about returning to the continent.

"This looks like it," Mayhew said, as a paddock planted with turnips came into view.

Willie agreed: It did look very much like Old John Plum's paddock.

They started across. Willie picked her way carefully, holding her hem up. *Squelch. Squelch.* Within a dozen steps, her half boots were heavy with mud. It was almost like ice skating—slip and slide, slip and slide.

Her half boots became heavier, her slips and slides more erratic.

"Perhaps this wasn't the wisest idea," the lieutenant said.

"Perhaps not," Willie admitted.

The lieutenant stopped. "Your choice, Miss Culpepper: keep going, or turn back."

Willie looked at what lay ahead, and then glanced behind them. It was a mistake; one of her feet slid sideways.

Lieutenant Mayhew caught her upper arm in a strong grip. "Steady, there."

Willie's other foot slid in the opposite direction. She clutched the lieutenant's green jacket and tried not to fall.

He set down the basket, but didn't release his grip on her arm. "I think we'd best turn back."

"Yes." Willie planted her right foot firmly in the mud, and then her left.

"Got your balance?"

"Yes." She cautiously let go of his jacket.

Mayhew waited a moment, then released her and reached for the basket—and skidded wildly, windmilling his arms.

Willie grabbed one of his elbows and he grabbed one of hers. He gave a great, sliding, sideways lurch, and she lurched with him, and it was as if they were dancing a clownish jig. The lieutenant's feet slid and her feet slid and they swayed left and then right and then left again.

Finally, they both caught their balance, clutching each other in the middle of the muddy field. Willie bit her lip and tried not to giggle, and failed.

The lieutenant grinned at her. "May I have this dance, Miss Culpepper?"

"It would be my pleasure, Lieutenant," Willie said, and she would have dipped him a curtsy if she'd been more certain of her footing, but she didn't quite dare let him go yet, let alone dip funning curtsies.

The lieutenant's grin faded, and his expression changed slightly. Not the casually appreciative look he'd given her when he'd climbed aboard the stagecoach in London, but something warmer and faintly regretful.

Willie felt that regret, too. If she and Lieutenant Mayhew had met under other circumstances, if she wasn't going to Vienna, if he wasn't going back to his regiment . . .

But these were the circumstances under which they'd met, and the likelihood of them ever seeing each other again after today was infinitesimally small—and there was nothing at all that could be done about that.

Willie released his arm.

"Back to the lane?" the lieutenant said.

"Back to the lane."

Lieutenant Mayhew let go of her. He shifted his weight. His left foot shot out from under him. His left hand shot out, too, grabbing her again. Together, they toppled over backwards into the mud.

Willie blinked up at the sky.

"Well, that was unfortunate," the lieutenant said, after a moment of silence. "Please accept my apologies, Miss Culpepper."

Willie began to giggle, and then to more than giggle. She laughed —laughed from her belly, laughed until her ribs ached and tears streamed down her face—and the lieutenant lay alongside her in the muddy turnip field and laughed, too.

Finally, Willie stopped laughing. She caught her breath and wiped her eyes and sat up.

The lieutenant sat up, too, alongside her. "Thank heavens you have a sense of humor, Miss Culpepper."

"It's just mud," Willie said, smiling at him. "It will wash off."

"So it will." He smiled back at her, and there was such warmth in his brown eyes, such approbation, that her breath caught in her throat and she realized that she didn't just like him, she liked him *a lot*.

And he liked her a lot, too.

Which didn't change the fact that she was headed to Vienna and he was headed back to his regiment.

The last of Willie's amusement snuffed out. She felt rather sad.

She looked around for the basket. It was sitting where the lieutenant had left it, lid firmly fastened. "It's fortunate you weren't carrying the kittens when you fell."

"Yes." The lieutenant carefully climbed to his feet, extended a hand, and helped her to stand. Then he picked up the basket. Together they slipped and slid their way back the way they'd come. Ironically, now that they were both caked in mud, neither of them fell over.

"The farmer must have hobnails on his boots," the lieutenant said, when they reached the lane.

"Undoubtedly." Willie looked around for a stick, found one, and set to work removing the mud from her half boots. That task accomplished, she took off her bonnet and examined it. It was liberally besmirched, as was her shawl and, yes, even her reticule. She only needed to look at the lieutenant's filthy rifleman's jacket to know what the back of her gown looked like.

But it was only mud, and mud could be brushed off and washed off. Nothing was ruined. The next time she wore these clothes, the mud would be just a memory.

As would the lieutenant and his kittens.

Willie tried not to sigh. She put the bonnet back on and retied the ribbons.

"Right," the lieutenant said, after he'd scraped the worst of the mud off his boots. "Let's get to Winchester as quickly as we can."

They set off at a brisk pace. Willie didn't bother trying to keep her hem clean anymore. The lane curved right, then left, then dipped down to a ford where water flowed swiftly.

They halted. "This would be why the farmer recommended the paddock," Lieutenant Mayhew said.

Willie eyed the water and tried to estimate how deep it was. Six inches? Twelve?

"I'll piggyback you across," Mayhew said.

"Piggyback?" Willie said. Her voice sounded a smidgeon higher than it usually was.

"Would you prefer wet feet?"

Willie bit her lip. No, she wouldn't prefer wet feet, but being piggybacked by a man she barely knew while on a public lane where anyone might see—being piggybacked *at all*—was not something that a respectable lady would do.

But neither was traveling in farm carts carrying pigs.

Or falling over in muddy turnip fields.

The lieutenant was still looking at her, eyebrows slightly raised, waiting for her decision.

"I would prefer to keep my feet dry," Willie admitted.

Mayhew grinned at her, and set down the basket. "Let me just check how deep it is, Miss Culpepper." He waded into the ford and cast about to find the shallowest spot. Willie was relieved to see that the water didn't come over the top of his boots.

The lieutenant returned and hunkered down with his back to her. "Climb aboard," he said cheerfully.

Willie glanced over her shoulder, made certain that the lane was empty of spectators, hiked her gown up past her knees, and scrambled onto Lieutenant Mayhew's back.

"Hold tight," he said, and stood.

Willie held on tightly, her arms around his shoulders, and the lieutenant held tightly to her, too, his hands gripping her legs just above the knees, where her garters were tied, and Willie realized that if he hadn't been wearing gloves, his hands would have touched her *bare skin*.

She shivered at this thought. Not a shiver of revulsion or unease, but a tingling, warm shiver that made her pulse accelerate. She held her breath as Lieutenant Mayhew navigated the ford, not merely because she was afraid he might lose his footing, but also because he was *touching her legs* and it felt deliciously exciting.

Once he'd gained the other side, the lieutenant crouched again. Willie scrambled down and smoothed her gown hastily past her knees again. She knew she was blushing; her face felt quite hot.

The lieutenant didn't notice. He was already heading back for the kittens. Willie watched him. He was very well put together, with those long limbs and those broad shoulders, and—as he turned around—that cheerful grin, a flash of white teeth in his tanned face.

Mayhew picked his way back across the ford, holding the basket. One of the kittens was mewing indignantly. "Poor Scout," he said. "She wants out, and I can't say I blame—"

He sat down suddenly in the water.

Willie stood frozen for a brief second, her mouth open in a soundless *Oh* of shock, and then she cast aside her reticule and splashed into the ford, dry feet be damned.

"Your shoes—"

"Kittens are more important than dry shoes," Willie told him, taking the basket, which he fortunately hadn't dropped. She heard two tiny voices, wailing their disapproval at the sudden change in elevation.

She waded back to dry ground and set the basket down. "It's all right, little ones," she said soothingly, and then she splashed back to the lieutenant. Her wet hem wrapped itself around her ankles.

She held out her hand. Mayhew took it and climbed to his feet. "Are you all right?" she asked.

"I believe my uniform's a little cleaner, now," he said.

Willie laughed, and he laughed, too, and as she laughed her foot slipped and she abruptly sat down.

The lieutenant was still holding her hand, so he sat down again, too.

There was a loud splash, and then silence. Willie bit her lip, and glanced at the lieutenant, sitting alongside her in the ford. His lips twitched. Her lips twitched, too, and then they were both laughing again, because really, what else *could* one do when one had just sat down in a ford?

"Well," the lieutenant said, when he'd caught his breath.

"Well," Willie agreed.

They helped each other to their feet. Willie's gown was quite sodden. Water streamed off it. "Are you all right?" the lieutenant asked.

"I believe my gown's a little cleaner, now," Willie said.

He grinned, recognizing his own words, and she grinned back at him, and then his grin faded, and hers did, too, and they just stood there in the ford, with water flowing around their ankles, looking at each other.

He's going to kiss me, Willie thought, and then she thought, *And I'm going to kiss him back.*

But at that moment a farm cart came around the corner, heading towards them.

Willie and the lieutenant stepped away from each other and sloshed to dry ground. The cart slowed, splashed through the ford, and halted alongside them. A stout, grizzled farmer man gazed down at them, a pipe clamped between his teeth. He removed the pipe. Its stem was well-chewed. "Dearie me," he said. "Dearie, dearie me."

CHAPTER SIX

The farmer took them home with him, where his wife fussed over them and bore Miss Culpepper off to the inner reaches of the farmhouse. When they returned, Miss Culpepper was wearing one of the farmer's wife's dresses. It wasn't just two sizes too large for her, it was *ten* sizes too large. Miss Culpepper looked as if she was wearing a tent.

But at least it was a dry tent.

The farmer loaned Mayhew a shirt and breeches, and they were tent-like on him, too, and they sat in the kitchen and drank cowslip wine while their clothes dried by the fire.

They stayed for three hours. Mrs. Penny, the farmer's wife, fed them bread and butter and the last of a knuckle of ham, and apologized that she had nothing better to give them. Mayhew told her of the time the commissariat's wagons had taken the wrong route and he'd had to eat acorns for his dinner, which made Mrs. Penny cluck with dismay. She stopped apologizing for the plainness of her fare, but she pressed bread and butter and ham on them until Mayhew feared that he would burst.

He could have stayed in that warm, cozy kitchen forever, seated at the table alongside Miss Culpepper, eating bread and butter and sipping cowslip wine, while Mr. Penny chewed on his pipe and Mrs. Penny bustled to and fro.

He watched Scout explore the kitchen, watched Bellyrub curl up and fall asleep on Mr. Penny's lap, watched Mrs. Penny knead dough and chop vegetables, but mostly he watched Miss Culpepper. He watched her eat, he watched her smile, he watched her enjoy being in this rustic kitchen, he watched her simply be *happy*.

She was good at being happy, Mayhew thought. Good at taking things in her stride. Today she'd missed a stagecoach, become separated from her luggage, traveled with pigs, fallen over in a muddy turnip field and again in a ford, and now she was wearing a coarse, country dress that didn't fit her—and she was happy.

Most young ladies would have had the vapors given any one of those events, let alone all of them, but Miss Culpepper hadn't. She hadn't even complained. Not once. Instead, she'd *laughed*.

Right now she was chuckling as Mrs. Penny described the time her children—three daughters—had decided to wash the hens. "A bigger mess you never did see. Feathers everywhere. Wet as fish, they all was. Wet as fish."

Mayhew watched the dimples come and go in Miss Culpepper's cheeks. He watched her sip cowslip wine and nibble bread-and-butter. She was enchanting. Utterly enchanting. The most enchanting female he'd ever met, and even though she was a colonel's daughter and he was merely a lieutenant, a tiny seed of hope flowered in his breast.

The Pennys had a nephew in the 2nd Regiment of Foot, and they asked about the Peninsula campaign. Mayhew told them stories of Spain and Portugal and France, and then he said, "But Miss Culpepper's been further afield than I have. Tell us about South America, Miss Culpepper."

She did. And then she told them about Constantinople and Russia, about chandeliers dripping with diamonds and plates made from gold, and she told them about dining with the tsar and dancing with princes.

The Pennys listened, openmouthed. Mr. Penny forgot to chew on the stem of his pipe. Mrs. Penny forgot to knead her dough.

Mayhew listened, too, and quietly let go of the hope that had flowered in his breast. To think that a colonel's daughter would marry a lowly lieutenant was foolish. To think that a diplomat's daughter who'd danced with princes and supped with the tsar might marry a lowly lieutenant wasn't merely foolish; it was laughable.

"Lordee," Mrs. Penny said, when Miss Culpepper had finished. "I'm quite betwattled! To think that you're sittin' at me own table, and you've dined with *royalty*."

"Your cowslip wine is better than anything I had in Russia," Miss Culpepper assured her.

Mrs. Penny went pink with pleasure.

"Do you miss diplomatic life?" Mayhew asked, even though he already knew the answer. Of course she missed it. She missed it so much that she was taking steps to return to it. As companion to Sir Walter's daughters, she would move in diplomatic circles again. She'd rub shoulders with attachés and ambassadors, and before very long a diplomat destined for a lifetime of dining off golden plates would snap her up.

"No." Miss Culpepper shook her head, a decisive movement that set her ringlets dancing. "It's army life that I miss."

"It is?" Mayhew said doubtfully.

She nodded.

"Why?"

Miss Culpepper frowned and gave the matter some thought, and even frowning she was enchanting. "Life is plainer in the army. Simpler. More real."

"More uncomfortable," Mayhew pointed out.

Laughter flashed across her face. "A great deal more uncomfortable!" The amusement faded, and Miss Culpepper's expression became serious. She looked down at the scrubbed wooden tabletop and circled a knot with one fingertip. "I know this will sound silly, but . . . I think I *like* to be a little bit uncomfortable. If one is forever wrapped up in luxury, one forgets to appreciate things like being warm and dry and fed. You never forget to do that when you're following the drum. When you have food, you're happy for it. When you have a dry bed, you're happy for it. When you don't have lice or fleas or saddle sores, you're happy for it."

She rubbed her fingertip back and forth, tracing the grain of the wood. "Army life is frequently dirty and disagreeable, and sometimes it's terrifying and sometimes it's heartbreaking, and I know it's not sensible of me to miss it, but I do. It made me feel alive, and not only that, it made me feel *glad* to be alive."

There was a long moment of silence while they all digested her words. Mayhew heard the fire mumbling in the kitchen hearth. He heard Mr. Bellyrub purring. He heard a rooster crowing outside in the yard. And while he heard those things, hope began to cautiously flower in his breast again.

Miss Culpepper *liked* army life.

Mr. Penny removed his pipe from his mouth. "Ye've a soldier's heart, lass."

"I do," Miss Culpepper said, with a rueful laugh. "But alas, I can't be a soldier."

You could be a soldier's wife, Mayhew thought.

He glanced at his pocket watch, which had fortunately survived his impromptu dip, and saw, with a sense of shock, that it would be dark in two hours.

He tilted the watch toward Miss Culpepper, letting her see the time.

Her lips tucked in at the corners, a tiny, regretful movement, and he realized that she wanted to remain in this cozy kitchen as much as he did.

"We must be going," Mayhew told the Pennys. "Miss Culpepper needs to be in Twyford by nightfall."

All became hustle and bustle. Miss Culpepper gathered up her clothing and retired to dress. Mayhew gathered up *his* clothing and retired to dress. His shirt was dry, his rifleman's pantaloons merely damp. His jacket was rather more damp, as were his boots, but Mayhew was used to wet jackets and wet boots.

When he returned to the kitchen, the kittens were already in their basket. "I took them outside," Miss Culpepper told him cheerfully. "They both did their business, and Mrs. Penny has put butter on their paws, so they're perfectly content."

"Thank you," Mayhew said. He went out into the yard and discovered that the sky was dark with clouds. He also discovered that Mr. Penny had harnessed his cob to the gig again. "I'll take ye to the Morestead bridge," the farmer said. "It's but a mile to Twyford from there."

"That's very kind of you," Mayhew said, with another glance at those threatening clouds. He reached into his pocket and fished out a shilling.

"Put that bob away, young feller," Mr. Penny said. "No need to pay me. I'd take ye all the way to Twyford if I could, but ol' Dobbin here won't cross the Morestead bridge." He clapped the cob on the shoulder. "Took a fright there ten year ago and ain't crossed it since."

Mayhew laughed, and put the shilling back in his pocket. He heard footsteps behind him and turned. It was Miss Culpepper. "Mr. Penny has offered to drive us to Morestead," he told her. "From there, it's only a mile to Twyford."

CHAPTER SEVEN

It was nearing twilight when they reached Morestead. The gloaming hour. That was a word Willie had always loved: gloaming. It sounded a little magical, a time of lingering daylight and long shadows and dusk slowly deepening in the hollows.

Morestead was too small to be called a village. It possessed a small church, a crossroads, a bridge, and that was all. The gig slowed as they approached the bridge, going from brisk trot to slow walk to complete standstill. The horse planted its hooves firmly, put its ears back, and refused to take another step.

Lieutenant Mayhew laughed. "I see what you mean."

"Aye," Mr. Penny said, around his pipe stem. "Stubborn as an ox, our Dobbin. Ain't no doin' nothin' about it."

Mayhew jumped down from the gig and held up a hand to Willie. She took it and jumped down, too.

"See that spire?" the farmer said, with a nod to the west. "That's Twyford, that is. Ye'd best walk fast, though. I don't like the look of them clouds."

"Thank you," the lieutenant said, lifting down the kittens' basket.

"There's another ford, jes' round the corner, but there's a foot-bridge alongside. Don't fall in, now."

The lieutenant laughed, and so did Willie. "We shan't," she assured Mr. Penny.

"Thank you," Lieutenant Mayhew said again. "We're very much obliged to you. You've been prodigiously kind, you and your wife."

The farmer chewed on his pipe and looked both pleased and bashful. "Godspeed."

By the time they'd crossed the humpbacked little bridge, the gig had turned around and was headed back towards Winnall. Willie watched it out of sight. "There are some very nice people in the world."

"There are." The lieutenant smiled down at her. "Come now, let's get to Twyford before it rains."

They turned right at the crossroad, walking briskly. No sound came from the basket. The kittens were snugly asleep.

Willie saw a line of oak trees ahead, and behind those, a church spire. Twyford.

She took a deep breath and set herself to enjoying this last mile of her journey—the gloaming, the mud and the puddles, the hedgerows on either side of the lane, the fields beyond that, the clouds heavy with approaching rain, the warm summer's breeze. And most of all, Lieutenant Mayhew's company.

"Here's the ford," he said.

"Yes." Willie eyed it as they approached. The ford was shallower than the one they'd fallen in, but wider and a great deal muddier.

"Footbridge," Mayhew said, with a tilt of his head.

Footbridge was perhaps too fine a word for that single, warped wooden plank, but at least their footwear wouldn't get wetter than it already was.

The lieutenant went across first, carrying the basket. He paused at the end of the plank, then took a long, leaping stride. He set the basket on the ground and turned to back her. "Have care, Miss Culpepper. It's wobbly, and there's a great puddle at the end."

Willie picked up her skirts and stepped onto the plank. It *was* a little wobbly, but not enough to upset her balance. She crossed quickly—and discovered that the puddle at the far end was not only larger than she'd thought, but also most unfortunately situated, precisely where she needed to step.

"Take my hand," Lieutenant Mayhew said.

Willie took hold of his outstretched fingers. "If I fall short, it's no matter. My shoes are still wet."

She jumped, but she didn't jump quite far enough. Her left foot landed in the puddle, and it wasn't merely a puddle, it was a *hole.*

Willie went in it up to her knee, lost her balance, and sat down. Fortunately, she let go of the lieutenant's hand, so she didn't pull him in, too. Muddy water enveloped her to the waist.

"Miss Culpepper!" Mayhew exclaimed, and he looked so aghast that Willie had to laugh.

"Are you all right?" he asked anxiously, crouching.

"Perfectly," Willie said, and then she shook her head and laughed again, because honestly, what else *could* one do when one had just sat in a muddy puddle in front of a man one was attracted to? She gave him her reticule and took his hand.

Mayhew helped her to stand. Water streamed off her. "Are you *certain* you're all right?"

"My pride has received a mortal blow," Willie told him. "But other than that, I'm perfectly well." And then she put her weight on her left foot and discovered that she wasn't perfectly well. She couldn't hide her wince.

The lieutenant saw it. "You're hurt?"

Willie bit her lip, and then confessed, "My ankle."

Mayhew picked her up as if she were a bride being carried over a threshold, crossed the lane to where there were no puddles, and set her down on the grass verge. "Let me see."

Willie sat silently while he knelt and unlaced her half boot and removed it. "Where does it hurt?" he asked.

Willie pointed.

Mayhew examined her ankle through her muddy stocking, probing with his fingers, testing the joint. There was no levity on his face now; his eyebrows were drawn together, his eyes slightly narrowed, his mouth a flat line. This was his serious face, Willie realized. His soldier's face.

"Does it hurt when I do this?" he asked, and flexed her ankle, watching her face as he did so.

"No," Willie said, and thought how *very* nice his eyes were. Quite the nicest eyes she'd ever seen. And then she scolded herself for mooning over Lieutenant Mayhew's eyes while he was examining her ankle. If one thing was certain, it was that at this moment *he* was not mooning over *her*. Not while he was kneeling in the mud and holding her foot in its wet, filthy stocking. If anything, he was probably annoyed at her for being so clumsy.

Willie shook her head at herself.

"What?"

"Just telling myself off for being so clumsy." She wrinkled her nose and attempted a joke: "This will teach me not to try to impress people with my athletic prowess."

He grinned at her. "You were trying to impress me, Miss Culpepper?"

Willie felt herself blush. "No, of course not."

The lieutenant's grin widened, and she had a horrible feeling that he didn't believe her, but he said nothing. He returned his attention to her ankle, rotating the joint carefully. It hurt, but not too much.

Willie told him that, and then she said, "I think it's just a sprain."

"So do I." He released her foot and sat back on his heels. "Thank God. I was afraid you'd broken it." He smiled ruefully at her. "Today has been a chapter of accidents, hasn't it? One catastrophe after another."

"They've been trifling catastrophes," Willie said. "Not full-grown ones."

Mayhew cocked his head. His smile changed, becoming faintly playful. "*Kitten*-astrophes?"

Willie's heart actually skipped a beat. How was it possible for a man to be so attractive? Especially when kneeling in the mud uttering appalling puns? But attractive he was. Incredibly attractive. Not because of the symmetry of his features, but because of the boyish tilt of his head, the twinkle in his eyes, that impish smile.

Willie tried to pretend that she wasn't flustered. She shook her head at him, uttering a chuckle that absolutely did *not* sound breathless, and said, "Allow me to inform you, Lieutenant, that puns are not your forte."

He shrugged, unabashed. "It made you laugh."

"Because it was so *bad*."

Mayhew grinned at her, and then his expression sobered and he climbed to his feet. "I'll run ahead to Twyford and fetch a carriage. You can't walk half a mile on that ankle, let alone a mile."

"I might be able to," Willie said.

The lieutenant looked doubtful, but he helped her to stand—and Willie took a few steps and discovered that her ankle actually did hurt rather a lot. She tried not to wince, but she knew that she *had* winced—and she also knew the lieutenant had seen it. "You're not walking to Twyford," he said, in a voice that brooked no argument.

"No," Willie said, with a sigh.

A puff of warm wind gusted along the lane. In its wake, a fat raindrop hit the ground. *Plop.* A moment later, came another one. *Plop. Plop. Plop.*

Mayhew frowned, and looked around. Willie looked around, too. She saw trees and hedgerows and that distant church spire, and on the other side of the nearest hedgerow, a small barn.

The lieutenant saw the barn, too. He picked Willie up and set off for it at a brisk pace.

"The kittens," Willie protested.

"I won't let them get wet," Mayhew said. "I promise."

A few raindrops pattered down while he carried her—*plop, plop-plop*—erratic and desultory, vanguard of the approaching storm. Willie eyed those dark clouds as Mayhew rounded the end of the hedgerow and headed across a rutted stretch of muddy ground, but it was difficult to pay attention to clouds or raindrops or even sprained ankles while Lieutenant Mayhew was carrying her. He was so *strong*. So steady on his feet. He smelled of wet wool. Perhaps it could be argued that one damp woolen garment smelled like another, but her nose told her that his green jacket smelled of *soldier,* and the familiarity of that scent brought a rush of home-sickness.

"Roof looks sound," Mayhew said, when they reached the barn.

The barn was small and dark and smelled of hay and turnips, even though there were no turnips that Willie could see. There was a lot of hay, though. Several piles of it.

Mayhew crossed to one pile, crouched and settled her carefully atop it, then said, "Won't be a moment," and headed back to the ford at a jog. Two minutes later he returned, panting, with the basket, Willie's half boot, and her reticule. He set all three items down. Outside, wind gusted, rattling the shutters.

"I'll run in to Twyford," Mayhew said. "Are you cold? The storm's almost upon us."

Willie shook her head. "It's a warm wind."

"Even so, take my jacket. It's not dry, but it's dryer than what you're wearing."

Willie wasn't at all cold, but her gown was soaked from the waist down, and part of her shawl was, too, so she made no protest when he peeled off his jacket. Mayhew crouched and settled it over her shoulders, not with brisk indifference but gently and almost tenderly, as if her comfort was important to him. As if he *cared* about her.

Willie slipped her arms into the sleeves and felt emotion tighten her throat.

The jacket was far too large, damp and heavy and warm from his body. The *soldier* smell of it was strong—and that made her throat tighten even further.

Mayhew looked at her, an anxious crease on his brow. "How do you feel? Warm enough?"

Willie didn't quite trust her voice. She pulled the jacket closed at her chest and nodded.

"Good." He stood. "I'll be back as soon as I can. Should be less than twenty minutes." But he didn't depart. He stood looking down at her, frowning. "I don't like leaving you on your own, Miss Culpepper."

"I'll be perfectly fine," Willie said firmly.

His frown deepened. She saw conflict on his face, saw that he truly *didn't* want to leave her, saw how much it worried him—and saw, too, that he knew he had to if he was to help her.

"Go," she said.

Mayhew hesitated a moment longer, then gave a curt nod, and as he nodded the wind gusted so strongly that it made the shutters bang against the walls and sent scraps of hay dancing madly across the dirt floor. On the heels of that mighty gust of wind came a burst of rain. Heavy rain. *Very* heavy rain. A downpour, in fact.

Willie raised her voice to be heard over the drumming on the roof. "You can't go out in that!"

Lieutenant Mayhew grinned, and shrugged. "It's a warm rain," he said, echoing her earlier words. "I'll be as fast as I can. Half an hour at the most." Then he plunged out into the deluge and was gone.

Willie opened the basket. The kittens blinked up at her. Did that loud roar of rain frighten them? She thought it probably did. "Hello, sweethearts," she said. "Come and sit with me while we wait."

Her gown was wet, but her shawl was still mostly dry, so she wadded it up and made a bed for the kittens on her lap and settled them there. Scout mewed up at her, but Mr. Bellyrub was silent. Willie petted them and murmured reassurances, "You're safe, I promise," and then she drew the damp green rifleman's jacket snugly around them all. She couldn't hear the kittens purring over the rain, but she felt it in the palm of her hand.

Gloaming was past, full night swiftly approaching. It was difficult to make out the interior of the barn—the piles of hay, the rusty implements, the abandoned buckets—but Willie wasn't afraid. She'd only been acquainted with Lieutenant Mayhew for a few scant hours, but she knew that if he said he'd be back within half an hour, he would be. Until then, she'd sit and enjoy the kittens on her lap and the smell of Mayhew's jacket and the noisy, turbulent drama of the storm. It reminded her of the humid, sultry storms she'd experienced in South America—

A figure loomed out of the semi-darkness. Willie started violently and let out a squeak of alarm—and then she recognized that grinning face. It was Lieutenant Mayhew. Water streamed off him.

"Your ride is here, m' lady," he said, with a flourishing bow.

"But you were gone barely two minutes!"

"Met a wagon in the lane." Mayhew crouched and helped her swiftly return the kittens to the basket. Poor Mr. Bellyrub squeaked his displeasure at this change in circumstance—or at least, Willie *thought* he did. She saw a flash of white teeth as his mouth opened, but couldn't hear anything over the rain. "Driver didn't want to stop for us," Mayhew said. "But I persuaded him to." He stood and held out a hand to her.

Willie climbed to her feet. Her left ankle gave a sharp twinge of protest.

Mayhew swept her up in his arms and carried her out into the storm. Warm wind gusted and warm rain poured down. When they reached the lane, a shape materialized in the gloom: a horse and wagon. Willie saw to her relief that the wagon was covered.

Mayhew lifted her over the tailboard, deposited her carefully in the wagon, and disappeared into the gloom. He was back in less than a minute with the kittens and her reticule and half boot.

Willie heard him shout something to the driver. The wagon lurched into motion, and they were off. Mayhew scrambled up into the wagon, wet and panting. "We'll be at Twyford in a few minutes, Miss Culpepper." She thought he was grinning, but it was too dark to be certain.

Willie felt a pang of regret. Which was absurd. How could she possibly regret arriving in Twyford, where a bath and a soft bed awaited her, and a trunk filled with dry clothes?

Willie frowned to herself, and examined her emotions.

She *was* relieved to be reaching Twyford—but not nearly as much as she ought to be, considering how wet and filthy she was.

It appeared that she didn't want this misadventure to end. If her father were still alive, he'd shake his head and laugh at her.

Willie did it for him: a shake of her head, a silent inner laugh. *Idiot,* she told herself. *Be thankful for the clean clothes and dry bed you'll soon have.*

And she was grateful for those things, she *was,* it was just . . .

She would miss Lieutenant Mayhew, miss his smile and his warm, brown eyes and his sense of humor and his chivalry.

Willie sighed at her foolishness, and as she sighed, she heard a crash that was louder than the storm.

The wagon halted abruptly.

"What was that?" she said, alarmed.

"I'll find out," Mayhew said, jumping down from the wagon.

He disappeared into the storm. Rain drummed down on the canvas overhead. Willie heard shouted voices, and then Mayhew returned. "A tree's come down across the road."

"Thank heavens it didn't fall on us!"

"Indeed." His voice was slightly grim. "It's an old oak, too big to move and we can't go around it. I'm going to help turn the wagon. Hold tight."

Willie nodded, but he was already gone. After a moment, the wagon began to move slowly backwards.

It took five minutes to turn the wagon, then Mayhew scrambled up alongside her again. "Where are we going?" Willie shouted over the roar of the storm.

"Morestead," Mayhew shouted back. "We'll see if we can find someone to take us in for the night."

Willie nodded, although it was too dark for him to see it.

Three minutes later the wagon was back to the ford—where it

halted again. Mayhew jumped down. Willie stayed where she was, clutching her reticule and the basket, listening to the rain beat on the canvas. She heard Mayhew shout something, heard the driver reply, and then Mayhew returned. "Too deep to cross. We'll have to stay the night in the barn."

"The barn?" Willie stared at his dark shape in dismay. Now that a dry bed and clean clothes were impossibilities, she discovered that she *did* rather want them.

"I'm very sorry, Miss Culpepper."

Willie reminded herself that she was a soldier's daughter. "It's not your fault, Lieutenant," she told him, as cheerfully as she was capable of. "We're fortunate that there *is* a barn for us to stay in."

CHAPTER EIGHT

The wagon driver was as big as a bear—and as surly as one. When Mayhew asked him to unhitch his horse and ride to Twyford for help, he refused. The horse was a massive beast, with powerful hindquarters and a great deal of feathering on its lower legs. A draft horse. Mayhew eyed that broad back. "Then let me and Miss Culpepper ride to Twyford," he said. "We'll stable your horse there overnight and I'll bring him back in the morning."

"Me 'orse ain't goin' nowhere," the wagon driver growled. "No while there's trees a-blowin' down."

Frustration flared in Mayhew's chest, but he held his tongue. In his experience, losing one's temper never helped a situation. He turned his attention to Miss Culpepper: lifting her down from the wagon, carrying her into the barn, carefully setting her on a pile of hay.

"At least the roof doesn't leak," she said, in the buoyant tone of someone determined to make the best of things. "And we have all this hay to sleep on. We're really very lucky!"

Water trickled down Mayhew's cheek and dripped off his nose

and chin. He wiped his face and reminded himself that they *were* lucky: they could be lying squashed under an oak tree right now.

He mustered a smile, because even if it was too dark for Miss Culpepper to see it, she'd hear it in his voice. "We are indeed lucky," he agreed. "I've slept in worse places in my time." And it was true; he'd slept in *far* worse places while on campaign.

Come to think of it, Miss Culpepper probably had, too.

He fetched the kittens, then helped the driver maneuver his wagon out of the rain as much as was possible, and then, praise be, the man produced a lantern and lit it.

The barn became almost cozy in that flickering golden light.

The wagon driver unhitched his horse and set to work rubbing the beast down with handfuls of hay. After a moment, Mayhew joined him. They worked in silence, while the rain hurled itself at the barn and the lantern cast dancing shadows. *Thank God it's summer,* Mayhew thought as he rubbed his way down the horse's hind leg. *Thank God it's warm.* The night was going to be uncomfortable, but if it had been winter and they were stranded here, soaked to the bone, it wouldn't have been merely uncomfortable, it would have been dangerous.

There was no risk of anyone freezing to death tonight. If anything, he was almost too warm.

He glanced across at Miss Culpepper. She'd removed her bonnet and gloves, but she still wore his jacket, so perhaps she was a little cold?

She didn't look cold. Or miserable. Or in pain. She was smiling, dimples dancing in her cheeks, her attention on something in her lap. A kitten, he guessed.

Thank God her ankle isn't broken, Mayhew thought, and then: *Thank God she's who she is. Thank God she's taking this all in her stride.*

In fact, there were a great many things to be thankful for tonight —the most important being that the oak tree hadn't fallen on them.

He crouched down to rub the long, wet hair that feathered the horse's lower leg, then stood and wiped his sweaty brow. "Done?" he asked the wagon driver.

The driver grunted and turned away, heading for his wagon.

Had the man *no* manners at all? Mayhew huffed out a soundless laugh and tossed away his handful of hay. He crossed to Miss Culpepper and crouched. "How's your ankle?"

She looked up at him and smiled, and despite the damp, bedraggled ringlets he thought she was the most beautiful woman he'd ever seen. "It doesn't hurt as long as I don't move it."

"I'm relieved to hear it."

Mr. Bellyrub was curled up in Miss Culpepper's lap, his eyes half closed, an expression of blissful contentment on his tiny face. Of his sister, there was no sign.

"Where's Scout?"

"Doing what she does best," Miss Culpepper said. She pointed, and he spied Scout investigating one corner of the barn, where a rusted hoe and several battered buckets lay discarded. "You were right; she ought to be a reconnaissance officer. She's absolutely fearless."

The driver had been rummaging in the back of his wagon; now, he returned with a rough woolen blanket, which he laid over his horse's broad back.

"Do you have another one of those?" Mayhew asked.

The man scowled at him, and produced a second blanket, which he handed over so grudgingly that Mayhew was hard put not to laugh. "Thank you," he said, and shook it out.

The blanket smelled strongly of horse, but it was thick and warm and dry. Mayhew placed it carefully around Miss Culpepper's shoulders.

"Thank you," she said, and then she pointed and said, "Look."

The wagon driver turned to look. So did Mayhew. He watched, incredulous, as Scout approached the draft horse. Her tail was high and her ears were pricked. She looked alert and inquisitive and wary. The horse saw her and pricked its ears, too, and dipped its great head for a closer look. Scout froze, every hair on her body bristling with cautious curiosity.

Their noses touched. Kitten and horse sniffed one another.

Scout stopped bristling.

The great horse nudged Scout gently, knocking her over.

Scout scrambled upright. She didn't retreat; instead, she frisked around the horse's front hooves, discovered the long feathering hairs, and reached out a daring paw and patted, as if those hairs were playthings.

Mayhew hastily retrieved her. The horse's hooves were far larger than Scout was. One misstep and the kitten would be dead.

Miss Culpepper was smiling. So was the wagon driver, although he scowled and turned away as soon as Mayhew caught his eye.

Mayhew deposited Scout on Miss Culpepper's lap. "Best keep her close. I'd hate for her to be squashed."

Scout wanted to continuing exploring, but Miss Culpepper distracted her with a long strand of hay. Soon the kitten was leaping and pouncing. Mr. Bellyrub joined in and they had a grand game. Miss Culpepper was laughing, and Mayhew was laughing, and he was pretty certain that the kittens were laughing, too, as they dashed around in the hay.

He didn't think the wagon driver was laughing, although he couldn't be certain because the man had his back to them. Mayhew kept an eye on him, watching as he gave his horse two armfuls of hay, then picked up one of the discarded buckets and went outside to fill it with water.

He lowered his voice: "Miss Culpepper, I promise I won't leave you alone with him for so much as one second."

"I don't think he's dangerous," she whispered back. "Just ill-tempered."

That was Mayhew's assessment, too, but he wasn't going to take the risk.

The driver returned and set the bucket in front of his horse. Then, he clambered up into his wagon. A minute later he emerged and crossed to where Mayhew and Miss Culpepper sat. "Here," he said brusquely, holding something out. "For the tibbies."

Mayhew held out his hand—and received a small piece of cheese. He blinked at it, too astonished to speak.

"Thank you," Miss Culpepper said.

The driver grunted and turned away.

Miss Culpepper's lips twitched, as if she found the man's complete lack of manners amusing.

Mayhew broke the cheese into crumbs and laid it down for the kittens. Mr. Bellyrub found it first, his little nose twitching. Soon both kittens were eating ravenously.

He glanced at Miss Culpepper. She was biting her lip. Her dimples were deep. She looked as if she was trying not to laugh.

"What?" Mayhew asked her.

She leaned close and said in an undertone, "He fed the animals, but not *us,*" and then she went into a peal of laughter.

Her laughter was contagious. Mayhew had to laugh, too, because it really *was* damned funny, but when he'd stopped laughing he climbed to his feet and went across to where the wagon driver was gathering a pile of hay, presumably for his bed.

"Do you have any more food?" he asked. "We'll pay you for it."

The man scowled, and grudgingly produced more cheese and some coarse bread.

"Thank you," Mayhew said. "What's your name? Mine's Mayhew, and my companion is Miss Culpepper."

"Williams," the man said gruffly.

With anyone else, Mayhew would have commented that his given name was William, and Miss Culpepper's was Willemina, and what were the odds of all three of them having variations on the same name? With this man, he didn't bother. He simply returned to where Miss Culpepper sat and offered his spoils.

"Excellent!" she said.

They ate their meal while the wagon driver finished assembling his bed. Mayhew didn't fail to notice that the man had chosen to sleep as far from them as was possible. Had he done that out of misanthropy? Or courtesy to Miss Culpepper?

He decided it didn't matter what the man's reason was. Even if the wagon driver *had* located his bed with Miss Culpepper's sensibilities in mind, there was no way in Hades that he was going to leave her alone with the man for twenty seconds, let alone the twenty minutes it would take to run in to Twyford and bring a horse back—always supposing he could find his way there and back in the dark *and* that he could get a horse past that fallen tree.

They were only half a mile from Twyford, but they might as well be on the moon for all the likelihood they had of reaching the coaching inn tonight. His most pressing concern at this moment—his *only* concern—was to keep Miss Culpepper safe.

Mr. Bellyrub climbed into Miss Culpepper's lap again. Mayhew watched her stroke the kitten. Lord, but she looked beautiful, the lantern light playing softly over her face. She looked happy, too. As happy as Mr. Bellyrub was right at this moment—which was exceedingly happy. Despite the storm, despite her wet clothing, despite her sprained ankle, despite the series of catastrophes that had befallen them today, she *glowed* with contentment. If she were a cat, she'd be purring right now.

She's remarkable, Mayhew thought. *Quite remarkable.* And then he shook that thought out of his head. He wasn't in this barn to make sheep's eyes at Miss Culpepper; he was here to keep her safe. And if he could make her laugh while doing so, so much the better.

To that end, he said, in a mock-lugubrious tone, "Has it occurred to you, Miss Culpepper, that we're doomed never to reach Twyford?"

She glanced sideways at him, still stroking Mr. Bellyrub. A dimple appeared in her cheek. "Doomed?"

"Doooomed," Mayhew repeated, drawing out the word.

Her lips twitched into a smile. "We are *not* doomed," she told him. "This is merely another kitten-astrophe."

Mayhew leaned back on one elbow in the hay and smirked. "I knew you liked that pun."

"It's a *dreadful* pun."

"Dreadful?"

"*Monstrously* dreadful. *Prodigiously* dreadful."

He laughed. "Please, don't spare my feelings."

Miss Culpepper rolled her eyes at him. He could tell from her dimples that she was struggling not to smile.

Mayhew laughed again. And then he stopped laughing. This felt dangerously like flirting, and he couldn't flirt with Miss Culpepper. Not under circumstances like this. Not when she was injured and dependent on his protection. Only a cad would do that, and he was not a cad.

Scout climbed up on his damp knee, her claws digging into his green pantaloons. Mayhew winced and carefully detached her. He sat up again, laid some hay on his lap, and let her settle there. She turned around three times, curled up in a tight ball, and closed her eyes.

Mayhew cupped a hand over her and felt the warm vibration of her purr. He glanced at Miss Culpepper. *No flirting,* he reminded himself. "How's your ankle?"

"Not bad at all."

"Are you warm enough?"

"Yes. Are you?"

He was. Wet, but warm. He cast about for a subject. "Where else have you been, Miss Culpepper, other than South America and Constantinople and Russia?"

Her face lit up. "We were in Egypt for four years. I was only a girl, but I still remember it."

They talked about Egypt, and briefly about South Africa, where Miss Culpepper's mother had died of a fever, and then she told him about Kingston upon Thames, the village outside London where her aunt lived, and where she'd spent the past year.

"You don't like it there," Mayhew said, when she'd finished.

Miss Culpepper pulled a wry face. "Is it that obvious?"

He nodded, and stroked Scout.

Miss Culpepper hesitated, and then said, "Kingston upon Thames is very picturesque and very quiet—and I know that most people would love to live somewhere picturesque and quiet—but my parents didn't, and I don't either." She sighed, and looked down at Mr. Bellyrub, asleep in her lap. "It would be much easier if I did. I could be married and settled there right now."

Mayhew's hand hesitated in its stroking of Scout. "Married? You had a suitor in Kingston Upon Thames?"

Miss Culpepper nodded. "They did me a great honor, but . . ." Her lips pressed together regretfully.

They?

Mayhew waited for her to continue, but she didn't. "They?" he prompted carefully.

Miss Culpepper colored. "Yes."

"How many is 'they'?" he asked, even more carefully.

She looked away. "It sounds braggish."

"I promise I won't think you're puffing yourself off."

Miss Culpepper looked back at him and hesitated, and then said, "Six."

Mayhew felt his eyebrows rise. "Six?" His voice might have risen a little bit, too.

Miss Culpepper had had *six* suitors in Kingston Upon Thames?

"Yes." Her lips pursed regretfully again. "First was the vicar. Then the squire's son. Then Mr. Hanslow, who's secretary to Baron Allen. Then the baron's youngest son. Then Sir Peter Frost, and the very last was Mr. Mannering."

Mayhew digested that list for a few moments. *Six.* "May I ask why you didn't wish to marry them? If it's not too impertinent?"

Miss Culpepper frowned down at Mr. Bellyrub and stroked him several times and then said, "They were all perfectly nice men, respectable and amiable and upstanding and . . . and well-born and . . . and . . ."

"Boring?"

"Yes." She sighed. "They all want to live in Kingston upon

Thames. Forever! And you may tell me that I'm a fool for not wanting that—my aunt certainly told me often enough—but unfortunately, I'm my parents' daughter. I felt as if I was *suffocating* in that village."

"There's nothing unfortunate about it," Mayhew said firmly. He ran through the list of suitors in his head: vicar, secretary, squire's son, baron's son. "Your suitors sound very much like my brothers."

She cocked her head at him. "They do?"

"My father's a baron," Mayhew told her. "My oldest brother will make a worthy successor when it's his turn. My next oldest brother is a rector, and the one after that is a vicar, and the one after that, too. And the youngest one, John, is secretary to an earl."

"You have *five* brothers?"

"Five brothers and one sister. Do you have any?"

She shook her head.

"Well, my brothers all live in the same county—in fact most of them live within ten miles of each other." He smiled at her. "They're exactly like your suitors: amiable and upstanding, and they don't want to leave Wiltshire, let alone leave England."

"But you're not like that."

Mayhew shook his head. "I want to see the world, and I want to be *challenged*." He hesitated, and then said, "What you said to the Pennys . . . that's how I feel, too. I love army life. Even when it's awful and heartbreaking." He rubbed between Scout's ears, gently and meditatively. "Waterloo was worse than awful. It was . . ." He grimaced at memory of that carnage. "A lot of fellows sold out afterwards, and I considered it myself, but . . . I couldn't. A soldier is what I'm meant to be. It's who I *am*."

Miss Culpepper nodded, as if she understood exactly what he was attempting to say. "It's who my father was, too."

He rubbed Scout's little head again. "I wish I'd met him."

"He would have liked you," Miss Culpepper said.

"I hope so." He stroked Scout once, twice. "From what I've heard, your father was everything a good commander should be. He led from the front, he was scrupulously fair, and he kept a cool head. Colonel Barraclough says that your father always said it was better to fix things than lose one's temper over them."

Miss Culpepper's smile was soft, a little sad. "Yes, he did say that."

"And Barraclough says he didn't play favorites." Which was, in Mayhew's opinion, almost as important as courage and cool-headedness in a commanding officer.

"Father? Heavens, no! Which isn't to say that people didn't try to pour the butter boat over him, because they most certainly *did*." Miss Culpepper chuckled, as if at some memory, and then her smile slowly faded, becoming soft and sad again. She looked down at the folds of rough blanket spilling around her and plucked a horse hair from the coarse weave. "That was the hardest thing for him when he moved in diplomatic circles—all the flummery and the puffery. Father much preferred bluntness."

Lamplight caressed her face. She plucked another horse hair from the blanket, and another, and she looked rumpled and lovely and pensive, and it struck Mayhew suddenly that she was an orphan, and not just an orphan but an only child, too, and that she was alone in a way that he, with five brothers and one sister, could never be. Her aloneness seemed suddenly so dreadful, so terrible, that his throat clenched and his heart clenched and the urge to put an arm around her was almost overwhelming. He wanted to tell her that she wasn't alone, tell her that he thought he'd fallen in love with her, that he wanted to marry her, and that if she married him she'd never be alone again, that she'd have him and the whole of the Rifle Brigade as her family.

But only a cad would put his arm around a young lady under circumstances like this, when she was vulnerable and under his protection, and only a fool would blurt out a proposal after an acquaintance of only a few hours.

Mayhew swallowed past the lump in his throat and looked away. "What sort of man is this baronet who's hired you?"

"Sir Walter Pike? He's . . ."

He glanced back at her. Miss Culpepper's expression was no longer pensive, but thoughtful, as if she was searching for a word. "He's very genteel," she said, finally.

Genteel? Mayhew gave a soundless snort. If Sir Walter Pike was so damned genteel, why was Miss Culpepper traveling by stage-coach? Surely a *genteel* employer would hire a post-chaise for his daughters' companion?

Dare he ask her that question?

He gave a mental shrug, and decided that he would. "Why are you traveling to Twyford by stagecoach?"

"Sir Walter was going to book me on the Mail," Miss Culpepper said. "But the waybill was full."

"If the Mail was full, why didn't he hire a post-chaise for you? Or send one of his own carriages?"

She shrugged. "More expensive."

Mayhew gave another soundless snort. Sir Walter might be genteel, but he was also a damned penny-pincher. "What time is he meeting you tomorrow?"

"Ten o'clock."

"You'll be in Twyford before that, Miss Culpepper. I give you my word." He'd make certain of it. Even if he had to carry her, she'd be there on time. *Before* time, because she needed to wash and change her clothes before she met Sir Walter.

He hoped to God that her trunk had been set down at Twyford. That would be a disaster he couldn't mend by ten o'clock.

Mayhew sent up a brief prayer for Miss Culpepper's trunk to be where it was meant to be, then glanced over at the wagon driver. Mr. Williams appeared to be asleep on his pile of hay. The great horse had one hip cocked as if it was sleeping, too.

He looked back at Miss Culpepper. "Why don't you get some rest? I promise that you'll be safe."

"What about you?"

Mayhew shook his head. "I'll keep watch."

Miss Culpepper leaned closer, lowering her voice so that he barely heard it over the hammering rain. "You should sleep, too, Lieutenant. Our friend may possess a churlish disposition, but I don't believe he'd harm us."

Mayhew didn't think the wagon driver would harm them either, but he wasn't prepared to risk Miss Culpepper's safety. "I'll keep watch," he repeated, firmly.

Miss Culpepper must have heard the implacable note in his voice, because she didn't try to persuade him to change his mind. She simply nodded, and said, "Here," and shucked his jacket and gave it to him.

"I'm not cold—"

"I have the blanket, so you must take this."

Mayhew heard the implacable note in *her* voice, and decided not to argue. He accepted the jacket.

Miss Culpepper removed the single half boot she was wearing, placed it alongside its mate, and settled herself and Mr. Bellyrub on their bed of hay, beneath the heavy horse blanket. She smiled at Mayhew, a cheerful smile, as if she wasn't wet and muddy, as if she didn't have a sprained ankle, as if this day hadn't been one disaster after another, as if she was *happy* to be in this barn with him and England's surliest wagon driver while a storm raged outside.

Mayhew smiled helplessly back at her.

Miss Culpepper snuggled deeper into the blanket and closed her eyes.

For some reason the fact that she'd closed her eyes made a lump grow in Mayhew's throat again.

Miss Culpepper trusted him not to touch her. She trusted him to keep her safe.

She *trusted* him.

Mayhew looked away and found that he needed to clear his throat and blink a little moisture from his eyes, which was rather embarrassing. He was a soldier, for heaven's sake. He didn't get mawkish over something as simple as someone closing their eyes.

Unless that someone was Miss Culpepper.

He glanced back at her. Emotions surged through him. Protectiveness was foremost, but there were a multitude of others: admiration, tenderness, longing, hope, respect. Love.

Mayhew lifted his jacket to his nose and inhaled, hoping to catch Miss Culpepper's scent. All he smelled was wet wool.

Idiot, he told himself, with a self-conscious glance around the barn. But no one had seen him. Not the wagon driver. Not Miss Culpepper. Not even the horse.

CHAPTER NINE

Willie woke to the sound of low voices. She blinked her eyes open and saw hay and daylight. Memory came sweeping back. She sat up hastily, dislodging Mr. Bellyrub. He uttered a squeaking meow, clambered to his feet, and shook himself from head to toe.

"Sorry," Willie said, stroking his tiny head, and it appeared that Mr. Bellyrub wasn't one to hold grudges, for he butted against her fingers and purred. Then he yawned widely and shook himself again.

Willie yawned, too, and rubbed her face and put her hand to her hair, which felt as tangled as a briar patch. Lieutenant Mayhew and the wagon driver were at the barn door. The lieutenant said something, his voice too low for her to catch the words, but it sounded like a question. The driver replied gruffly.

Willie plucked out her hairpins. She ran her fingers through her ringlets and found them as snarled and messy as she'd feared. She needed a mirror and a comb if she was to repair that, but neither of those things was available right now, so she replaced the hairpins as best she could and made inventory of her situation.

One: chaotic hair.

Two: her gown was still damp, the muslin stained with mud and puckered into a thousand wrinkles—but she could do nothing about that, so there was no point worrying about it.

What *was* worth worrying about was her ankle.

Cautiously, Willie flexed it. The resultant twinge barely qualified as pain.

So, that was all right. In fact, it was *better* than all right.

A bath, a comb, and fresh clothes, and she would almost be as good as new.

Lieutenant Mayhew turned his head, saw that she was awake, and crossed swiftly to her. "Miss Culpepper. Good morning."

"What time is it?" Willie asked.

"Nearly seven o'clock." He crouched alongside her, smiling. He looked rumpled and disreputable—hair disheveled, golden stubble roughening his cheeks—but not nearly as rumpled and disreputable as she knew that *she* looked.

Willie told herself there was no point in vanity in situations like this, but she did wish she could wash her face and tidy her hair.

"The rain stopped about an hour ago," Mayhew said. "Mr. Williams has been out to check the road. The ford's still flooded, so we can't go that way, and the oak that came down is too large for his horse to move, but he thinks that you and I can climb over it, and from there it's less than half a mile to Twyford."

Willie nodded.

"We'll be in Twyford by eight thirty," he promised. "I'll carry you."

"I don't think that will be necessary. My ankle feels much better today."

His eyes lit with hope. "May I examine it? Do you mind?"

"Of course not." Willie extended her leg and pulled up her hem a few inches, revealing her filthy stockinged foot and ankle.

The lieutenant examined it as he had yesterday, probing gently with his fingers. It felt ridiculously intimate. Willie's pulse hammered in her throat and her face felt hot. No, it wasn't just her face that felt hot; her whole *body* felt hot.

Lieutenant Mayhew carefully rotated her ankle joint through its range of movement, a thoughtful frown on his face.

"It really doesn't hurt much at all," Willie told him, and to her relief her voice was steady, not breathless.

"Let's see how it feels when you put weight on it," Mayhew said, releasing her ankle. "Let me put your half boots on." He did just that, carefully sliding them onto her feet and lacing them up. Willie should have felt like a child, to have him do that, but she didn't. She felt . . . a little self-conscious and desperately aware of him—his proximity, his deft fingers, the way his eyebrows drew together as he concentrated—but mostly, she felt cared for, a sensation that she hadn't felt since her father had died. A sensation that made her throat constrict and her eyes sting.

Willie blinked several times and looked away, then back. The glinting golden stubble on Mayhew's cheeks made him look more flesh-and-blood man and less dashing lieutenant. It made him look older, too. She caught herself wondering how old he was. Twenty-seven? Twenty-eight?

Mayhew tied the laces into neat bows, stood, and extended his hand to her. "Here, I'll steady you."

Willie let him pull her to her feet—and realized that neither of them was wearing gloves any longer. Her fingers tingled at his touch.

Willie held on to his hand and tried to ignore the tingle and the way it elevated her heart rate. She took a cautious step. Her ankle gave a throb of discomfort, but that throb was nothing like the raw, stabbing pain of yesterday. "It feels a thousand times better. I don't think you'll need to carry me, Lieutenant." And *that* was a blessing for which she was deeply thankful. If her fingers tingled when he touched them for a few seconds, imagine how she'd feel if he carried her half a mile?

Mayhew released her hand and Willie should have felt relieved, because the tingle snuffed out, but perversely she felt sorry for that loss of contact.

"I'd feel better if you had a crutch or walking stick." Mayhew cast a frowning glance around the barn, then his face brightened. "How about that hoe, Miss Culpepper?"

He brought it to her, flipping it so that the blade pointed to the ceiling. "Blade's rusted, but the handle looks strong."

Willie accepted the hoe and leaned on it and took a careful step.

"Well?" the lieutenant asked, a hopeful note in his voice.

"It will do perfectly," Willie said.

Mayhew grinned at her—a grin that took her breath away—and rubbed his hands together briskly and said, "Right, let's be off!" And then he lost his grin and went faintly pink and said hesitantly, "Or, do you need to, *er* . . ."

Yes, Willie did need to, *er*.

She hobbled outside and around to the back of the barn, thanking God for the hoe with every step that she took. Imagine if Mayhew had had to carry her out here to do this?

She spent her penny, as the saying went, and hobbled back, and discovered that Lieutenant Mayhew had fetched a bucket of water for her to wash her hands and face in. The thoughtfulness of that shouldn't have made her eyes sting, but it did.

She also discovered that the wagon driver had put down some cheese for the kittens, which was no surprise—the man clearly liked animals more than he liked people. What *was* a surprise was that he offered her and the lieutenant food without being asked.

They ate quickly, then Mayhew fetched fresh water and they drank, and it was time to go. Mayhew folded up the horse blanket she'd slept under and gave it to the wagon driver while Willie caught Scout and put her in the basket. She closed the lid and looked around for Mr. Bellyrub.

"All set?" Mayhew said, turning to her with a smile.

"Once we find Mr. Bellyrub, yes."

"Ah." He lost his smile.

Mr. Bellyrub wasn't where the cheese had been. He wasn't in the nest of hay where Willie had slept. He wasn't in the nest of hay where the wagon driver had slept, either. He wasn't making the acquaintance of the draft horse. He wasn't under the wagon. He wasn't in any of the four corners of the barn.

The sense of déjà vu was strong. This was how it had all started: searching for a kitten while precious minutes ticked away.

Willie began to feel slightly frazzled. She thought the lieutenant was feeling frazzled, too; she heard him mutter something that was probably a curse as he pawed through the hay.

"Perhaps he went outside?" Willie said, after it seemed that every strand of hay in the barn had been turned over at least three times.

Mayhew strode out and made a hurried circuit. He shook his head when he reentered the barn. "We'll leave the kittens here."

"But—"

"I'll come back for them, Miss Culpepper. I promise. But I need to get you to Twyford. That's the most important thing right now."

"He's here somewhere," Willie insisted, rifling urgently through the hay.

"Miss Culpepper," the lieutenant said, in the sort of stern voice her father had used when telling her to do something he knew she wouldn't like.

"Five minutes!" she begged.

It took four and a half minutes, and it was the wagon driver who found Mr. Bellyrub. He was fast asleep inside a bucket that lay abandoned on its side. A bucket that Willie *knew* both she and Mayhew had checked earlier. "You little rascal," she told him sternly.

Mr. Bellyrub twitched his ears, but didn't bother to open his eyes.

"Into the basket, little man," Mayhew said, scooping the kitten up.

Mr. Bellyrub didn't object to his change in circumstance; he purred as he was placed in the basket. His sister tried to scramble out. Mayhew closed the lid ruthlessly. Willie heard Scout's indignant squeak.

Mayhew fastened the strap, sat back on his heels, and blew out a breath. Then he stood and checked his pocket watch. "Quarter to eight. We'll be in Twyford by half past, Miss Culpepper, I *promise* you." He turned to the wagon driver. "Thank you, Mr. Williams. We're extremely grateful for your help."

Mr. Williams grunted and turned away.

Willie almost burst into helpless giggles. She met Mayhew's eyes and saw laughter leap across his face. His lips twitched and a muscle jumped in his jaw. He said, with barely a quiver in his voice, "Shall we depart, Miss Culpepper?"

"Yes," Willie said, and her voice was almost as steady as his. "Let's." She picked up her reticule and looped it over her wrist—and then her amusement snuffed out, because this was the end of their adventure together.

The lieutenant carried her across the rutted, muddy stretch of ground between the barn and the lane, set her carefully on her feet, and ran back for the kittens and the hoe. He returned, grinning, and handed her the hoe with a flourish. Willie tried to grin back, but it felt unnatural on her face, an imitation of cheerfulness.

They set off together, Willie using the hoe as a walking stick, the lieutenant slowing his pace to match hers. Water sparkled on grass blades and tree leaves and hung in spiders' webs in bright, trembling drops. The world seemed fresh and new and clean. Birds sang and grasshoppers chirped and with every step that Willie took her spirits should have risen; instead, they sank.

All too quickly, they reached the fallen oak. It was bigger than Willie had thought, a colossus of a tree, its trunk thicker than she was tall.

She looked at that great trunk and the shattered branches and the squashed hedgerows on either side of the lane. "We're very lucky," she said soberly.

"Yes," Mayhew said, equally soberly.

The oak lay squarely across the road. There was easy no way around, not unless they backtracked and ventured into the muddy paddocks on either side of the hedgerows. "We'll climb over it," Mayhew said, setting down the basket.

And that was what they did: they climbed over the great, slain oak, finding a path through the tangle of branches, clambering and crawling, and always Mayhew was there with a hand outstretched, ready to steady Willie, to brace her, to help her.

He jumped lightly down on the other side and held up both hands to her. "Slide. I'll catch you."

Willie perched for a moment on the gnarled trunk, and then did as he bid, sliding, her gown snagging on the rough bark. Mayhew caught her, his hands around her waist, and set her carefully on the muddy ground. "All right?" he said, smiling down at her.

"Yes," Willie said breathlessly, terribly aware of his hands at her waist.

Mayhew released her, and scrambled back up into the oak. "Won't be a minute," he said, and he was true to his word: less than a minute later he reappeared, with the hoe and the kittens and her reticule.

He lowered all three items to her, then jumped lightly down. "How's your ankle?"

"I barely notice it," Willie said.

"Good," he said, and glanced past her. "We're almost there."

Willie followed his gaze: the curve in the lane, the church spire peeking from behind the trees. "Yes," she said, and felt a pang of something that might have been sorrow.

The bell in the church spire struck the quarter hour—eight fifteen —and as the echo died away, a horse and cart came around the bend in the lane.

"Cross your fingers, Miss Culpepper," Mayhew said. "We may not have to walk."

The cart was small and crude and filled with firewood, but there was room for them to both perch on the tailboard.

Mayhew lifted her up, handed her the basket, then helped the driver to turn the vehicle. "Our luck has finally turned," he said, climbing up alongside her.

"Yes," Willie said. But she didn't feel lucky as the cart rattled towards Twyford; she felt an absurd sense of loss, and a sadness that was close to grief.

Mayhew sniffed, scenting the air, then sniffed again, and she saw that he'd caught the lingering aroma of cow dung.

He glanced at her, clearly hoping she hadn't recognized that smell.

"And they rode into town in a dung cart," Willie said jauntily.

Lieutenant Mayhew huffed a surprised laugh and Willie laughed, too, at the expression on his face—but deep inside, she felt like crying.

CHAPTER TEN

Five minutes, Mayhew told himself. They'd be in Twyford in five minutes. And that was good. It was better than good; it was excellent. Miss Culpepper's trunk would be waiting for her, and she'd have time to bathe and change into clean clothes. Right now, she looked as if she'd been dragged backwards through a hedge, but by ten o'clock she would once again be the respectable, faintly aloof young lady he'd met yesterday morning: her hair tidy, her gown unwrinkled, everything about her pristine and immaculate.

He preferred her as she was now, perched alongside him on this dung-cart-turned-firewood-cart, with her messy ringlets and her grubby clothes. This young lady was the Sweet Willie he'd heard so much about, the girl everyone in the second battalion had loved for her spirit and her resilience and her *joie de vivre.*

Not that the respectable Miss Culpepper of yesterday morning hadn't been attractive. She had been. Just not as attractive as this muddy, messy, vividly alive young woman beside him.

The horse's hooves clopped and the wheels turned and the cart jolted and splashed its way through ruts and puddles, and now it was only four minutes to Twyford, probably less.

Resolve had been gathering in Mayhew's belly for hours, slowly accreting into something solid and weighty, but now that Twyford was mere minutes away, it put out claws and took hold of his innards and grabbed hard, no longer resolve, but *urgency*.

Urgency, because once they reached the coaching inn, they would say their farewells.

Urgency, because Miss Culpepper was off to Vienna next month.

Urgency, because he might never see her again.

Another fifty yards rattled away beneath the cart wheels, while his urgency grew until he simply *had* to speak, even if it was foolish and even if he had no chance.

Mayhew took a deep breath. "Miss Culpepper? I know it's irregular, but . . . while you're in Vienna, may I write to you?"

It was more than irregular. It was, in fact, verging on improper. Single young ladies and single young men did not correspond with one another. Not without the permission of the young lady's parents. Not unless there was an acknowledged connection between them.

But Miss Culpepper had no parents and she was perfectly capable of making her own decisions.

She didn't reply immediately, but she did look at him. Her gaze was serious and he saw that she understood that he wasn't merely asking to correspond with her; he was asking to court her. A year of letters, perhaps two years, and then, when she'd fulfilled her commitment to the Pikes and he'd obtained his captaincy, he would ask for her hand in marriage.

Mayhew held his breath. His heart thumped loudly with hope. Miss Culpepper had turned down six offers in the past year and she could very well turn him down, too. She hadn't wanted to marry a baronet, or a baron's son, or a vicar, but maybe, just maybe, she *did* want to marry a soldier.

He tried to look as if her answer wasn't desperately important to him. If she said *No,* he'd smile and say something light and friendly, and then in three minutes' time, when they reached the inn, he'd help her down from the cart and bow politely over her hand and let her go. A chance lost forever.

"Yes," Miss Culpepper said. "I would like that."

Mayhew's heart gave a great leap. "You would?"

"Yes."

A smile grew on his face. Miss Culpepper liked him. She liked him so much that she'd agreed to correspond with him. She *wanted* to correspond with him.

Mayhew felt jubilant, felt like laughing aloud, and then he *did* laugh out loud, because it really was too absurd to have made the equivalent of a proposal while perched, damp and filthy, on the tailboard of a dung cart.

Miss Culpepper laughed, too, dimples dancing in her cheeks, and then their laughter faded and their grins faded and they just sat there, looking at each other, smiling ever so faintly.

Mayhew had never felt anything quite like this—the warmth in his chest, the joy, the hope, the sheer wonder that he'd met this particular woman out of all the women in the world and that possibly, hopefully, in a year—or perhaps two—they would marry.

If Miss Culpepper didn't meet someone else in Vienna. *If* she didn't lose interest in him. *If* nothing untoward or—heaven forbid—disastrous happened to one or the other of them.

He suddenly wanted, quite desperately, to ask her to marry him *now,* right this very instant. Mayhew bit the words back. He couldn't ask her to marry him today, or even this week or this month. Not when Miss Culpepper was bound for Vienna. Not when he was still merely a lieutenant.

But if he couldn't ask her to marry him now, he could take her hand, and so he did.

Miss Culpepper didn't object. On the contrary, she gripped his hand back, a firm grip, a grip that said *I am yours and you are mine,* a grip that made him feel even more hopeful about the future. The world glowed with sunshine and happiness. They could do this, he and Miss Culpepper. It would be hard, a year apart, perhaps even two years, but they could do it. He *knew* they could do it.

The first houses of Twyford came into view. Mayhew released her hand, because it wasn't acceptable for unmarried young ladies to be seen to be holding hands with unmarried young men. "When do you leave for Vienna?" he asked.

"In two weeks."

"I'll write to you before then," he promised. "I'll write to you tomorrow. Where should I address it?"

She barely had time to tell him before the cart slowed to a halt. Mayhew looked up at the sign swinging overhead in the breeze. This was it, the place they'd been trying to reach for what seemed like forever: the coaching inn in Twyford, where Miss Culpepper would meet Sir Walter Pike in . . . He pulled out his pocket watch and saw, with relief, that she still had an hour and a half before that appointment.

He shoved the watch back in his pocket and jumped down from the cart, lifted Miss Culpepper down and set her carefully on her feet, then retrieved the basket and the hoe. One of the kittens mewed plaintively. Most likely Scout.

Mayhew checked that Miss Culpepper had her reticule, then raised his hand in thanks to the farmer.

The man nodded back, flicked his reins, and the cart clattered off, with its load of firewood and its aroma of cow dung and the tailboard upon which Mayhew had sat while he'd asked what was perhaps the most important question of his life.

"Do you need the hoe?" he asked Miss Culpepper. "Or will my arm suffice?"

She smiled up at him. "Your arm will suffice. It's only a few steps."

Mayhew leaned the hoe against the brick-and-plaster wall, made a mental note to have one of the ostlers return it to the barn, and gave Miss Culpepper his elbow. Together they entered the inn. It was low-ceilinged, warm and dimly lit and fragrant with the smells of coffee and baking bread.

The plump, smiling innkeeper welcomed them and confirmed that yes, Miss Culpepper's trunk had come yesterday on the stage-coach and was upstairs, and that yes, her room was ready for her, and that yes, water would be heated immediately for a bath, and that yes, he did have a walking stick that she might use while she was here.

Mayhew inhaled the smell of baking bread and knew that finally, after nearly twenty-four hours of mishap and misfortune, things were going their way.

He placed the basket on the floor and took Miss Culpepper's hands, while the innkeeper bustled off to fetch the walking stick. This moment felt like an end, but he knew it wasn't. It was a beginning. *Their* beginning. His and Miss Culpepper's. He could wait a year for this woman. Two years, if he had to. Because she was worth it.

"Well," he said. "I guess this is good-bye."

"It's au revoir," Miss Culpepper told him. "*Not* adieu."

They smiled at each other a little foolishly, and Mayhew wished that he could bend his head and kiss her, but he couldn't. Not with the innkeeper standing there, plump and smiling, holding out a walking stick.

Reluctantly, he released Miss Culpepper's hands. Reluctantly, he picked up the basket again. Reluctantly, he took a step back.

"I'll write to you every week," he said, and what he actually meant was, *I'm madly in love with you.*

"It'll write to you, too," Miss Culpepper said, taking the walking stick from the innkeeper.

She looked utterly disreputable, with her uncombed hair and her grubby shawl, her wrinkled gown and those filthy half boots—and at the same time, she looked extraordinarily lovely. Sweet Willie. *His* Sweet Willie. The Sweet Willie who'd be his wife in a year. Or perhaps, two.

If everything went well.

Mayhew didn't want to say goodbye. He wanted to blurt a proposal, wanted to beg her to marry him today. But marriage today wouldn't have been possible even if she *hadn't* been going to Vienna with Sir Walter Pike's daughters. Not without a special license, not without his commanding officer's permission.

Mayhew took another reluctant step back. One of the kittens squeaked faintly in the basket. "Goodbye, Miss Culpepper."

"Goodbye, Lieutenant."

He managed a smile. "Enjoy Vienna."

A door opened behind her, giving Mayhew a glimpse of a private parlor. A stout, well-groomed man emerged—and halted abruptly. "Miss Culpepper!" he exclaimed.

CHAPTER ELEVEN

Miss Culpepper jerked around. Her face paled. She looked as appalled as the man did.

Mayhew didn't need an introduction to know who this newcomer was. It was blindingly obvious. The man was Sir Walter Pike.

What was also blindingly obvious was that their disasters weren't over yet. In fact, the expression on Pike's face told Mayhew that the greatest disaster of all might be upon them.

Miss Culpepper clearly realized that, too. She put a hand to her damp, misshapen bonnet, as if she wished she could somehow hide her appearance, but it was no use. Everything about her was unkempt. And bedraggled. And grimy.

Mayhew put the basket down on a wooden bench and took a hasty step forward. "Sir Walter Pike? I can explain everything."

The man looked him up and down, visibly dismissed him, and turned his attention back to Miss Culpepper. *"You,"* he said, a whiplash of anger in his voice. "You are *dismissed,* Miss Culpepper."

"It's not what it looks like," Mayhew said, and in contrast to Sir Walter, his voice was calm and reasonable.

Sir Walter ignored him. "You were meant to arrive last night!" he snapped at Miss Culpepper.

"We missed the stagecoach at Abbots Worthy," Mayhew said. "It was my fault."

Sir Walter paid him no attention. "You are *late*," he said, his voice sharp with accusation. "Late and untrustworthy and *slatternly* and—"

Rage ignited in Mayhew's chest. "And *you* are out of order, Sir Walter. You know absolutely nothing about what befell Miss Culpepper yesterday!"

"I know enough that I don't want her anywhere near my daughters," Sir Walter Pike said, and his tone wasn't merely disrespectful, it was *exceedingly* disrespectful: a verbal sneer of contempt.

Mayhew took a step closer. "You would be *lucky* to have Miss Culpepper as companion to your daughters," he told the man. "She's the most outstanding female I've ever met. She has more fortitude and more character than you will *ever* have! She's too *good* for you and your daughters, you small-minded, pompous *prat*."

Sir Walter stopped glaring at Miss Culpepper and glared at Mayhew instead. He drew himself up. "You are out of order, Lieutenant!"

"No, *you* are!" Mayhew thundered back. "You've jumped to conclusions—*offensive* conclusions—without even *asking* what happened, and *then* you've had the insolence to insult a lady *to her face*. Heaven help the Empire if you're an example of His Majesty's diplomats, because you're an ill-bred, ill-mannered *buffoon*."

Sir Walter flushed an ugly shade of red. "Who the devil are you?" he demanded, trying to look down his nose at Mayhew, which, given that he was a good four inches shorter than Mayhew, didn't work.

"Lieutenant William Mayhew," Mayhew informed him. "*Lord* Mayhew's son." And he enjoyed saying that 'Lord,' because this stout, pompous man was merely a baronet. "*I* am the person responsible for Miss Culpepper missing the stagecoach, and *I* am responsible for her appearance. She is entirely blameless! Which you would *know*, if you'd bothered to *ask* her what happened, instead of assuming the worst!"

Sir Walter flushed even redder, and glared at Mayhew.

Mayhew glared back at him and realized, suddenly, that they had accumulated a sizable audience. At least a dozen people were watching agog from the doorways to taproom, coffee room, and kitchen.

Sir Walter came to the same realization a split second later. The color in his face mounted until it was almost puce. He took a step sideways, towards the street.

Mayhew stepped sideways, too, planting himself firmly in the man's path. "Apologize to Miss Culpepper," he said, in a hard voice.

Sir Walter firmed his jaw. "Out of my way, Lieutenant."

Mayhew didn't move. "*Apologize to her.*"

Sir Walter glowered at him, and then turned to Miss Culpepper and said, stiffly and insincerely, "I apologize if my words were offensive, Miss Culpepper."

She nodded coolly. "Your apology is accepted, Sir Walter."

Sir Walter turned back to Mayhew, his face still puce with rage and humiliation. "Your commanding officer will hear about this, Lieutenant," he said in a low, threatening voice.

"I hope so," Mayhew said. He bared his teeth at the man in a smile. "Colonel Barraclough, of the Rifle Brigade. He's a stickler for *gentlemanly* behavior."

Sir Water flushed even redder, which Mayhew hadn't thought possible. He lifted his chin, sidled around Mayhew, and headed for the door to the street. His gait was more scurry than strut.

Mayhew watched until the door swung shut behind the man, then turned back to Miss Culpepper. His audience was still staring at him, agog. Miss Culpepper was staring at him, too. He couldn't quite discern her expression. She didn't look angry, although she had ample reason to be. Not only was he the author of every misfortune she'd experienced in the past day and night, he had just subjected her to an extremely unpleasant and very public scene.

"I beg your pardon," he told both Miss Culpepper and the innkeeper.

"Not at all," the innkeeper said, and Mayhew had the feeling that the man held no very high opinion of Sir Walter.

Miss Culpepper said nothing.

The innkeeper clapped his hands briskly. "Back to work."

Half their audience disappeared. The other half didn't.

Mayhew looked at Miss Culpepper, and at those lingering spectators, and at the open doorway to the private parlor that Sir Walter had occupied.

"May we?" he asked the innkeeper, tipping his head at the parlor and the privacy it offered.

"Of course," the innkeeper said. "I'll set the water heating for you, Miss Culpepper. Your bath will be ready shortly."

"Thank you." Miss Culpepper glanced at Mayhew, her expression still indecipherable, then turned and entered the parlor, leaning lightly on the walking stick.

CHAPTER TWELVE

Mayhew made to follow Miss Culpepper, remembered the kittens, and caught up the basket. He stepped hastily into the parlor, closed the door behind him, set the basket down again, and turned to face her.

Miss Culpepper had crossed to the small diamond-paned window casement and was looking out. Her back was to him and he could see every mud stain, every wrinkle, every snagged thread.

No wonder Sir Walter had assumed the worst.

"I'm very sorry," Mayhew said contritely. "I shouldn't have said half of what I said and I *definitely* shouldn't have said it so loudly and so publicly."

Miss Culpepper turned to face him. To his astonishment, he saw that she was smiling. It was a small smile, not enough to set the dimples dancing in her cheeks, but enough to tell him that she wasn't furious with him.

Which she really *ought* to be.

She'd been harangued in public because of him. She'd lost her chance to go to Vienna because of him.

"I'm very sorry," Mayhew said again. He felt a rising tide of shame, and on the heels of shame, dismay. He'd accused Sir Walter of ill-breeding, but *he'd* been ill-bred, too, losing his temper like that.

It's better to fix things than lose one's temper—Colonel Culpepper's maxim, that, and Mayhew had indisputably lost his temper. Even worse, he couldn't fix this mess. Miss Culpepper's position with the Pikes was irrevocably lost.

But he *would* fix the things that *could* be fixed.

"May I escort you back to Kingston upon Thames, Miss Culpepper? That is . . . if my behavior hasn't given you a repugnance of me."

Miss Culpepper cocked her head at him. "Repugnance?"

"Your father disapproved of displays of temper. I must presume that you do, too."

Miss Culpepper's dimples finally made an appearance. "Do you think my father never lost his temper, Lieutenant? You'd be wrong, then, for he most certainly did!"

"You're not angry with me?" Mayhew asked cautiously.

"Angry?" Miss Culpepper's dimples deepened. "Lieutenant, you were shockingly uncomplimentary to Sir Walter, but you were *exceedingly* complimentary to me."

Some of the tension in Mayhew's chest eased.

"If my father had been here, he'd have given Sir Walter exactly such a raking down as you did," Miss Culpepper said.

"He would have?"

"Yes." She pursed her lips thoughtfully. "Although he probably would have been louder."

"But . . . your position in Vienna—"

"It would have been interesting to live in Vienna for a spell," Miss Culpepper said. "But I doubt I would have enjoyed being part of Sir Walter's household. As you so eloquently put it, he's a pompous prat."

Yes, he had called Sir Walter that. Loudly.

Mayhew didn't know whether to grimace or laugh, so he did both. Then his laughter faded and his grimace faded and he just stood in the middle of the private parlor, looking at Miss Culpepper.

"I meant it," he said quietly. "You are the most outstanding female I've ever met."

Miss Culpepper's cheeks became an adorable shade of pink. She looked down at the muddy toes of her half boots.

"The last eighteen hours have been both irksome and uncomfortable. Most people would have complained, but you haven't. Not once! Not when you missed the stagecoach. Not when you got muddy and wet. Not even when you *hurt* yourself and had to sleep in a barn! You've borne everything with fortitude and good humor."

Miss Culpepper's cheeks became even pinker. "You make me sound like a paragon, but the sad truth of it is that I've enjoyed it, Lieutenant." She glanced up at him through her eyelashes, not flirtatiously, but a little uncertainly, as if she was doubtful of his reaction. "Even the mud. Even the storm."

"I'm shocked," Mayhew said, a smile growing on his face. "Deeply shocked." He took a step closer. "And extremely relieved. And . . . enchanted."

Miss Culpepper blushed ferociously at that last word. She fixed her attention on her half boots again.

Mayhew laughed softly and reached out and tipped up her chin.

Her eyes met his shyly, and Mayhew felt an almost overwhelming urge to bend his head and kiss those rosy lips.

The urge was so strong that he almost succumbed to it—but he'd just comprehensively upended Miss Culpepper's life and he needed to mend that before he did anything else.

"What would you like to do now?" he asked her. "Tell me, and I'll make it happen. Would you like to return to your aunt? Or would you like to come to Southampton with me? You can stay with my sister and her husband—there would be no impropriety, I assure you!— they're *very* respectable. He's a magistrate, you know."

"Southampton?" Miss Culpepper said.

"Yes." Mayhew's lungs squeezed tight. "And . . . if you wish . . . I can apply for permission to marry you." He felt himself blush, and continued resolutely on: "But I'll only do that if it's what you truly want, because we don't know each other very well and perhaps we ought to correspond for a while, and I *am* only a lieutenant."

"My father was only a lieutenant when he married my mother," Miss Culpepper said.

Mayhew's heart gave a hopeful leap. Did that mean what he thought it meant? "Tell me what you'd like to do, Miss Culpepper. What you would *most* like to do."

She smiled at him. "What I most want to do is marry you."

"Now?" he said cautiously. "Or in a year—"

"Now."

Mayhew's heart didn't just leap in his chest, it soared. "Are you certain?" He searched her face for doubts, for hesitancy.

"I'm certain," Miss Culpepper said. "Maybe I don't know everything about you, but I *do* know that we're cut from the same cloth, you and I."

"Indeed, we are." He lifted one hand and touched her cheek, ghosting his thumb over the spot where her dimple was hidden.

"I think I could search all of England and not find someone who suits me as well as you do," Miss Culpepper told him.

"Nor I you." Mayhew stroked her cheek again, lightly, reverently, marveling at the softness of her skin.

She smiled, and a dimple sprang to life beneath his thumb. "And it's not just because you're a soldier. I think I should wish to marry you even if you weren't."

"You do, do you?" he teased her. "Are you certain about that?"

The dimple deepened. "Yes."

"I'm very pleased to hear it," Mayhew said. "Because I've decided to sell my commission and become a farmer. A pig farmer. In Wiltshire."

Miss Culpepper laughed. "No, you haven't."

"No, I haven't," Mayhew agreed. He gave in to temptation and tipped up her chin and kissed her lightly. Her lips were exactly as he'd imagined, soft and warm, but also shy and trembling, which he hadn't expected, and a sudden realization flashed through him: Willemina Culpepper had never been kissed before.

Mayhew drew back slightly and looked down at her.

Miss Culpepper gazed back, shyness written on her face, and it made his heart squeeze in his chest to think that he was the first man to kiss this remarkable woman.

Shyness wasn't the only thing written on her face. Trust was there, too, but trepidation and fear weren't—which didn't surprise him, because his Willie didn't have a timid bone in her body. His Willie was brave and confident and indomitable—and gazing at him not just with shyness and trust, but also with *expectancy*.

Mayhew could see that she wanted him to kiss her again, so he did, bending his head, touching his lips to hers. It was a kiss that was gentle and tender and friendly, affectionate. A kiss that said *hello* and *I love you* and *this is our beginning*. Then he drew back and took both her hands in his. "I know I'm only a lieutenant, but I *have* been tapped for a captaincy. I'll be a major within five years, and a colonel before I'm forty. I promise you."

"I don't mind if you're a lieutenant forever," Miss Culpepper told him. "But I have no doubt that you'll be an excellent colonel."

"I hope to be."

"I *know* you'll be," she said. "I have confidence in you. And I have confidence in *us*. You and I were destined to be together."

Mayhew laughed at that and kissed her again, lightly, and whispered, "I have confidence in us, too," against her mouth, and then he kissed her again, not quite so lightly, and her lips parted for him and the tip of her tongue touched the tip of his and a shiver went through him from head to toe.

Mayhew drew her closer. He kissed her in wonder and joy and delight, and she kissed him back eagerly. His arms were around her, drawing her close, and her hands were fisted in his jacket, pulling him even closer, and the dance of their mouths became deeper and more intimate, more urgent . . .

Mayhew reluctantly broke the kiss. He lifted his head and tried to catch his breath, tried to catch his wits, but it was practically impossible to do either when Miss Culpepper was clutching his jacket and gazing up at him, looking flushed and breathless and utterly adorable.

Much as he wanted to keep kissing her—much as he wanted to do a *lot* more than merely kiss her—now was not the time and here was not the place.

It took effort to let her go, effort to uncurl her fingers from his jacket, pick up the walking stick from where it had fallen on the floor and hand it to her, effort to take a half step back.

Miss Culpepper looked as disappointed as he was, but she didn't protest. She knew as well as he did that a servant could enter the parlor at any moment.

Mayhew took her free hand in his. "A postponement," he said, sealing the promise by laying a light kiss on her knuckles. "Hopefully not a long one, but I *do* need permission to marry. I can't imagine Barraclough will refuse. He knows you, after all! He is in France, though, and it'll take time." He grimaced at thought of exactly how *much* time. Weeks, damn it. "But I'll try at the Horse Guards first. It's possible someone there will give me permission. General Seaton is a family friend. He sponsored me into the Rifles. He might—"

"General Sir George Seaton?"

Mayhew nodded.

"Seaton was a good friend of my father's."

"Was he?" Mayhew began to feel more hopeful. "I'll apply to him first, then. If he feels he can't sanction it, we'll have to wait for Barraclough's permission, but I *know* we'll get that."

Miss Culpepper nodded. She'd grown up in the army; she understood how these things worked. Officers couldn't marry without permission.

Mayhew released her hand and made himself take another step back, when what he really wanted to do was step closer and gather Miss Culpepper in his arms and kiss her until they were breathless and dizzy. "What's going to happen now is that you're going to go upstairs and have a bath and change into dry clothes," he told her. "And then we'll go to Southampton, and tomorrow I'll return to London and speak with General Seaton." He waited a beat, and then said, "If that meets with your approval?"

She nodded. "It does."

"Good." Mayhew crossed to the door and took hold of the handle.

Miss Culpepper came to join him, leaning on the walking stick. Her nearness, the smile on her lips, the smile in her eyes as she gazed up at him, made his heart feel as if it had grown several sizes in his chest.

"May I call you Willie?" he asked.

She nodded.

"May I call you *Sweet* Willie?"

She blushed, and nodded again. "If you wish."

He did wish. Very much. "I hope you'll call me Will," he said.

"Will and Willie." She laughed at that and shook her head, and then she tucked her free hand into his, a gesture of trust and familiarity that made Mayhew's heart leap absurdly. "We really *were* made for each other, weren't we?"

"We were."

"I'm glad we missed the stagecoach in Abbots Worthy," Miss Culpepper told him. "And that the horse cast a shoe. And that we fell in the ford and got caught in that storm and had to spend the night in a barn. I'm glad for *all* of it."

"So am I," Mayhew said, and he was. More glad than he'd ever been of anything in his life.

He gazed down at her, knowing that this was a moment to be treasured: the coaching inn, this parlor, Willemina Culpepper holding his hand. And then he realized that while this moment was wonderful, what was even more wonderful was that they'd be able to hold each other's hands for the *rest of their lives*.

Mayhew's throat tightened and it became ridiculously hard to swallow. He managed it, though, and then he released her hand and opened the door and said, "Go and take your bath. I'll wait here. Would you like me to order breakfast sent up to you?"

"Yes, please." Miss Culpepper smiled at him, grubby and bedraggled and vivid and beautiful.

Mayhew smiled back, feeling so damned *happy* and so damned *lucky*. How had this happened? This combination of mischance and pure good fortune? How had he ended up betrothed to Sweet Willie Culpepper?

A maid appeared and bobbed a curtsy. "Are you wantin' to go to your room, ma'am?"

"Yes, please."

Mayhew watched them cross the vestibule and climb the stairs— the tidy maid in her apron and mob cap, and the unbelievably messy colonel's daughter in her mud-stained dress and bedraggled bonnet, limping ever so slightly, leaning on the walking stick. Miss Culpepper sent him a smile before disappearing from sight and Mayhew smiled helplessly back. Then he uttered a laugh of disbelief and wonder and sheer joy, and went in search of the innkeeper to arrange for a hot breakfast for Miss Culpepper, and a hot breakfast for himself, and milk for the kittens, and a carriage to take them the ten miles to Southampton, where *his* dry clothes were waiting.

CHAPTER THIRTEEN

Six days later . . .

When Mayhew had said that his brother-in-law was a magistrate, Willie had pictured someone serious and stern, with gray sideburns. Sir John Belton *did* have gray sideburns, but thereafter reality had diverged from what she'd imagined. Sir John was jolly rather than stern and his eyes twinkled with good humor. His wife had twinkling eyes, too, and their six-year-old twins were giggling, harum-scarum delights.

The Beltons had welcomed her into their home without question, and it should have been awkward, staying with people who were practically strangers, except that after the first half hour the Beltons hadn't been strangers at all. They'd been friends. They'd been *family*.

The time while Mayhew was in London had passed swiftly. Willie had rested her ankle for the first day, then spent the next two days in a blur of kittens and hide-and-seek and building forts out of furniture. They'd been good days, wonderful days even, but nothing had equaled the moment when Mayhew had returned, and she'd run down the sweeping curve of the marble staircase and seen him standing in the entrance hall, handsome in his green Rifleman's uniform.

Willie had laughed and cried when she'd greeted him, and she'd laughed and cried some more when Mayhew had told her that he had a special license in his pocket and General Seaton's permission to marry. And then she'd hugged him again, and again, and *again*.

She'd kissed him, later that afternoon, when they'd had a moment alone together in the drawing room, and that was how she'd measured the rest of their time in Southampton: by kisses. Two the day he'd arrived. Three more the next day. And then yesterday, six. *Six*. Because yesterday had been special. The day before their wedding, the day the Beltons had hosted a dinner party in their honor.

There'd been dancing after the dinner, with a small orchestra, and Willie had stood up with Sir John Belton twice, but she'd danced all the other dances with Mayhew, because it was a private ball and it was the night before her wedding and she could dance every single dance with her fiancé if she wished to—and she *had* wished to.

Mayhew had kissed her after the ball, and he'd kissed her this morning before the wedding ceremony, and again afterwards, and he'd kissed her quite a few times in the six hours since they'd departed from Southampton. So many times, in fact, that Willie had quite lost count of today's kisses.

Last week, when she'd left London on the stagecoach, she'd been so excited that she'd been hard pressed not to wriggle in her seat. Today, as she sat in a post-chaise while afternoon ripened into early evening, she wasn't excited in a wriggle-in-her-seat way; she was excited in a huge, uplifting way. She almost felt as if she was floating.

As of ten o'clock this morning, she was *married*.

She was no longer Willemina Culpepper. She was Willemina Mayhew, and she was sitting in a post-chaise with her husband, en route to Oxfordshire to meet Mayhew's parents and brothers, and then they were going to Kingston upon Thames so that he might meet her aunt, and *then* they were going to France. Home to the army. Home to the Rifle Brigade.

Willie turned her head and found Mayhew watching her. "Hungry?" he asked. "Tired?"

Willie shook her head. "Neither. Happy."

He grinned at her and leaned in for another kiss. "So am I," he whispered against her lips.

The post-chaise slowed to a trot while they kissed, and then slowed further. The wheels rattled over cobblestones. They drew apart. Mayhew looked out the window. "We're coming into Nettlebed."

Nettlebed, where they'd break their journey for the night. Nettlebed, where they would consummate their marriage.

Willie gave a tiny shiver that was equal parts anticipation and excitement, with a dash of nervousness thrown in.

She gave another of those delicious little shivers when they climbed down from the carriage, and yet another when the innkeeper showed them to their bedchamber. It was a handsome room, with a washstand and a dressing table and a four-poster bed hung with green curtains.

"Does it meet with your approval?" Mayhew asked, smiling down at her.

"It does," Willie said, and another tingling shiver ran through her, from her scalp to the tips of her toes.

"The private parlor is taken, but you'll be quite comfortable dining in the coffee room," the innkeeper said, and showed them where the coffee room was, and while he was doing that more travelers arrived, an elderly man and his wife.

The man could have been anything in his younger days—a clerk, a farmer, an apothecary—but Willie looked at his weather-beaten face and his bearing, upright despite the way age had curved his spine, and thought *soldier*.

"We're full, sir," the innkeeper said. "Try one of the other inns."

"We have. We've tried them all." The old soldier's voice held a Yorkshire brogue and an indefinable hint of something that Willie's ears identified as *sergeant*.

"Then I'm afraid you'll have to drive on to Nuffield, sir."

"We'll take anything," the old sergeant said. "Even truckle beds in the stables." He looked exhausted, and his wife even more so.

The innkeeper hesitated. "I have a room up in the attic, but it's only fit for servants."

Willie exchanged a glance with Mayhew. He lifted his eyebrows fractionally, a silent question to which she returned a nod.

"We'll take it," the old soldier said.

"No, *we'll* take it," Mayhew said. "You and your wife may have our room."

Three pairs of startled eyes swung around to look at him.

"Thank you, Lieutenant," the old man said, assessing Mayhew's rank with the merest glance at his shoulder. "But it's not necessary."

"We insist," Mayhew said. "Which regiment were you?"

The man hesitated, and then said, "The Fifty-First."

"You were a sergeant?" Mayhew asked.

"Yes."

"Well, Sergeant, we'd be pleased if you would take our room."

"You'd prefer not to climb all those stairs, I think," Willie said, with a smile at the elderly couple.

The old soldier wavered for a few more seconds, then gave a stiff, courteous bow. "Thank you, we would be most grateful."

THEIR ORIGINAL BEDCHAMBER had been well-appointed. Their new one was not. The ceiling sloped so steeply that Mayhew had to duck his head, the floorboards were bare, the bowl in the washstand was chipped and the four-poster bed was missing one of its posts, but the room had the quaintest of tiny-paned windows through which the setting sun cast a golden glow.

There were dust balls on the floor and the bed linen wasn't clean, a fact that discomfited the innkeeper greatly. He went as red as a lobster, promised to have the floor swept and the sheets changed immediately, and hurried back down the steep, narrow stairs, shouting for his servants.

Mayhew glanced at her. "What do you think?"

Willie looked at that delightful little window and the bed with its three posts. "I love it," she declared.

He laughed, and said, "Of course you do," and she could tell from his expression that he was thinking about kissing her again.

Willie stepped closer and tucked her hand into his. "Thank you for changing rooms. You don't mind, do you?"

"Mind? Of course not." Mayhew drew her even closer and bent his head—and then stepped back as someone clattered up the uncarpeted stairs. A maid hurried into the room with a broom. On her heels was another servant bearing an armful of bed linen.

Willie and Mayhew retreated downstairs. The coffee room was comfortably snug, with a low-beamed ceiling and a small fire burning in the grate. Two of the little tea tables were occupied by other travelers, and the hearth was occupied, too—by a basket containing half a dozen kittens.

"Look!" Willie said, and headed for the kittens.

Dusk fell, that magical gloaming hour. Willie sat near the fire with her husband alongside her and a tortoiseshell kitten on her lap, drinking home-brewed cider. The cider was crisp on her tongue, tart and sweet at the same time. She sipped it and felt happy enough to burst.

They ate a raised pie for their dinner, and the pastry was buttery and the meat tender and fragrant, and while they ate, Willie said, "I think the Fates were watching over us the day we met."

Mayhew smiled at her over the rim of his tankard. "The Fates?"

"Yes," Willie said, and although she was joking, she also wasn't *quite* joking. "I think they made certain that we had enough time to become properly acquainted."

"They did, did they?"

"Yes," she said again. "Because if those things hadn't happened—the horseshoe and the storm and the tree falling over—then we'd have sat in the same carriage for a whole day and never known we're meant to be together." Her throat tightened at that thought.

Perhaps Mayhew's throat tightened, too, because he didn't laugh at her; instead, he raised his tankard. "To the Fates," he said. "And to *us*."

They touched brims and drank, and despite that fact that it was mostly a joke, the moment felt weighty and ceremonious.

Servants cleared their plates, lit the candles, and closed the shutters. Other guests came and went, eating, drinking, reading the *Gazette* beside the fire. A kitten found its way onto Willie's lap again, the same kitten that had been there before: a tortoiseshell with one ginger paw. She stroked it and listened to the tiny vibrato of its purr and thought that no one had ever had such a good wedding day as she was having.

A faint melody crept into the coffee room, teasing her ears. "Where's that music coming from?" Mayhew asked, when a servant came to place more coals on the fire.

"Taproom," the woman said. "The Barrett brothers brought their fiddles in again."

Mayhew glanced at Willie. "Would you like to listen for a while?"

If Willie had been by herself she would never have dared venture into a taproom; in the company of her husband, she did. A rollicking jig spilled out when Mayhew opened the door. Willie looked around with interest, but the taproom was no dangerous den of iniquity; it looked very much like the coffee room, although the furniture was a little rougher, trestle tables and wooden benches instead of tea tables and chairs. The clientele was a little rougher, too, and quite a lot rowdier. Not rowdy in a bellicose way, but rowdy in a loud, cheerful way, people stamping and clapping in time to the music.

They found space at a bench and a servingman brought them

more home-brewed cider. Willie settled in to enjoy herself. The
tunes weren't tunes she knew, but they were lively and infectious,
and she sipped her cider and tapped her feet to the music and felt
happiness bubble in her veins.

Mayhew got up to speak with one of the fiddlers, and when he
returned to their bench he didn't sit, but held out his hands to her.

Willie let him pull her to her feet.

The fiddler struck up a new tune, and called out, "A dance for
the newlyweds! Married today, they was."

A whoop went up, and the second fiddle joined the first, and thus
it was that Willie danced her first dance as Mrs. Mayhew.

She had danced in a private ballroom last night, wearing pearls in
her hair and silk slippers on her feet. Those dances had been formal—
the waltz, the quadrille, the cotillion. Tonight's dance wasn't formal
at all. It was fast and foot-stomping. Mayhew whirled her around and
around, while the fiddlers fiddled and their audience clapped and
stamped and whooped, and when it was over, Willie clung to her
husband, breathless and laughing, and she just *knew* that no one had
ever had such a marvelous wedding day as she was having.

They returned to their wooden bench. Mayhew put an arm
around her shoulders and Willie leaned into the heat of his body and
enjoyed this gift of an evening: the strangers, the music, the
good cheer.

She sipped the last of her cider and smothered a yawn.

"Time for bed?" Mayhew asked.

"Time for bed."

They went up the steep, narrow stairs and discovered that their
luggage had been brought up, the candles lit, and the bedclothes
turned back. Mayhew eyed the three-poster bed somewhat dubiously.
"We can wait, you know. It doesn't have to be tonight."

"It's good luck to consummate one's marriage in a three-poster
bed," Willie told him.

His eyes creased at the corners with amusement. "Is it, now?"

"*Very* good luck. Quite auspicious, in fact."

Mayhew laughed. "Auspicious?"

"Exceptionally auspicious."

He took both of her hands in his and smiled fondly down at her. "Well, then. Let's not wait."

CHAPTER FOURTEEN

Mayhew had undressed a woman before, but it had never been like this, unhurried, a sweet and slow disrobing, minutes slipping by in quiet murmurs and gentle touches, in the whisper of fabric sliding over skin, in the feather-light brush of his fingertips across the nape of Willie's neck, in reverent kisses placed on her bare shoulders.

When they were both standing naked Mayhew couldn't help but gaze at Willie, because she was so damned beautiful, all creamy skin and slender curves, sweet rosy lips and sweet rosy nipples.

Willie gazed back, taking him in from head to toe, a blatant perusal that made his balls tighten and heat flush beneath his skin. Then she tilted her head and said, "You look very fine, Lieutenant Mayhew."

Mayhew laughed—somewhat breathlessly, and said—somewhat hoarsely, "You look a great deal more than fine, Mrs. Mayhew."

She laughed, too, and Mayhew realized in that moment that his hands were trembling slightly. He wasn't sure whether the tremble came from his eagerness to make love to Willie or his fear of hurting her. He swallowed past the sudden lump in his throat. "It might hurt a little bit."

"I know," Willie said. "Your sister told me about it."

Mayhew blinked at her. "My sister did?"

Willie nodded. "She said it would probably hurt the first time, maybe even the first few times, but after that it would become a lot more enjoyable."

Mayhew stared at her, bemused. His *sister* had talked to Willie about *sex*?

His expression appeared to amuse Willie, because she laughed, and then she climbed up on the three-poster bed, giving him a tantalizing glimpse of her derrière as she did so. "Come to bed, Lieutenant Mayhew."

Mayhew did.

He'd never felt shy when making love to a woman before, but he found himself a little shy tonight. Willie was shy, too, of course—shy and blushing, but she was also eager and trusting. She laughed at him while he worshiped every one of her fingertips with kisses, and she giggled when he nipped and teased his way down her throat, and she gasped and squirmed as he kissed his way up her inner thighs.

He did his best not to hurt her, entering her more slowly than he'd ever entered a woman before, more carefully. He watched her face intently while he sank in those final inches and he thought that he'd mostly succeeded. Willie looked flushed and wide-eyed and a little disconcerted, but not pained.

"How does it feel?" he asked.

Her lips pursed thoughtfully. "Odd."

It didn't feel odd to Mayhew; it felt unbelievably good.

Willie shifted her hips slightly, making the breath catch in his throat. She heard it, and grinned up at him. "How does it feel to you?"

"Good," Mayhew said, and the word was almost a groan. He was trembling—the muscles in his belly, in his thighs, in his arms as he braced himself above her. Trembling with the need to move and the equally strong need to stay still until he was certain he wasn't hurting her.

He bent his head and kissed Willie. Their lips clung together for a long moment, and then he began to move—slow slide, slow glide—coaxing a rhythm between them.

Willie enjoyed it. He could tell from the way she gasped and the tiny, guttural moans she uttered, and also from the way that she moved, clutching his arms, arching into him—and he could tell from the way she laughed at the moment of her climax. Mayhew laughed when she laughed and climaxed when she climaxed, because it was impossible not to do either, and then he held her tightly while they both floated down from that soaring high.

He would have liked to have stayed inside her all night, but he couldn't, so he carefully withdrew and cleaned her with a handkerchief, and then he blew out the candles and crawled into bed and tucked Willie into the curve of his body, her back pressing snugly to his chest, his arm securely around her waist.

They lay curled together in the cozy warmth of the three-poster bed. Willie stroked the back of his hand. "I know your sister said it would get better, but I honestly can't imagine it."

Mayhew couldn't imagine it either.

WHEN HE WOKE, it was dawn and his wife was still in his arms. He pressed his face into her hair and inhaled her scent—orange blossom—and wondered how he'd been so damned lucky as to meet Sweet Willie Culpepper, let alone marry her.

Mayhew tightened his arm around her, but only a little bit; he didn't want to wake her. But it appeared that she was already awake, for her fingers intertwined with his. "Careful," she whispered. "Don't disturb the kitten."

"Kitten?" He lifted his head and peered over her, and there on the pillow was a tortoiseshell kitten, curled up asleep. He found that he wasn't surprised. It felt almost like fate. "How long has it been there?"

"I don't know. It was there when I woke."

Mayhew was fairly certain it was the same kitten that had sat on Willie's lap in the coffee room. "It must like you."

Their voices woke the kitten. It blinked its eyes opened and yawned, pink-tongued and sharp-toothed. It looked adorable. Almost as adorable as Willie.

Willie slipped her hand free from his clasp and reached out and stroked the kitten. "It was born a marmalade tabby, I think, but someone took it by the paw and dipped it in a cauldron of magic and stardust, and now it looks like the night sky."

Mayhew huffed a laugh. "Very poetic." And accurate, too; the kitten's coat did look like a night sky speckled with stars. Except for that one golden paw.

Willie carefully rubbed between the kitten's ears. Mayhew heard the tiny rumble of its purr. "My brigade major had a kitten that looked a bit like that," he told her. "He found it at Badajoz, carried it around with him for months."

"He did?" Willie said, and he heard her surprise.

"He did. His name's Reynolds. Major Reynolds." Mayhew smothered a yawn. "Actually, it was Reynolds who rescued Scout and Mr. Bellyrub." Or Princess Plum Blossom and Prince Purr-a-lot, as they'd been renamed by the twins.

"Is he on furlough, too?"

"Sold out after Waterloo. Henry Wright's our brigade major now. He's first rate. You'll like him."

"I'm sure I will," Willie said, and then, "Colonel Barraclough didn't mind one of his officers keeping a kitten while on campaign?"

"Not at all. He was rather fond of it. Was forever bringing scraps for it to eat."

"Was he now?" Willie said, her tone thoughtful.

Mayhew yawned again. "I think Barraclough likes cats."

Willie was silent for a moment, and then she said, "Good," and tickled the kitten under its chin with a fingertip.

Mayhew watched her fingertip and heard that tiny purr and

made a belated realization. "We're taking the kitten with us, aren't we?"

"Yes," Willie said. "It's our wedding gift from the Fates."

Mayhew didn't laugh at that statement because he had a feeling she might be right. "What shall we name it?"

"Stardust," Willie said, and tickled the kitten under its chin again.

Mayhew pressed his face into his wife's hair and inhaled her orange blossom scent, and then he laughed softly, his breath stirring her messy ringlets. "I love you," he told her.

Willie stopped stroking the kitten. Her fingers intertwined with his again. "I love you, too."

Mayhew inhaled another orange-blossom-scented breath and thought that he couldn't possibly be any happier than he was at that moment, lying in a three-poster bed, holding his wife, while a kitten purred on the pillow alongside them.

Then he remembered that this was the first of many such mornings together, and he discovered that it *was* possible to be even happier. He gathered Willie closer, tucking her warmth and her soft, slender curves in tightly to his body. "This is going to be so good," he whispered in her ear. "Us, together, forever."

"It most certainly is!" Willie said.

And it was.

AUTHOR'S NOTE

The kittens in *Lieutenant Mayhew's Catastrophes* are based on a litter of day-old kittens that I found several years ago. I raised them until they were old enough to be rehomed, and I found it fascinating how quickly they developed strong and disparate personalities. One of them was an utterly fearless and very fluffy little girl whose greatest desire was to explore. Her adventures were often quite hair-raising. She had an extremely laid-back brother who adored lying in my hand and having his belly rubbed. He would close his eyes and purr blissfully.

Scout, Mr. Bellyrub, and their siblings made their debut in **Lady Isabella's Ogre** (excerpt below). Lieutenant Mayhew made his debut in that novel, too. I've always wanted to know what happened to him when he headed off with two kittens in a basket, and I'm delighted to finally have the chance to tell his story.

If you'd like to be notified whenever I release a new book or have deals and discounts, please sign up for **my newsletter** or follow me on **BookBub**. My latest novel is **Primrose and the Dreadful Duke** (excerpt below), and the next one, **Octavius and the Perfect Governess**, will be out in early 2020.

Happy reading!
  Emily

PRIMROSE AND THE DREADFUL DUKE — EXCERPT

Primrose and the Dreadful Duke by Emily Larkin

An irrepressible duke, a bookish spinster, a devious murderer ... Regency house parties have never been so hazardous!

Oliver Dasenby is the most infuriating man Primrose Garland has ever known. He may be her brother's best friend, but he has an atrocious sense of humor. Eight years in the cavalry hasn't taught him solemnity, nor has the unexpected inheritance of a dukedom.

But when Oliver inherited his dukedom, it appears that he also inherited a murderer.

Oliver might be dreadfully annoying, but Primrose doesn't want him dead. She's going to make certain he survives his inheritance—and the only way to do that is to help him catch the murderer!

Oliver's next partner was Lady Primrose Garland, the sister of his oldest friend, Rhodes Garland—and the only unmarried young lady in the room whom he knew *didn't* want to marry him.

"Lady Prim," he said, bowing over her hand with a flourish. "You're a jewel that outshines all others."

Primrose was too well-bred to roll her eyes in public, but her eyelids twitched ever so slightly, which told him she wanted to. "Still afflicted by hyperbole, I see."

"You use such long words, Prim," he said admiringly.

"And you use such foolish ones."

Oliver tutted at her. "That's not very polite, Prim."

Primrose ignored this comment. She placed her hand on his sleeve. Together they walked onto the dance floor and took their places.

"Did I ever tell you about my uniform, Prim? The coat was dark blue, and the facing—"

"I don't wish to hear about your uniform."

"Manners, Prim. Manners."

Primrose came very close to smiling. She caught herself just in time. "Shall we discuss books while we dance? Have you read Wolf's *Prolegomena ad Homerum*?"

"Of course I haven't," Oliver said. "Dash it, Prim, I'm not an intellectual."

The musicians played the opening bars. Primrose curtsied, Oliver bowed. "I really *must* tell you about my uniform. The coat was dark blue—"

Primrose ignored him. "Wolf proposes that *The Iliad*—"

"With a red sash at the waist—"

"And *The Odyssey* were in fact—"

"And silver lace at the cuffs—"

"The work of more than one poet."

"And a crested Tarleton helmet," Oliver finished triumphantly.

They eyed each other as they went through the steps of the dance. Oliver could tell from the glint in her eyes and the way her lips were tucked in at the corners that Primrose was trying not to laugh. He was trying not to laugh, too.

"You're a fiddle-faddle fellow," Primrose told him severely.

"Alliteration," Oliver said. "Well done, Prim."

Primrose's lips tucked in even more tightly at the corners. If they'd been anywhere but a ballroom he was certain she'd have stamped her foot, something she'd done frequently when they were children.

"Heaven only knows why I agreed to dance with you," she told him tartly.

"Because it increases your consequence to be seen with me. I *am* a duke, you know." He puffed out his chest and danced the next few steps with a strut.

"Stop that," she hissed under her breath.

"Stop what?" Oliver said innocently, still strutting his steps.

"Honestly, Daisy, you're impossible."

Oliver stopped strutting. "No one's called me that in years."

"Impossible? I find that hard to believe." Her voice was dry.

"Daisy." It had been Primrose's childhood nickname for him, in retaliation for him calling her Lady Prim-and-Proper.

Oliver had been back in England for nearly a month now, and that month had been filled with moments of recognition, some tiny flickers—his brain acknowledging something as familiar and then moving on—others strong visceral reactions. He experienced one of those latter moments now. It took him by the throat and wouldn't let him speak for several seconds.

Because Primrose had called him Daisy.

Oliver cleared his throat. "Tell me about that book, Prim. What's it called? Prolapse ad nauseam?"

"*Prolegomena ad Homerum.*"

Oliver pulled a face. "Sounds very dull. Me, I much prefer a good novel. Especially if there's a ghost in it, or a headless horseman."

And they were off again, arguing amiably about books, the moment of emotion safely in the past. Primrose knew a lot about books. In fact, Oliver suspected that she preferred books to people—which would be why she was still unmarried at twenty-seven. Primrose was a duke's daughter *and* she was pretty—that ash-blonde hair, those cool blue eyes. If she wanted to be married, she would be.

Therefore, he deduced that she didn't want to marry. Which made her unique in a ballroom filled with young ladies on the hunt for husbands.

Order your copy of **Primrose and the Dreadful Duke**, and read on for an excerpt from **Lady Isabella's Ogre**.

LADY ISABELLA'S OGRE — EXCERPT

Lady Isabella's Ogre by Emily Larkin

Lady Isabella Knox enjoys her independence. She collects strays— dogs, kittens, runaway brides—but she has no intention of collecting a husband.

Major Nicholas Reynolds returns from the Battle of Waterloo a hero. He's had enough of soldiering; all he wants now is a bride . . . but his scarred face sends young ladies fleeing—literally.

When a slip of her tongue brands the major an ogre—and his chances of marriage disintegrate—Isabella sets out to undo the harm she inadvertently caused. How better to revive the major's marriage prospects than for the two of them to indulge in a make-believe flirtation? They both know it's not real, so where's the danger?

But Isabella is soon in over her head—and so is Major Reynolds.

"If you'll forgive my impertinence, Major Reynolds . . . what is it you're looking for in a bride?"

"I want peace and quiet," Nicholas said. "I want a marriage with no arguments."

"Quiet," Lady Isabella said. She glanced around the ballroom, a thoughtful crease on her brow. "Have you considered Miss Thornton? She's—"

"Too old."

"Too old?" Her eyes flew to his, startled. "But she's barely twenty-two!"

"I want a young bride." Too late, Nicholas realized that Lady Isabella was well past the age of twenty-two.

But Lady Isabella appeared not to have noticed the unintended insult. "Why?" she asked, frankly.

Nicholas concentrated on his steps for a moment. He chose his words judiciously, careful not to give offense. "While I was in the army, I observed that the more youthful a recruit was, the more easily he could be molded into a soldier one wanted to serve with."

Lady Isabella surveyed him, the thoughtful crease still on her brow. "You wish to mold your bride into a wife who suits you."

Stated so baldly, it sounded . . . arrogant. "Yes," Nicholas said firmly. *I have nothing to be ashamed of,* he told himself, and yet his cheeks felt faintly hot, as if he flushed.

"And would you expect your wife to mold you into the husband she would like to have?"

"Mold me?" he said, affronted. "Of course not!"

Lady Isabella's lips tucked in at the corners, as if she suppressed a smile.

"My wife would have no need to mold me," Nicholas said stiffly.

Her lips tucked more deeply in at the corners. "You have no flaws, Major?"

Nicholas eyed her with suspicion. Was she laughing at him? "None that a wife should care about," he said, even more stiffly. "Apart from the scar."

Lady Isabella's mouth lost its tucked-in look. Her gaze touched his left cheek. "The scar is unimportant," she said. "A woman who didn't see that would be a poor wife."

Nicholas found himself without any words to utter.

"Quiet and malleable," she said, glancing around the ballroom again. "And young. Are those your only criteria?"

He nodded.

Her eyes lighted on someone to his left. "How about Miss Bourne? Have you considered her?"

He didn't turn his head to follow her gaze. He knew precisely what Miss Bourne looked like: hazel eyes, light brown hair, shy smile. She had been on his list of suitable brides. "Unfortunately Miss Bourne's mother seems to believe I *am* an ogre."

Lady Isabella's gaze jerked back to his face.

"No smoke without a fire, as they say." His tone was light and wry, but it didn't elicit a smile. Instead, Lady Isabella frowned and said tartly, "Mrs. Bourne is a very foolish woman!"

"She merely conforms to public opinion. And she's not the only mother in this room to do so."

Lady Isabella's frown deepened. "But surely—"

"Would you wish your daughter to marry a man rumored to be an ogre?"

Lady Isabella bit her lip.

"No," Nicholas agreed. "Neither would I."

Order your copy of *Lady Isabella's Ogre*!

CATNIP AND KISSES

By Grace Burrowes

CHAPTER ONE

"You have mice." Three words, laden with judgment. The sentence wasn't spoken so much as intoned, a *Dies Irae* rumbling in masculine tones across the library's quiet.

Because the speaker held a cat, and because that cat peered at Lady Antonia Mainwaring from her eye level, it seemed to Antonia as if the cat had spoken. Antonia had a ferociously firm grip of the English language and a firmer grasp of common sense. To shake free from fanciful notions of talking cats, she nonetheless needed the moment it took to remove her spectacles and fold the earpieces.

"I beg your pardon, sir?" She remained seated, as was a lady's prerogative.

The cat—a large, long-haired gray tom with a grumpy green gaze—switched its tail. The beast reposed in the arms of a tall man with light brown hair. The fragrance of a bakery clung to him, and his clothing suggested he worked for whatever daily bread he consumed. His coat was heavy wool, rumpled, and none too new. He wore no hat and the red plaid scarf about his neck was missing half of its tassels.

"Mice," he said, in the same inflection a preacher used when referring to original sin. "They delight in books. They chew the bindings to feast on the glue, shred the pages to make their nests, destroy wisdom itself for their furry little comfort."

This big, unkempt man and his disgruntled cat tempted Antonia to get to her feet, the better to run from any stray thunderbolts.

"I have seen no evidence of mice on the premises. Are you a library patron, sir?"

Winter was bearing down in all its unrelenting bitterness, and the library was a refuge for the homeless. Antonia's emotions on that point were mixed. In a city that considered itself the jewel of civilization, nobody ought to die of exposure to the elements, but she was at a loss for what one said to a person in such straits. "May I help you find a book?" seemed unforgivably insensitive, and yet, who deserved the comfort of great prose more than those tempted to despair?

And must London's unfortunates be so formidable?

"I am a patron," he said. "Lucifer cannot say the same."

The cat commenced purring, as if the beast enjoyed mention of his name. His expression made clear that the library was poorer for not extending to felines the privileges of membership.

"Where do you see evidence of mice?" Antonia asked.

"Come," the fellow replied, supporting the cat with one arm and striding off in the direction of the biographies. The only patrons at the library today were the Barclay sisters, a pair of white-haired spinsters who pretended to read Fordyce's sermons by the hour. Antonia suspected they were conserving coal while hiding from their neighbors, for they never took Reverend Fordyce home with them.

The gentleman with the cat disappeared between two rows of shelves and then took the spiral steps up to the mezzanine. Antonia rose and followed him. His pace was deliberate, and for a big man, he moved quietly.

The sisters exchanged a glance as he passed them. Miss Dorothy wrinkled her nose. He seemed impervious to this rudeness, though the cat sent a glare in Miss Dorothy's direction.

"Here." Still holding the cat, he knelt at the back of the H through T row of biographies. "Mice."

He pointed to what could only be mouse droppings.

His fingernails were clean, which struck Antonia as odd.

"Lucifer can solve your problem, madam. He'll expect the occasional saucer of milk and a bit of fish for his wages. If you crack a window for most of the day he'll come and go as nature demands. Feed him on the premises, and he'll defend the books all night from any and all rodents."

The man passed Antonia the cat before she could step back. In the narrow space between the bookshelves, that left her and Lucifer's owner exactly one cat-width apart.

One surprisingly light cat-width. "You are nothing but skin and bones, you poor fellow," Antonia cradled the beast to her chest, enjoying the feel of his purring. "You look formidable, and you make a prodigious noise, but you've missed a few meals."

The shameless creature licked her chin. The sensation was odd, halfway between a scrape and a tickle. The cat was too light, a ball of fluff where a muscular predator should be.

"He'll do the job God intended him to do," the man said, "your books will be safe, and the mice will decamp for less perilous surrounds."

Antonia had grown up with the requisite progression of pantry mousers, though she didn't particularly like cats and certainly hadn't been permitted anywhere near the kitchen. Cats lacked a dog's loyalty, lacked sufficient size to discourage intruders, and—probably their worst failing—lacked an adoring gaze.

"I don't have the authority to permit a cat to live on the premises," she said. "I'm a volunteer, and I'm sure the manager and the board of directors will have to convene a meeting and discuss—"

The man stroked the cat's head, which meant his hand was very close to Antonia's person. She wasn't frightened, but neither was she accustomed to biding so near a fellow unless he was standing up with her before a ballroom full of chaperones.

"By the time the Board of Fossils assembles," Lucifer's friend said, "by the time they conclude their dithering, you will have lost a dozen bound volumes to the ravages of the rodents. Who will pay to have those books replaced, assuming you can find copies of the damaged titles? Which would you rather explain, the minuscule expense of feeding Lucifer, or the ongoing drain of resources a plague of mice will effect?"

His speech was educated, for all his hair was untidy. He was, in fact, a handsome man, now that Antonia studied him. His eyes were an arresting shade of blue, closer to periwinkle, and the stubble on his cheeks was golden. He struck her as a book with its pages bound in the wrong order.

He smelled of the bakery, but was built to handle a plough.

His hair needed a trim, though his diction was precise.

He wore a laborer's rough clothing, while his touch on the cat's head was gentle.

Lucifer's friend dressed as an unlettered workingman, but his eyes held intelligence... and even a hint of humor?

Or challenge. He was challenging Antonia to accept this feline.

"I make no promises," she said. "You may leave the cat with me for now, and the chophouse can oblige with some sustenance for him. I'll have to discuss this with Mr. Kessler."

Lucifer preened under one last, slow caress.

"Be vigilant, my friend," the man said. "The literacy of Bootjack Street depends upon your courage and devotion to duty."

Antonia led the way back to the steps, and while she could have put the cat down, she didn't. He was a comfortable sort of cat to hold, not the kind that struggled and clawed against being carried.

"If the board should disapprove of Lucifer, how can we return him to you?" Antonia asked.

The day was frigid, but at least no precipitation fell. The weather alternated between sleet, snow, and rain of late, and sometimes all three at once. Lucifer's friend paused by the main door and rewrapped his scarf about his neck.

"You'll remember to crack a window for him?" he asked.

"I know that cats must heed the call of nature. I'll leave instructions that the window by the service door is to be cracked during daylight hours. Mr. Kessler will likely have an apoplexy, but we don't heat the back passage in any case."

Lucifer rumbled along, the most placid mouser Antonia had ever encountered.

"He likes haddock," the man said, his hand on the door latch.

"Very well, but how can I return him to you? I must have a name and a direction."

She had the sense that leaving Lucifer behind was difficult, which implied the man didn't intend to see his cat again. That bothered her, and not because the board of directors was likely to evict the cat. They wouldn't, not when the alternative was to spend money on a rat catcher.

"Don't bother the board," he said. "Tell Kessler you got the idea from the Countess of Bellefonte, who keeps mousers in all of her libraries. Show Kessler evidence of the infestation, and he'll soon decide that acquiring a cat was his own idea."

Mr. Kessler was nothing if not fastidious. Mouse droppings would horrify him. "I need your name and direction," Antonia said. "You clearly care about this cat, and he's not fared well recently. If he's turned back out on the street, he likely won't last the winter."

Now the wretched beast was butting his head against Antonia's chin, while Miss Dorothy was doing a poor job of pretending to browse the travelogues as she eavesdropped.

The man bent near. "Max Haddonfield. My rooms are above the bake shop on Dinwiddie Lane."

He left on a gust of frigid air and pulled the door firmly closed behind him.

"BUT DID SHE *LIKE* HIM?" Dagger asked, trotting at Max's heels.

"You didn't just *leave* him there, did you? Poor old sod, down on his luck, and winter setting in. You probably dropped him behind the dustbin without a bleedin' Happy Christmas or a—"

"Lucifer was purring in the lady's arms as I left," Max said. "Snuggled into the warmest embrace he's known in his miserable, lazy life."

Dagger slowed. "You're sure? You could hear him purring?"

"Like thunder." Beelzebub would be next, though Max would have to give him a different name. Lucifer, in addition to connoting the fiend, also brought to mind the dawn star, a happy image.

"What if the library patrons decide Lucifer's bad luck?" Dagger asked. "They'll toss him into the snow, and we'll never be the wiser."

Max understood the boy's emotions all too well. Next to the hope that one more helpless creature had found a safe, warm, happy station in life, was the gaping wound of saying good-bye to a friend, a friend one had chosen to entrust to the world's kindness.

Dagger well knew the world was not kind to the helpless, much less to skinny old cats too slow to catch a regular meal.

"If Lucifer fails to win the hearts of the patrons, I suspect Miss Antonia will intercede. She is kind." She was also starchy, prim, and a great believer in the fantasy that *rules must be obeyed*, but her heart had gone out to Lucifer, just as Max's had.

"Was she old?" Dagger asked. "Old ladies die, and nobody looks after their cats. It's a bleedin' disgrace. Dogs is always safe, because they're too stupid to manage on their own, but a cat's got to look out for his self."

"Dagger, the library is two streets from our rooms. If Lucifer is cast out, he will eventually toddle back to us, probably two stone heavier."

"You're being *unscientific*. No cat weighs that much." Dagger had learned to whip that five-syllable word around as lightly as he skipped down the street at the sight of a watchman.

Unscientific was a good modifier, having much applicability in a chaotic and hypocritical world. Dagger would cultivate that term for a time, then move on to another. Max had heard him, late at night, slowly pronouncing any number of learned words.

Corollate. Indicate. Verification. Variability. Lovely words.

"How old was she?" Dagger asked. "You say the old ones are most likely to take pity on a miserable cat, but Miss Antonia doesn't sound like a white-haired name."

The scent of baking bread wafted up the street, and though Max knew the notion was ridiculous—the bakery was a commercial enterprise—the smell brought a sense of homecoming.

"Miss Antonia has decades of life yet to enjoy," Max said, "if the Deity is merciful."

"Which He seldom is. What sort of Deity sends us weather like this and then tells us we're to have a holiday while we freeze and starve?"

Max turned down the alley. "When better to celebrate an occasion that reminds us to be kind and generous, than in the darkest week of winter?" That was the answer his brother-in-law Daniel might have offered, but then, Daniel was former clergy and a happily married man who, *unlike Max*, enjoyed the company of children.

"Fetch the day-olds," Max said, passing Dagger a coin. "And now that Lucifer is settled, we can start looking for a home for Beelzebub."

"Right-o. Day-old bread, coming right up, and after Yuletide we can start looking for a library for Beelz."

Sorry, my boy. "Beelz will soon be too hearty a specimen to pluck at anybody's heartstrings, Dagger. We will find him a new home in the next week." The library on Constable Lane was large enough to keep a cat happy, and the Thursday through Saturday librarian was a lovely aging Scotswoman who knew more about whiskey distillation than any old dear ought to.

"*Next week?* That's too soon. We just got him, and he's great friends with Hannibal, and Edward likes him, and *why next week?*"

The boy kicked a pile of slush, spreading cold and wet in every direction. Once upon a time, Max had been an angry boy, then he'd been given a copy of Newton's *Principia*, and anger had faded into curiosity and wonder.

"Next week, Dagger, because people are at their most charitable as the holidays approach. The shopkeepers are being paid for a year's worth of custom, the preachers are encouraging us to be generous. The streets are full of carols and kindness. Beelz is shy. He'll need a patient librarian who doesn't give up on the fussy patron. Next week is his best chance."

Dagger left off murdering the slush pile. "I hate this. Why do we always have to give them away?"

"We don't give them away like a pair of old boots. We find them respectable addresses and good company. The libraries get safety from mice, the cats earn good homes. We can't take them all in, Dagger. We've had this discussion. If you'd seen Lucifer, cuddled in Miss Antonia's arms, rubbing his head on her chin. . ."

Dagger wiped his nose on his sleeve. "Like that, was it? Flirting with her?"

"Not flirting." Max hadn't been able to watch it, whatever it was. "Getting acquainted, settling in. Making a new friend. Letting me know he'd handle matters on his own from now on."

The boy's shoulders slumped. "Least old Lucifer can be respectable." Not so, a climbing boy who'd grown too large for his occupation.

"Keep working on your vocabulary—your words—and you can be respectable, too." *If you'll just stop with the thievery.* "Best get the day-olds before they're all gone."

"My vo-cab-u-lar-y." Dagger took off up the narrow space between the bakery and the neighboring pub. His penchant for stealing puzzled Max, because by an urchin's standards, Dagger was well provided for. He slept in the warmth of the inglenook beside Max's hearth. He had enough to eat. He had clothes to wear and boots on his feet.

And yet, an inventory of Dagger's pockets at the end of the day had become necessary. He'd taken to snatching monogrammed handkerchiefs from the coats of dandies. Many talks, and the exercise of returning three stolen handkerchiefs to the various victims, hadn't stopped the habit.

Max climbed the steps to his rooms and unlocked the door. Leaving the cats at their new homes was hard, coming home to the remaining members of the household was harder.

Hannibal stropped himself around Max's boots, though the cat's eyes held a question. One-eyed Edward, who was curled up in a basket on the hearth, had been through the drill often enough to treat Max to the worst hurt of all, utter indifference. Shy Beelzebub peeked out from under the sofa, while the three others gazed at Max expectantly.

"Lucifer won't be coming back." Talking to cats was unscientific in the extreme; ergo, Max was talking to himself. "He's found a good home. He'll be better off, and his leaving makes a place for another here. Dagger will doubtless start searching tomorrow."

Hannibal squinted up at him.

"She's pretty, she's young, she's kind," Max went on, "and if the library won't have him, Miss Antonia will." Max hoped. Spinsters were a self-possessed lot, much like cats but not half so prone to purring. That she was Miss Antonia at her age, not Miss Smith or Miss Whoever, suggested an even older unmarried sister. In some families, that meant the younger sisters waited in vain for a match, or perhaps in her case, they contented themselves with the company of books.

Beelzebub and Hannibal touched noses, and Hannibal joined Beelzebub under the couch.

"Fine, then," Max said, unwrapping his scarf and trailing it slowly over the carpet. "I'll check on him next week, only because you insist and only the once."

Edward yawned, stretched, and squinted at Max out of his one good eye, then joined the other two under the couch. Max suffered an unaccountable urge to go back to the library and check on Lucifer at that very moment, but that would set no sort of example for Dagger.

He tossed his scarf onto a peg behind the door and added half a bucket of coal to the fire.

MR. PAXTON SLAPPED the book down on Antonia's desk loudly enough to wake the cat, who was curled in a basket beside the fireplace.

"I specifically told Mr. Kessler to locate a *first* edition of Richardson's treatise," Mr. Paxton snapped. "This is not a *first* edition."

Across the reading room, the Barclay sisters peered at Antonia over their sermons. They'd intervene if she indicated a need for assistance, so she ignored them and met Mr. Paxton's glare with a calm eye.

"This is a fourth edition, sir, though your request was made only the day before yesterday. We'll be happy to notify you if and when a first edition arrives. You are welcome to borrow this copy until then."

Antonia remained seated, while Mr. Paxton drew himself up, a hot air balloon of male self-importance preparing to lift into a flight of indignation. The bell on the front door tinkled and Lucifer left his basket. He greeted each patron as conscientiously as a butler would, then went back to his basket, almost as if he were expecting one caller in particular.

"What sort of librarian," Mr. Paxton began, "cannot tell a first edition from subsequent printings? What sort of institution employs staff who cannot fulfill a simple loan request? Was I not clear that I wanted a *first edition?*"

He braced his hands on the desk and leaned closer. "Did I not complete your form to Mr. Kessler's satisfaction? Did he perhaps allow Mr. Lincoln Candleford to have the first edition before I was permitted to see it? I know the library on Constable Lane has one, but it's lent out, and they won't tell me who has it."

Mr. Paxton needed a closer acquaintance with several sheaves of fresh parsley. His breath reeked of the tobacco habit, which did not blend well with the excessive rose pomade in his hair.

"Libraries value the privacy of their patrons," Antonia replied. "If Constable Lane had a first edition available to lend, I'm sure they'd have sent it around. Did you seek to research a particular topic covered by Mr. Richardson's treatise?"

Mr. Paxton's gaze crawled over Antonia's feminine endowments. He might have been any one of a hundred half-drunk, blond, blue-eyed fortune hunters forgetting himself in a Mayfair ballroom, and in that setting, Antonia would have known what to do about him.

The cut direct, a raised eyebrow, a knowing glance to the chaperones waiting to pounce on a man's reputation from among the potted ferns. He'd find himself in want of invitations for the remainder of the Season, which was a fortune hunter's version of doom.

"Young woman, are you listening to me? Is your female brain overtaxed by a patron's request when that request is plainly and succinctly put before you? Must I complain to Kessler about his paltry collection *and* his dimwitted staff?"

Antonia rose, standing eye to eye with Mr. Paxton, the desk between them. "Your request has been submitted to our sister institutions. Is your male brain too limited to grasp that Mr. Richardson's treatise was published in 1788, and first editions have had nigh three decades to become lost, damaged, or destroyed? Locating one might take more than two days, though I suggest you retrieve your manners in the next thirty seconds."

His gaze roamed over her in a manner so far beyond insulting that had Antonia been at one of polite society's social functions, she would have slapped him.

He obviously knew she couldn't. Not here, where she was a volunteer on probation until a paying post became available. Not now, with only a pair of old women to gainsay Paxton's version of events. At the library, Antonia was simply "young woman," not an earl's daughter with a private fortune. For the first time since embarking on this literary adventure, Antonia understood why her cousins had tried to dissuade her from it.

She wasn't afraid, exactly, but she was uneasy.

"You were a governess, weren't you?" Paxton said. "A long meg like you was passed over by the bachelors. You probably lost your position because you got above yourself. You think a little French and a smattering of Italian make you an *intellectual*. What you need is—"

The smell of freshly baked bread gave Antonia an instant's warning that her conversation had acquired another witness.

"What *you* need," Mr. Haddonfield said, positioning himself at her elbow, "is to leave. Now."

Paxton put a hand on his hip. "Who might you be and what gives you the right to intrude here?"

"Max Haddonfield, at your service. Your rudeness invites any gentleman in the vicinity to intercede. Apologize to the lady for behaving like a petulant brat and find another library to patronize."

"Please do leave, Mr. Paxton," Antonia said. "You've disturbed the other patrons, and contrary to your imaginings, librarians are not magicians. Finding a thirty-year-old first edition will take some time."

"Go," Mr. Haddonfield said, making a shooing motion.

"And are you a librarian, sir, to be so dismissive toward a man of my academic credentials?" Paxton sniffed, picking up the book.

Mr. Haddonfield plucked the book from Paxton's grasp. "I'm a chemist." He smiled at Paxton as if being a chemist was better than having put Wellington on his first pony. "Haven't blown anything up in more than two weeks. I grow short-tempered when I can't blow something up."

Paxton took two steps back. "Kessler will hear about this."

Mr. Haddonfield crossed his arms, which made his coat stretch over broad shoulders and muscular biceps. "He certainly will. Your rudeness toward both the staff and the other patrons will doubtless result in revocation of your lending privileges."

"Other patrons? I assume you refer to yourself?"

Mr. Haddonfield twirled his finger. Paxton glanced over his

shoulder, to where the Barclay sisters were no longer even pretending to read. Miss Dottie waggled her fingers. Miss Betty smiled over a bound volume of the Reverend Fordyce's wisdom.

"Other patrons," Mr. Haddonfield said. "Away with you. Be gone." He clapped his hands rapidly at Mr. Paxton, like a housekeeper impatient with a sluggardly maid.

Paxton leapt back, jerked his coat down, and marched for the door. The silence in his wake was broken by bells on a passing gig tinkling, a merry sound.

"Do you really blow things up?" Antonia asked.

"Yes, but usually only on purpose."

CHAPTER TWO

Max was a scientist, which to his siblings meant he indulged in a quaint hobby, sometimes breaking things, sometimes arriving late to social gatherings with odd smells lingering on his clothes. He read a lot of books and liked to go for long walks by himself.

His brothers and sisters were kind people. If he'd told them he chose to arrive late because explosives were simply more interesting than polite society, they would have been puzzled, if not hurt. Chemistry, physics, natural science—the world that could be studied and understood—held far more fascination for Max than the world that waltzed and swilled tea.

Miss Antonia was an item of anomalous data. She was clearly not of a species native to the workaday surrounds of the library's neighborhood. Her height set her apart, height usually being characteristic of the reliably well fed classes. Her diction had finishing school crispness about the consonants, and her attire was not only made from excellent cloth, but up to the moment in style.

Other features contradicted the hypothesis of a lady fallen on hard times or doing a charitable bit at a lending library.

Her clothing, while stylish and well made, was plain to a fault. No ruffles called attention to her curves, no fanciful embroidery flattered her blue-gray eyes. Her bearing was a conundrum as well: Somebody had taught her perfect posture, but they had neglected to teach her perfect confidence in the face of loutish behavior.

"Are patrons like Mr. Paxton common here?" Max asked. And where was Lucifer?

"I would not know," Miss Antonia replied. "I am new to my position, but the records indicate Mr. Paxton is a frequent borrower and occasionally tardy about his returns."

"Then you must never give quarter where he is concerned. Do not back down, do not blink when he stares at your—your person. Regard him as you would an unruly child much in need of a stint on the dunce stool, for that's exactly what he is."

"I have no experience with unruly children." Miss Antonia regarded the book in Max's hands. "Would you like to check out that volume?"

"I have little interest in the illegal brewing of beer and ale," Max said, holding tome out to her.

"Is that what—? Oh, I see." She took the book. "Is that what Mr. Paxton is about?"

"I cannot say for a certainty. He has no estate that I know of, he dwells in a rooming house that I very much doubt has facilities for home-brewing, and his last commercial venture—crossing the Channel by balloon—failed spectacularly."

Paxton was not a scientist. He was one of the many opportunists looking to science for personal gain rather than for the betterment of humanity. Richardson's treatise, which purported to teach the use of the saccharometer for establishing consistent results when making beer, had been a basic text among brewmasters for decades.

"People die flying hot air balloons," Miss Antonia said. "From what I recall, one can sail by boat from Dover to Calais in a few hours. Are balloons really so much faster?"

Had she been to France herself?

"The issue is the return journey," Max said. "When the winds oblige, the trip from Dover to Calais can be made speedily by boat, but Calais to Dover is often a much longer journey. Balloons can search at various altitudes for favorable winds, if the pilot is skillful. Then too, the views from several thousand feet in the air are splendid."

She studied him for a curious moment before marching off with Mr. Richardson's treatise. "You have flown in hot air balloons?"

"Frequently," Max said, following in her wake. "People think of explosions as violent occurrences, but in truth, a balloon expanding or a loaf of bread dough rising are simply explosions that happen over a longer time. If we can harness the energy of an explosion—as we do every time a bullet is propelled down the barrel of a gun—we will have great power that has until now been supplied only by the sweat of our brows."

"What was it like?" Miss Antonia asked. "To be in that balloon?"

"The preparation can last longer than the flight. One must first pump cold air into the balloon itself, then heated air to expand the volume of the cold air, and all without the flames doing any mischief. The launching must be timed to avoid anything but the slightest breeze, and—"

"No," she said, pausing at the bottom of the spiral steps. "I mean, what was it *like*, to fly so high, to see the world as only God and the birds have seen it previously?"

I'll show you. The words sprang to Max's mind without any rational provocation other than the longing in Miss Antonia's eyes. A woman who let Paxton's blustering intimidate her would be terrified to see the world from two thousand feet up, but Miss Antonia apparently longed for that view.

"The perspective is amazing," Max said. "Full of odd contrasts. The world is at once small and enormous. Mighty forests look like squares on a quilt, France is right next door, not twenty miles away.

Because the balloon is moved along by the wind itself, there's an odd sense of stillness despite traveling at a good clip. One moment, all is quiet majesty, then next, the firebox is roaring and you're trying to avoid a disobliging hillside."

"Women fly," Miss Antonia said quietly. "A few women."

Women not only flew hot air balloons, they did so spectacularly. Max could not picture this tidy, prim librarian manning the firebox and delighting in the vagaries of the wind.

"Would you like to fly, Miss Antonia?"

She took off up the winding steps. "I am flying, Mr. Haddonfield. This library, full of flights of imagination and wisdom, is my sky and the books are my wings. I need not risk my neck on a lark involving silk, flame, and foolish fancies."

The spiral stairs were constructed of metal, and her half boots made quite the racket as she ascended. Max followed more quietly, wondering what disobliging male hillside had blighted Miss Antonia's sense of adventure.

His conjecture was hardly scientific, and yet, it had the ring of a solid hypothesis. "What will you do if Paxton makes trouble?"

"Trouble, Mr. Haddonfield?"

"If he returns for another round of attempted bullying or he complains to your superior?"

She moved down a row of bound volumes and shoved Richardson back among his fellows, then remained gazing at worn book spines of brown, red, and black leather.

A boring sky, by Max's lights, though one meriting some study.

"You need not be concerned, Mr. Haddonfield. I will have a word with Mr. Kessler when he drops by on Thursday. He has more than a dozen libraries under his management, and one rude patron won't deserve much notice from such a busy man."

Max had four sisters whom he loved dearly. They had mothered him when his own mama had gone to her reward, interceded for him when his older brothers became too overbearing, and prevented his father from sending him to boarding school at a tender age when Max's experiments had nearly set the stables ablaze.

Women paid attention in ways men often did not, and yet women were often not afforded attention in ways they deserved, particularly when that attention was owed them by a *busy man*.

"You complain first," Max said. "You inform Kessler that his library has attracted a bad sort, one intent on exploiting the learning to be had here for criminal gain. You make it plain that Paxton's rudeness to you and to the ladies at the reading table is a sorry disappointment to your feminine sensibilities and will not be tolerated."

Miss Antonia gave him another one of those considering looks. He could not read her gaze, but he sensed a prodigious intellect coming to careful conclusions.

"I'm to be the offended lady?"

"Aren't you offended?"

She folded her arms and faced him. "What if Mr. Paxton was to become personally troublesome?"

Over the scents of old books, leather, and coal, Max detected a grassy fragrance laced with mint. Coming from *her*.

"Troublesome, Miss Antonia?"

She stared at a spot beyond Max's shoulder as pink crept up her neck. "Troublesome, like a bachelor who has made one too many trips to the men's punch bowl."

Interesting analogy for a librarian. "You mean his hand accidentally glides over your bum when you're showing him where to find the brewing treatises? Or he passes too close to you, such that—"

"Yes," she said, a bit loudly. "Troublesome in that regard."

"Your knee," Max said. "A fine weapon when deployed in the vicinity of a man's falls. He'll drop like wet laundry if you look into his eyes while you're doing it."

Miss Antonia was bright pink now, even to her ears. "And if he should grasp my arm?"

Max circled her wrist with his fingers. "Get my smallest finger in a good grip and haul it smartly back and away from my hand. You can break my finger that way. Then jab your thumbs into my eyes while I'm whimpering in male outrage, and follow up with a heel stomped on my instep."

She looked down at his hand wrapped around her wrist. "Your smallest finger?"

"I grew up with older brothers of the big and boisterous sort. They sometimes didn't know when to stop teasing me, so my sisters taught me a few handy moves."

Miss Antonia smiled up at Max, her hand resting over his as he grasped her wrist. "Your *sisters* taught you how to fight?"

"How to defend myself." What lovely eyes Miss Antonia had, and how delightful that she was tall enough that Max didn't feel like a plow horse when he stood next to her.

"Like this?" She gave Max's finger a tug that would not have awakened a napping kitten.

"More firmly." Did her perfume include a hint of lemon?

She tugged again, still not very hard.

"Have you ever waltzed?" Max asked.

She looked down. "I have. I am considered too tall to be a suitable partner for most men."

"Madam, most men are too short to partner you effectively. When you dance with a partner who knows what he's doing, does he dither and hesitate or does he move decisively?"

"Most of them dither and hesitate while they stare—they mince about. There is an earl, though. Or there was. He's on the tall side, and I did enjoy dancing with him very much."

Had this earl been her disobliging hillside? Max's older brother Nicholas was an earl who was very tall, also very married. Though how did a librarian end up dancing with any earl at all?

"Be like that fellow when you yank on my finger. Know what you're about."

She looked up at Max, and he braced himself for another kitten-tug.

"'Zounds!" She'd nearly ripped his finger off. "Well done." He shook his hand, considering the hurt worth the reward, for Miss Antonia was beaming at him.

"Like that?" she asked.

"Exactly like that, and then flounce off in high dudgeon. That part's important because most men won't deal well with having been bested. Make your exit while you can, no lingering about to gloat."

Miss Antonia's smile was impish, filling her gaze with sheer glee. She gave Max's arm a glancing pat.

"High dudgeon will take some practice, but I will work on it. Mr. Paxton isn't the only patron inclined to haughty airs. Nobody warned me about that. Did you come here for a particular book, Mr. Haddonfield?"

"I came here to see how Lucifer is faring, though perhaps he's gone out on feline business."

Miss Antonia swished past him, which allowed Max to confirm that indeed, the luscious meadow-y, summery scent came from her.

"Lucifer rarely goes out during the day. He takes his responsibilities as a member of the staff quite seriously, though he apparently thinks he's been given the job of butler rather than mouser."

"He's settling in well?" Dagger would be disappointed.

"He has made conquests, Mr. Haddonfield. Come along." She descended the steps and continued on to the reading table. "Ladies, excuse the interruption, but has either one of you seen our Mr. Lucifer?"

One of the old dears lifted her book of sermons to reveal the top of Lucifer's head peering over the edge of the reading table, as if he, too, had been enjoying the reverend's spiritual guidance.

"Lukey is such a dear thing," she said. "A gentleman in every sense."

"He likes Betty best," the other added. "A pity the library has only the one cat. They are not the solitary creatures we make them out to be, you know. They enjoy company as much as we do."

Lucifer squinched his eyes at her, as if concurring in her opinion.

"One cat is more than enough," Miss Antonia began. "We have apparently eradicated the mouse problem, and that suggests—"

"You need another," Max said. "One should keep loyal patrons happy. As it happens, I'm in a position to help." He bowed to the ladies and departed before Miss Antonia could marshal any arguments.

"I CAN SMELL the books on you," Peter said, smiling as he bowed over Antonia's hand. "Very scholarly, my dear."

Antonia could nearly smell the amusement Peter's tone exuded. To him, her *little lending library frolic* was a passing fancy to be indulged until she came to her senses. Coming to her senses would involve marrying Peter, keeping Papa's fortune in the family—she and Peter were second cousins, once removed—and having Peter's babies. The title had gone to a first cousin, and that happy fellow was larking about somewhere in Italy.

Antonia was trying to reconcile herself to taking the sensible course. Peter was a decent man, good-looking, and not given to excesses. She might not be miserable with him and she would do her best to ensure he wasn't miserable with her. He was willing to over-look her great, hopeless age and her propensity to read at all hours. He was a known quantity who wouldn't expect her to manufacture any romantic effusions.

Was it possible to be *too* sensible?

"Have you rung for tea?" Antonia asked. "I could do with a cup myself."

Afternoons at the library were quiet and chilly, but then, after-noons at home this time of year were quiet and chilly—also dull.

"I did not want to presume," Peter said. "How goes your grand adventure at the library?"

Peter's reluctance to presume was a recent invention. Usually, when he was under Antonia's roof, he assumed the privileges of family and expected the deference owed a guest.

Antonia tugged the bell pull twice. "I do so enjoy having endless time to read."

"Some believe novels upset the delicate humors of a lady's imagination." He offered this observation while using a spill to light the silver candelabra on the piano.

"Some men."

"And many women." He shook out the flame on the spill and tossed the unused paper into the fire on the hearth.

At the library, nobody would have wasted a spill that had at least three more uses left. Here, the footmen would replenish the blue porcelain spill pot on the mantel daily.

"As it happens," Antonia said, "I was reading about how to make good beer. There's more to it than one suspects."

Peter's smile faded into perplexity. "*Beer*, Antonia?"

Every household consumed a quantity of beer. Most servants' compensation included allotments for ale, candles, and tea. The commodities could be of much greater value than the coin earned. Antonia had had a vague grasp of those realities—she did oversee her housekeeper's and butler's books—but hours of reading had enhanced her understanding.

"Beer, Peter. We both drink it, most larger households brew it. A bad batch can result in terrible ailments, while good beer and ale is an English point of pride."

"So you're honing your housewifely arts?"

Must he sound so hopeful? "I'm familiarizing myself with the library's inventory, also reading about the lady aeronauts. Napoleon's official balloonist was a woman, and—"

"And look what happened to Napoleon."

Antonia was beginning to find Peter's smile, which showed off perfect white teeth and made the corners of his eyes crinkle, irksome.

"The Corsican conquered most of Europe before suffering a defeat that many attribute to bad weather and worse luck."

Peter's smile disappeared. "Have you been reading *French histories* again, Antonia?"

That tone, which conveyed both disappointment and a touch of asperity, was part of why Antonia had yet to consent to the sensible match Peter proposed.

She took a seat, grateful for the deep cushion of the reading chair by the hearth. "Why insist that women learn French if we're not to use that skill to learn what the French know?"

"Learn French recipes," Peter said, pacing the width of the parlor. "Enjoy French opera, nip over to Paris to buy some French fashion, but don't trouble your pretty head with drivel spouted by failed revolutionists."

Antonia had no illusions about her looks. Her head, like the rest of her, was plain. Moreover, she was constructed on too grand a scale to ever qualify as pretty. Peter stood an inch taller than she did, only because she never wore heels unless she was on horseback, while he consistently trotted around in fashionably heeled boots. When she danced with him, they were the same height.

Max Haddonfield, by contrast, had a good six inches on her, and he was well muscled. If Antonia stood up for a waltz with him, he'd neither dither nor hesitate, and he didn't stare at her chest either. He had the most marvelous blue eyes, so calm and intelligent, but not too—

"I did not come here to argue politics with you," Peter said, slouching against the sideboard. "I came to extend an invitation. The sisters and I are to attend Lady Chalfont's ball on Wednesday and we'd like you to join our party."

The autumn entertainments were fewer and less crowded than their springtime counterparts. Many families had already departed for the countryside, where they would spend Yuletide and greet the New Year.

"I sent regrets to Lady Chalfont."

"Why would you do that? She hires excellent musicians and sets out a formidable buffet."

The first footman arrived with the tea tray, which—thank the good offices of a well trained kitchen staff—included some cheese rolls. Antonia used the delay to frame a reply to Peter's question, though she resented the need to explain herself to him.

"I would prefer to remain at home when the weather is so dreary."

Peter took the opposite chair and poured himself a cup of tea, adding milk and sugar, and putting two tea cakes onto his saucer.

"But you trudge off to the library in a frigid downpour, Antonia, there to impersonate a cit's spinster daughter while you fill your head with French political fairytales. What's the real reason you declined her ladyship's invitation? Do you fear to have an empty dance card?"

Five years ago she might have admitted to that error. Now she feared being late for her shift at the library the next morning.

"Few men have the height to partner me competently," she said, paraphrasing Mr. Haddonfield. "Putting up with those who enjoy leering at my bodice grows tedious."

"My dear, you must not fault a man for admiring nature's bounty when it's immediately before his eyes."

Antonia was almost certain Peter had meant that as a joke. "I fault a man for poor manners. I suppose both Diana and Athena are attending this ball?"

"Of course."

Antonia's female cousins were bright women whose company she honestly enjoyed. One or the other of them would sit out most of the dances with her, and they'd pass an enjoyable evening among the dowagers and wallflowers.

"Very well, I will attend, but do not expect me to make a late night of it."

"Save me your supper waltz, my dear." Peter finished his tea in a few gulps, stuffed the two cakes into his pockets, and scampered off without bothering to bow over Antonia's hand.

She sat alone in the parlor, grateful for the solitude, already regretting her decision to attend yet another ball when she'd rather be home curled up with a book. The one fellow whose company she honestly enjoyed—the Earl of Casriel—had made a love match at the end of the previous Season. He and his countess were rumored to already be in anticipation of an interesting event.

What would that be like? To conceive a new life in intimate congress with a man whom one loved madly? With a man who loved one madly in return?

Antonia could read every volume in her library and still not learn what such an experience entailed, an odd and lowering thought for a woman whose idea of bliss was a rainy afternoon spent reading in solitude.

"YOU'RE NEXT," Max said to Beelzebub, who purred contentedly amid the morning's calculations. The surest way to inspire a cat out from under the sofa was to spread work on the desk and commence measuring and recording. Wherever Max set down his pencil or ruler, there the cat was, looking as comfortable as a marmalade tom ever had.

Though Beelzebub wasn't a typical exponent of his gender. When the ladies called from the alley, he yawned and closed his eyes. When Dagger set out a saucer of milk, Hannibal and Edward both got their share at the same time, while Beelz hung back, waiting to lick up whatever the other two missed.

"You content yourself on scraps and leavings," Max said, scratching the cat behind the ears. "Maybe when you can settle into your own library, you'll regain some confidence."

Clearly, Beelz had been somebody's pet. He was tame to a fault and happiest curled up next to Dagger in the nook by the fireplace. Dagger had a way with the shy ones—or they had a way with him.

As if Max's thoughts had conjured the boy, the window banged open and he leapt into the room. "More day-olds," he said, setting a sack on a corner of the desk. "Stinkin' damned cold outside."

"Frigid," Max said, peering into the sack. "Did you eat half the samples?"

"Nah. Folk are buying more bread now the weather's turned. I know to wait until you've done the measuring before I eat 'em." He snatched a small loaf off the desk, tossed it in the air, and caught it. "You done with this one? I fancy some cheese toast."

"I'm through with it. I've found a home for Beelzebub."

Dagger left off tossing his bread about. "Already? It's too soon. Lucifer just left and Edward and Hannibal will mope. Beelz won't get fat—he'll never get fat as long as other cats are around."

"The library where Lucifer went wants another cat." Not exactly true, though the two old ladies who read there day after day would enjoy a second cat. Miss Antonia was another matter entirely.

Dagger gnawed a bite off the loaf. "Two cats in the same library?"

"Lucifer is friendly. He and Beelz get on well, and two cats are hardly more trouble than one." Max hadn't quite convinced Miss Antonia on that point, but her practical air hid a soft heart.

She was also pretty when she smiled, interesting when she didn't, and not a typical librarian. Max's curiosity where she was concerned refused to abate, even when he took up the pleasurable job of making the day's measurements.

"You having any luck with this batch?" Dagger asked, taking a quarter-round of cheddar from the window box.

"That was a half wheel of cheese only yesterday morning."

Dagger flipped out a blade much too lethal-looking for the innocent smile he aimed at Max. "Growing boys—"

"Don't use that filthy knife on your comestibles. Use a proper cheese knife." This lesson—different utensils for different situations—was an ongoing exercise in frustration. Dagger's world valued efficiency, meaning tools that served in multiple capacities.

The world Max had been raised in valued. . . he wasn't sure what. Having many specimens of the same item, and justifying the proliferation of possessions by decreeing one knife was for fruit, another for steak, another for bread.

And none of those would ever, ever be used for self-defense.

Neither world suited Max, and thus he escaped into the world that did, where measurements, hypotheses, and careful observation advanced the welfare of the species.

Dagger fetched the cheese knife from the sideboard. "If a body was hungry enough, he wouldn't bother over which knife he used. You lot don't get hungry."

"We do," Max said, setting aside the last of his figures. "When you've finished eating, you can copy my calculations into the journal. No luck so far, but we have many trials yet to go."

"I'm getting tired of eating bread," Dagger said, around a mouthful of cheese. "Never thought that day would come."

"Eat some apples with that bread and cheese, Dagger, or your bowels will seize."

Dagger paused in his chewing and farted. "They ain't seized yet."

"Haven't. They haven't seized yet." Max managed not to smile, but the boisterous, irreverent vulgarity of boyhood was cheering. Also ripe as hell.

"Let's see your pockets, Dagger. I'm off to call upon my sisters."

Anytime Dagger had been out by himself, Max subjected him to this indignity. Fortunately, the boy's pockets were empty —this time.

"I'll be back before dark," Max said. "Beelzebub goes to his new home tomorrow."

Dagger tossed the loaf of bread aloft again. "Not if he ain't here he won't."

"If he's not here, then Hannibal will go instead."

Max wasn't sure he could do that—Hannibal and Edward were a couple, and dear to him, but Dagger had a scheming mind and was attached to Beelzebub.

"He'll be here."

"See that he is."

Max bundled up against the elements and prepared for the trek to Mayfair, mentally considering the day's calculations. Walking was good for thinking, but today, science wasn't interested in keeping him company.

Instead he was distracted by a shy lady with fine gray-blue eyes, one who loved books and hadn't yet learned how to put a bounder in his place. She and Beelzebub would get along famously, which was some comfort when a man contemplated parting from yet another friend.

CHAPTER THREE

"You must join us at Lady Chalfont's ball," Susannah said. "You never get out anymore."

"Haddonfields are known to be charming," Della added, draping a linen towel over the porcelain teapot. "You can't be charming if you're always off doing your experiments and burying your nose in scientific treatises."

"Della is right." Susannah aimed a look at Max over her embroidery hoop. She was stitching a scene of gamboling puppies for what looked like a throw pillow cover. Her husband, Willow Dorning, was dog-mad, and Susannah in her quiet way was Willow-mad. Della was rumored to have set her cap for another of the Dorning brothers, but that rumor was apparently false—or premature.

Both sisters were biding for the nonce at the Haddonfield family town house. The owner of the dwelling and oldest Haddonfield sibling, Nicholas, Earl of Bellefonte, had taken his countess out for an ice. That excuse covered myriad deceptions, such as when Nick and Leah sought a private hour in his woodworking shop behind in the stables.

"One can be charming anywhere," Max said, "but what's the

point of being charming to a lot of young ladies who see me only as a means of marrying into a titled family?" He had a respectable competence from a deceased pair of great aunts, but he used that to fund his experiments.

Della rose to move the fire screen, though the parlor struck Max as cozy enough. Della was small and dark, the Haddonfield changeling. The rest of the siblings were tall, and but for Max, blond. He had been born blond, but as he'd matured, his hair had darkened. His brothers had claimed that was evidence of his brain curdling as he became more enamored of science.

He'd always felt that the lack of blond hair gave him something more in common with Della than with the rest of their siblings. She was the youngest girl, he was the youngest boy. She was as yet unmarried, and he was. . .

Running a foundling home for stray cats. "Why did you marry?" he asked Susannah. Of all his sisters, she'd been the most bookish and retiring, something of a Shakespeare scholar.

"Because I could not imagine life without Will. He saw me for who I truly am, and he became a part of my heart. If we live in a hut in the Outer Hebrides subsisting on cabbage soup, I want to be with him."

They did not dwell in a hut, but they did live a retiring life on a small country estate with a bloody lot of canines.

"I cannot imagine life without science."

Della passed him a tray. "Have another sandwich. Life with science left you peaky and gaunt."

Like Dagger, Max wasn't all that keen on eating more bread. His experiments left him awash in bread, most of which Max gave to Dagger to do with as the boy saw fit.

"There will be mistletoe at Lady Chalfont's ball, Max," Susannah said, resuming her stitching. "You could steal a few kisses."

"Not a Haddonfield male born who wasn't interested in that undertaking," Della added, taking the place beside Max. "Admit it."

Max liked kissing and he liked very well all that came after it. He did not like emotional complications, entanglements, or drama. When he'd first come down from university, one young lady had set her cap for him and nearly seen him compromised. Fortunately, his sisters had taught him to pick locks with a hairpin, and what could have become an awkward scene in a linen closet had passed without incident.

"If I were a lady," Max said, "I would not want the fellow who kissed me only under the safe passage of the mistletoe tradition. I'd want the fellow who asked my permission before he took liberties, the fellow who sought to kiss *me* rather than have a holiday lark beneath a bit of greenery."

"You are simply no fun at all, Max," Della muttered. "Have you considered that you might find sponsors for your investigations at the Chalfont ball? The card room will be full of older fellows who no longer want to stand up for every set. You can prose on to them about the ascendency of science and progress and all that other whatnot, provided you aren't rude about it."

Susannah held her puppies up to the firelight. "You can mention in passing that you've made progress, and when they politely reply, you suggest the matter might be better discussed at a fellow's club. You do still belong to some clubs?"

"Three." All of which were concerned exclusively with science.

"Say you'll come." Della's smile was a little forced, suggesting she wanted an ally. "If nothing else, you can partner me after Will has finished his duty set with me."

She was too small to be a good match for Max on the dancefloor. A pity Miss Antonia wouldn't be at the ball. Max would enjoy partnering her, but what were the chances he'd cross paths with Mayfair's only waltzing librarian?

"I suppose I can put in an appearance," he said, rising. "And in case you're wondering, my experiments are uniformly failing these days."

"Who was it that said the failed experiments often yield the most interesting results?" Susannah replied, getting to her feet. She linked arms with Max and escorted him to the door, tucking his scarf around his neck as if he were eight years old.

"Why don't we ever gather for a family meal, Susannah? Ethan, Will, and George all pass through Town regularly. We could get Beckman up here if we enlisted Sara's aid. Daniel and Kirsten could get away from headmastering for a few days if we asked it of them."

As the youngest son, Max barely knew Ethan, the firstborn half brother who'd been sent off to school and estranged from his siblings at a young age. Beckman, the spare, gloried in the life of a country squire near Portsmouth, while George was making a good start on the same role in Kent.

The Haddonfields were thriving, but must they thrive at such distances from one another?

"They would all come to Town for a wedding," Susannah said, patting Max's lapel. "If you married a well-to-do lady, your science would benefit."

This had become a refrain from his sisters, and their suggestion was sensible. Max could offer family connections, the lady would bring some means to the union, and everybody would pronounce it a fine match.

Though *some means* was hardly a compelling motivation to make a lifelong commitment. "I'll see you at the Chalfonts' do," Max said, tapping his hat onto his head. "Don't expect me to stay long."

"You haven't asked when it is."

"As it happens, my evenings are free for the foreseeable future. I'm guessing Wednesday, to avoid conflicting with parliamentary duties."

"Wednesday it is. See you then. And Max?"

"I know. Have my evening clothes pressed. Tuck a flower into my lapel, though no sensible flower blooms this time of year. Be charming."

He kissed her on the cheek and escaped into the cold smoky air, already regretting his decision to attend the ball.

"WHY DO I BOTHER?" Antonia muttered, fanning herself slowly. "Why did I let Peter talk me into this *again*?" To any onlooker, she doubtless appeared to be chatting pleasantly with her cousin. Diana had found them a bench among the potted palms, out of sight of the men's punch bowl.

"Dancing was never Peter's greatest strength," Diana replied. "Athena and I figured that out before he'd landed either one of us on our bums."

Peter had nearly sent Antonia sailing into an older couple, though the gentleman had neatly caught Antonia by the arm, winked, and set her back on her feet.

"As soon as the next set begins, I'm off to repair my hem. To think I nearly careened into Their Graces of Windham." The duke and duchess not only danced *on the beat*, an accomplishment that eluded Peter, they looked enormously happy to be waltzing with each other.

"Their Graces were a love match," Diana said, raising her fan to keep the words private. "My abigail said the duchess comes from modest wealth, but her antecedents weren't that impressive."

What did that matter, when Her Grace of Windham was so clearly the duke's partner in every regard?

"You will excuse me," Antonia said, passing Diana a nearly full glass of punch. "I must away to the retiring room." Not that any other man would ask her to dance, not after the near-fiasco with Peter.

She ducked through one of the ballroom's side doors and into the gallery. The cooler air was a benediction, as was the quiet. The guests raised their voices to be heard over the music and the thump of the dancers' feet. The musicians played more loudly to be heard over a hundred conversations, until the ballroom pulsed with sheer noise.

I miss the library.

That thought surprised Antonia and pleased her. She'd taken on the volunteer position in an effort to do something—anything—more meaningful than literary committee work, tatting lace, and calling on acquaintances. The job wasn't exactly thrilling, and Mr. Kessler had let his skepticism regarding Antonia's abilities be loudly known. Nonetheless, she was beginning to look forward to the library days and to hope that the paying post would be offered to her.

She rounded the landing on the way up to the retiring room and once again nearly landed on her bum. A pair of strong male hands on her arms steadied her, and she found herself gazing up into familiar blue eyes.

"Mr. Haddonfield."

"Miss Antonia. Good evening, and my apologies for not watching where I was going."

The men's retiring room was typically on the same floor as the ballroom, lest ladies and gentlemen encounter one another at awkward moments.

"Were you lost?" Antonia asked.

"Not lost." He bent nearer. "Lurking."

His evening attire was spotless and fit him very nicely, though the width of his lapels suggested his jacket was several years out of date.

"You are rather grandly proportioned to be successfully lurking anywhere, sir. Does the august company intimidate you?"

He offered his arm. "Spare me from august company. I don't mind small talk, and I came prepared for the hostess to inflict my dancing on a few of the wallflowers, but it's the flora that sent me fleeing to Lord Chalfont's library."

They reached the top of the steps, the music from the ballroom fading to a faint lilting melody. "Flora? The potted palms?"

He took Antonia by the hand and led her to the balcony that overlooked the main foyer. "The dread greenery is everywhere. Draped from the rafters, hanging over the punch bowl. It's even on the terrace where a man ought to be free to enjoy his cheroot in safety—not that I smoke. Even the card room isn't safe."

Scientists could be eccentric. The foyer was decorated in anticipation of Yuletide, with green and red ribbons spiraling around tall candles, red bunting wrapping the stair rail, and cloved oranges hanging in the windows. Lady Chalfont was anticipating the Christmas season by weeks but she—or her professional decorator— was anticipating it with exquisite traditional flourishes.

"What's everywhere?"

"*Viscum album*," Mr. Haddonfield replied, keeping Antonia's hand in his. "Mistletoe, in common parlance, though the name translates from the Anglo-Saxon as something like bird-dung-on-a-twig. Damned stuff can kill a mature tree, and what do we do with it? Make a parasite into an excuse for kissing complete strangers."

The supper buffet had concluded prior to the present set so neither Antonia nor Mr. Haddonfield wore gloves—not that he seemed aware of her hand in his.

"Once mistletoe gets a start," he went on, "the only way to get rid of it is to cut off all the limbs affected or shroud them in dark cloth. Mistletoe needs light, which is why it likes to grow far out on the highest branches."

"I thought you were a chemist. You sound like a botanist."

He dropped her hand. "One of my brothers has done some plant collecting. I'm surprised to find you here."

Did he mean here abovestairs, or here at the Chalfonts' ball? "I've torn a hem. I'm on my way to the retiring room to effect emergency repairs." Antonia brandished the tiny sewing kit she carried in her pocket. The attendant in the retiring room would have the essentials, but Antonia's gown was brown velvet, and not just any color of thread would do.

"I can stitch a hem," Mr. Haddonfield said, taking her sewing kit and striding off down the corridor. "Come along."

He had her sewing kit, so Antonia followed him, though what was a chemist doing at such a gathering? "Where are we going?"

"Not the library. At least two couples looking for a trysting place disturbed my reading. I'm supposed to be in the card room, but—here we are." He opened a door that led to a small unoccupied music room, perhaps more of a practice room. "Nobody should disturb us here."

He flipped the lock, and Antonia found herself, for the first time in her adult memory, alone with a man who was neither a close family friend nor a relation.

"This is most irregular, Mr. Haddonfield." Though instead of feeling unsafe, Antonia was relieved to have some near-solitude, and relieved to have found an ally of sorts.

"How is this any more irregular than disporting with you among the biographies?" he asked. "I am a gentleman, Miss Antonia, though some of what I've seen transpiring beneath the mistletoe this evening makes me rethink my definition of the word. Let's have a look at that hem."

Most irregular. "I can sew my own hem, sir."

"I can sew it more quickly." He gestured toward a chair beside the fireplace. "On board ship, we had little to do besides mend sail, play cards, and clean the brine off every surface exposed to fresh air."

Antonia took the seat, though she had the sense of having stepped out of the frilly, frothy world of Mayfair entertainments and onto an altogether more interesting plane.

"When were you on board a ship?"

"Expedition to the far north," he said, lowering himself to sit tailor-fashion on the carpet. He flipped open the sewing case and extracted a needle from the padded cloth wedged inside the lid. "Where is the damage?"

Antonia twitched at her skirts, shifting the material so that the part of her hem right of center was draped across Mr. Haddonfield's satin-clad knee. Antonia's riding habits and any outfit in a military style were created by male hands, and yet, the sight of Mr. Haddonfield's fingers measuring off her hem was unsettling.

"Were you avoiding the mistletoe by lurking in the library?" she asked, as he threaded the needle with brown silk.

"Absolutely. You?"

"If I'd known Lady Chalfont had already decorated in anticipation of the Christmas season, I would have developed a megrim. I vow some men count the exact number of paces they need to cover in order to nearly collide with a woman beneath a kissing bough."

Even Peter had ambushed her, though she'd turned her head at the last moment and escaped with a mere peck to the cheek.

"As do some ladies." Mr. Haddonfield knotted the thread and took up Antonia's hem. "My sisters dragged me here, then abandoned me, a sacrificial lamb among the vixens. This is lovely material."

"I like good quality. It wears better."

The moment should have been awkward, but with the fire crackling in the hearth, and the faint music from the ballroom, Antonia felt peace stealing over her. The fire found gold and copper highlights in Mr. Haddonfield's hair, while his evening attire showed off his broad shoulders quite nicely. There was an earldom held by a Haddonfield family. Perhaps Max Haddonfield was that handsome cousin pressed into escort service from time to time.

"You like fine fabrics," he said, bending over the material. "I like kissing, in the general case, but not when it's contrived as the next thing to an entertainment. The men lay bets in the retiring room, you know. Reminds me of public school and not in a good way."

"Bets?"

He paused in his stitching to send her a brooding look. "Will Lord Bollingbrook succumb to Miss Abbott's abundant charms? Will Mr. Peter Nagle endure Lady A's company beneath the kissing bough when Miss Huntly has been sending him melting glances all evening? I don't even know who those people are, but what sort of kiss can be had when only pagan tradition or matchmaking schemes inspire the undertaking?"

He focused again on Antonia's hem while she made herself take a slow breath. Exactly one Mr. Peter Nagle was in attendance, and Miss Huntly was both comely and well dowered.

"Male wagering has ever been the province of utmost folly," Antonia said, "though I agree that one ought to kiss because one pleases to, not because some dead leaves are hanging from the nearest rafter."

"Exactly." Mr. Haddonfield tied off the thread and used the tiny scissors to snip the loose ends. "All finished." He reassembled the contents of Antonia's sewing kit and passed it to her. "My sisters despair of me."

This was a confession rather than a passing remark. "My cousins despair of me."

He smiled up at her. "Maybe that's why I enjoy your company. Shall we return to the ballroom?"

Antonia rose and offered Mr. Haddonfield her hand. The gesture was inappropriate, but the man had been sitting literally at her feet, for the purpose of repairing her hem. *Appropriate* was apparently a lost cause.

He took her hand and rose easily. "I was regretting my decision to attend this ball. I regret it no longer."

He was so wonderfully solid and tall, and his smile was so unexpectedly merry. "What became of your regret?"

"Chased off by a sensible lady to whom I could render a small service." His smile faded with that admission, though again he kept hold of Antonia's hand. "I would like to kiss you. Here and now, no silly tradition to take the credit or the blame."

"I must ask, why me, Mr. Haddonfield?"

He stroked his thumb over her knuckles, and even his thumb had calluses. "I'm not sure why. Kissing is unscientific, but the best of my experiments have been illuminated by strong intuition as well as logic. My intuition tells me you are sensible. You don't babble. When you smile. . ."

To any other man, a sensible woman who didn't babble would be boring or invisible. "I have good teeth." Why on earth had those words come out of her mouth?

"What you have is a hidden capacity for mischief," Mr. Haddonfield said, stepping closer. "You guard a kind heart, you love books, your mind is lively, and you don't suffer fools. May I kiss you?"

Oh, to be asked. He'd wait all evening for her answer too. Under the mistletoe, Peter had puckered up like some great land-dwelling fish, using a public situation to extort acquiescence from his victim.

"May I kiss you back?" Antonia asked. "Not simply hold still while you demonstrate your mastery of the art?"

"I am no expert, but I suspect kissing is akin to waltzing. Success is most likely when both parties put their best foot forward." He slid a big, warm hand along the side of Antonia's neck and into her hair.

Any more brave questions evaporated from Antonia's mind on a cloud of wonder, because really, truly, Max Haddonfield intended to kiss her.

"Antonia?"

"Mr. Haddonfield?" Her heart was waltzing, as were the butter-flies in her tummy.

He pressed his lips gently to hers, and so Antonia, without hesitation—without any hesitation at all—kissed him back.

ONE MINUTE, Max had been spouting inanities about the botanical properties of mistletoe, the next, he'd been courting impropriety by closeting himself with Miss Antonia in an empty music room. He'd been seized with the need to use any pretext to spend time with her someplace quiet, where sensible people could hear themselves think.

Miss Antonia was quite sensible. Witness, she carried her own little perfectly organized sewing kit equipped with the exact colors of thread she might need to repair her ensemble. Max's sisters didn't do that, and he felt as if being trusted with Antonia's petite sewing kit was a very great boon indeed.

The lady also shared Max's disdain for the whole mistletoe farce, which was a damned shame for the scheming fortune hunters of polite society, because she had a delightful way with a kiss.

She maneuvered Max where she wanted him, using her fingers fisted in his hair to angle his head and her free hand on his jaw to hold him still—not that he was going anywhere. Max took a reciprocally firm hold of the Antonia, his hands grasping her sides in that tempting territory above her waist.

She sighed against his mouth, then swiped her tongue over his lips. Desire welled, surprisingly fierce—like the woman in Max's arms. She did it again, more gently, as if asking a question. Max answered and gathered her close as she twined her arms around his waist.

The fire in the hearth threw out a lovely heat, the music from the ballroom faded as the set ended, and Max's world became an investigation of how to pleasure Antonia. She liked a firm touch—on her sides, on her back, on her lovely muscular derriere. She liked sweet, slow kisses, and lots of them, and she liked to pause, cuddling closer, as if Max's kisses were too rich to be consumed all at once.

"Mr. Haddonfield, you have me in a state."

"Max."

She leaned her forehead against his shoulder. "Short for Maximillian?"

"Maximus, a deuced poor jest on a fellow with seven older siblings. I used a middle name growing up because my elders could not resist making sport of my first name." He stroked her nape, loving the combination of textures there. Warm, soft skin. Silky tresses. Delicate lace edging her collar.

"I feel as if I've had a bit too much cordial."

Oh, the things she said. "I feel as if you *are* the cordial, and I want to consume the whole bottle."

She smiled at him a little dazedly. A curl had come loose from her coiffure to coil at her shoulder, softening her appearance. A trill of laughter in the corridor had her stepping back, though she didn't go far.

"You have given me something to think about, Mr. Haddonfield. I need to make an early night of it, but like you, I was regretting my decision to attend this ball."

"And now?"

"I regret that I must leave this room."

She bussed his cheek and rustled away, pausing for a moment to smooth her skirts and assume a very correct posture before opening the door. She put Max in mind of an actress, taking a moment in the wings to don the persona of a character whom she must portray on the stage.

"I'll bring another cat by the library tomorrow," Max said, "if you'll be there."

"I'll be there all afternoon."

She slipped out the door, leaving Max to wonder what the hell had just happened, and how soon he could make it happen again.

ANTONIA HAD BEEN out past midnight, so she wasn't at her best rising for an early breakfast. She'd left the ball immediately after parting from Mr. Haddonfield, unwilling to spoil the memory of his kisses with bad punch or another inept waltz.

Recollections of time spent with him lingered as she poured her second cup of tea, warming her in a way that had nothing to do with the fire burning in the breakfast parlor's hearth.

"Shall I have the coach brought 'round, my lady?" Miller, the first footman, asked. "Looks like we could get rain or worse."

The library was all of five streets away, but two of those streets were not the most fashionable. Morning sun was making latticed patterns on the carpet, and Miller was being diplomatic.

"I'll walk," Antonia said. "If you'd accompany me, my passing will cause less talk."

For Antonia to walk without a chaperone was skirting impropriety, but then, she was also skirting spinsterhood. Her companion, an aunt of venerable years, never rose before noon and most assuredly never walked anywhere a coach could take her.

So Antonia walked when she could, where she could, and ignored the veiled questions and snide remarks. Then too, she wanted to have a peek at a certain bakery on Dinwiddie Lane and perhaps buy a hot cross bun or two.

"You sure you don't want the carriage, my lady?" Miller asked, lifting the lid over the warming tray that held the omelet. "Weather can turn quickly this time of year."

The scent of cheese and oregano wafted through the parlor, and Antonia's belly growled.

"No carriage this morning. I find the fresh air clears my head, though you are right about the weather. I'd best enjoy the sunny mornings when they come along."

And the sunny kisses. Who knew a kiss could be a source of joy? The poets maundered on about earthly love and passion and all manner of folderol, and Antonia had always attributed such effusions to literary excess.

She was rising to serve herself a portion of eggs when Peter strode into the parlor.

"Antonia, good morning. You there,"—he waved a hand at Miller —"set a second place for a hungry fellow."

Miller, may his wages ever increase, sent Antonia a questioning glance as she resumed her seat, her plate still empty.

"Please do set a place for my cousin, though I must say, Peter, this is an unexpected treat." An ambush. Peter was still in evening attire, which might mean he'd spent the night playing cards. Whatever the case, he didn't mind that Antonia knew he'd been out past dawn, which sat ill with her. In his way, Peter was trying to court her. Charging unannounced into her breakfast parlor while wearing rumpled evening clothes was disrespectful.

Miller finished arranging a second set of cutlery at Antonia's left elbow, then took up a place at the end of the sideboard, hands behind his back.

Peter helped himself to an enormous serving of eggs, did not ask if Antonia cared for any herself, and appropriated the teapot.

"We caused a bit of talk last night," he said, starting on his eggs. "You danced with only me, dear cousin. Should I be encouraged?"

You should be hiring a dancing master. "From one dance? I no longer need stand up with every shy bachelor or gouty uncle in Mayfair, Peter. You asked for a waltz, I granted that request. When you nearly cast me into the other dancers, my ankle took it amiss, and thus I left. Watching Miss Abbott make a fool of Lord Bollingbrook under the mistletoe is entertainment for inebriates and fools."

Peter sent her a curious glance, then scooped three spoonfuls from the jam pot and slathered them on his toast. "Do you have a megrim, Antonia? Perhaps your female humors are vexing you?"

Miller cleared his throat, the servant's equivalent of boxing a guest's ears, though if anything vexed Antonia, it was the thought of Peter encouraging Miss Huntly's melting glances.

"As long as I avoid the near occasion of waltzes with you, Peter, I enjoy excellent health." Antonia passed Miller her plate, and he served her eggs and two slices of ham, her usual fare.

"You are peckish first thing in the day," Peter said, chewing like a squirrel. "I will remember that. Diana is the same way. A veritable virago. I say, my good man, might you fetch us another pot of tea?"

He smiled at Miller, the eye-crinkling, jolly-good-fellow smile he frequently turned on Antonia.

Miller, again, waited for direction from Antonia.

"A pot of black," she said. "My cousin is not fond of gunpowder." Nor was Peter subtle in his machinations, for the teapot was still half full.

Miller pointedly left the door open when he departed with the teapot.

"I came here to apologize," Peter said, putting down his knife and fork to pat Antonia's hand. "I got a bit enthusiastic on the dance floor last night. Meant no harm, of course."

Beam, crinkle, grin.

"You have a spot of egg on your cuff, Peter. Right next to the wine stain."

His smile faltered, revealing an instant of mulishness in his eyes. "I should have gone home and changed, I know that, but I wanted to make things right with you. I ought not to have asked for your waltz. I know you don't care to dance, but people talk when a lady isn't asked to stand up even once."

"And people talk when she does stand up, apparently. I am not responsible for people talking."

"But you are responsible for breaking my heart, Antonia. I have paid you obvious attentions, I have broached marriage with you, and you must admit a match between us has many advantages. Many."

Antonia was torn between the desire to end Peter's hopes once for all, and the certain knowledge that he was making sense. She stared spinsterhood in the eye, Papa had always liked Peter, and days at the library were not a life.

She might have discussed her circumstances with the Earl of Casriel, who had once also offered for her. He was a sensible fellow, a gentleman to his bones, and he'd keep Antonia's confidences. When she'd rejected his suit, he'd insisted they remain friends.

And his dancing was lovely, though he'd married shortly after courting Antonia—a love match, of course.

Max Haddonfield wasn't courting anybody, but he'd given Antonia a reason to hesitate where Peter was concerned.

"I have not broken anybody's heart, Peter, and I don't care for manufactured drama. In point of fact, you have broached marriage, but you have never courted me, never sought my permission to pay your addresses, never presented yourself as a suitor rather than a cousin spouting platitudes and practicalities."

He consumed another three bites of omelet. "You are saying I have not courted you. Fair enough. Let the courtship begin. I'll call upon you this afternoon and we can take the coach out for the carriage parade. The park is much less crowded this time of year, and—"

"I am not free this afternoon." *And you still have not asked if you can pay me your addresses.* "As it happens, I must go out shortly."

Antonia was not about to leave Peter running tame in her house, though, so she poured herself another cup of tea from the fresh pot Miller brought in.

"Tomorrow then," Peter said. "Weather permitting. You can't call me out for a shortcoming and then leave me no opportunity to make amends. That's not sporting, Antonia."

And courtship was not a sport. Not a game to be played under the mistletoe. "Tomorrow, weather permitting, you may drive me about the park." If Aunt Emily came along, Peter would have to keep his talk of courtship to himself.

He gulped down the rest of his tea and rose. "I shall count the hours until then, my dear. The minutes and the seconds as well. If it's courtship you want, it's courtship you'll get."

Miller's brows rose nearly to his hairline. Peter bowed, blew Antonia a kiss, and sauntered out with a piece of buttered, jam-topped toast in his hand.

The silence in his wake could have toppled castles. "Does my lady have good news to share with the staff?" Miller asked after the front door slammed.

Brave of him. "No, I do not. My cousin presumes, and I haven't the heart to dash his hopes."

Miller collected Peter's empty dishes and cutlery onto a tray. He was typically the most discreet of men, and he was making a racket to wake the dead.

"Just say it, Miller. I won't turn you off, I promise."

Miller lifted the tray and headed for the door. "*He* would. He'd turn me off on any pretext and enjoy doing it. He'd cut Mrs. Pritchard or Mr. Davenport loose with even more relish because he knows your housekeeper, your butler, the lot of us, are all loyal to you, my lady."

Miller's observation, offered with calm certainty, gave Antonia far more to think about than any mishap on the dancefloor could. Peter was a problem, marrying him looked increasingly like no solution at all, and yet, the alternative was to become an object of pity.

What titled lady with a significant fortune could find no husband at all?

Every girl was raised to regard a family of her own as the fulfillment of her very purpose on earth. Antonia could reject that reasoning with the rational part of her mind, while still longing for somebody of her own to love.

Mr. Max Haddonfield wasn't a solution either—he was a chemist of limited means and he wasn't offering marriage, despite his luscious kisses—though Antonia would far rather dwell on Mr. Haddonfield than on Peter.

She was nearly at the library steps, Miller marching along a few paces behind her, when Miss Dottie trotted up to her side.

"Sister and I thought you should be warned, Miss Antonia. Mr. Kessler is inside, and he is not at all happy with you. He's waving some letter about and stomping around like a peevish bullock. Lukey-pie bolted for the back hallway, and I don't blame the poor dear."

"Splendid," Antonia said. "Just splendid. Two ambushes in one morning. What else could possibly go wrong?"

CHAPTER FOUR

When Max had returned to the ballroom the previous evening, Susannah had taken him by one arm and Della by the other. Five minutes later they'd introduced him to Henry, Viscount Hamblin, an older gent who professed to be an amateur chemist with a very great interest in "progress."

Max had spent twenty minutes listening to his lordship impersonate a harbor cannon on the topics of power looms, coal mines, and steam engines. Those subjects had very little to do with chemistry, but they all connected to the science of amassing a fortune.

The price of escape had been acceptance of a dinner invitation for tonight at Lord Hamblin's home. At midday, Max was still wishing he'd eluded his lordship's hospitality.

"Don't know when I last laid out your evening togs two days runnin'," Dagger said, skipping along at Max's side. "You will be a sar-tor-i-al wonder, you will. Should I fetch a posy for your lapel?"

"No, thank you. You shall fetch the day-olds and begin weighing and measuring them yourself. Mind you don't eat any samples until I've checked your work."

Dagger came to a halt, his gaze on the pickle vendor pushing his cart down the street. "You want *me* to do the measurements? All of them?"

"If you don't want to do the calculations of diameter based on circumference, I can do those when I'm through at the lending library."

Dagger speared him with a look. "I was supposed to help you at the library."

"I'll manage on my own. Measuring the samples is more important."

"You don't want me to see Lucifer. You think I'll steal him."

Max did not want Dagger making a bad impression on Miss Antonia. "A library is a genteel place, Dagger. It's a wipe-your-boots and keep-your-voice-down place where little old ladies and hopeless prigs like Alfred Paxton make themselves at home. If you'd like to peek in on Lucifer, you should, but the longer we wait to collect the day-olds the fewer of them there are. A smaller sample size means our results are less trustworthy."

"Which is why I'm not to gobble them all up. I know."

Dagger apparently pondered his options for the remainder of the distance to Bootjack Street. The afternoon was cold, not the bitter, biting cold of January, but to a skinny boy, the warmth of the bakeries would appeal on such a day.

"I'll say hello to Lucifer another time," Dagger muttered. "Let him settle in a bit more."

"I will give him your best regards, assuming I can pry him from the arms of his adoring friends."

Dagger sprinted off before Max could remind the boy to keep his fingers to himself, but the warning would likely have done no good. Dagger picked pockets like some men smoked a pipe—compulsively, for comfort, regardless that it made their clothing stink and resulted in foul breath and congestion of the lungs.

Libraries were good places. Dagger would figure that out for himself when he could keep still for more than two consecutive minutes.

Max let himself into Miss Antonia's domain, prepared to spread good cheer in all directions, but the two older ladies at their customary table weren't even pretending to read.

"Up there," the smaller of the two said, pointing to the mezzanine.

The other sister shook her head, as if a hopeless illness beset somebody in the house. "He is not a nice man, that Mr. Kessler. Not nice at all."

"He frightened the poor kitty," the first lady reported. "What sort of man menaces a dear, helpless creature like that?"

Lucifer was dear; he was far from helpless.

Max unwound his scarf and pulled off his gloves, stuffing them into his tool bag. He let his footsteps reverberate on the spiral staircase and unbuttoned his coat with one hand as he went.

"Miss Antonia?"

"Back here." Two words that conveyed a wealth of exasperation.

Max found her among the gothic novels, sitting on a low stool, surrounded by piles of bound books.

"Is something amiss?"

"Worse than amiss," she said, snatching a book from the stack nearest her knees. "Good day, Mr. Haddonfield, though *good* hardly applies. Nobody told me I was to catalog and shelve new books, nobody told me why those boxes were sitting by the back door. Then along comes Mr. Kessler, waving a vile epistle from Mr. Paxton, and three boxes and one shouted sermon later, my post is imperiled."

Max slid down along the bookshelves to sit opposite her in the cramped space between the rows. "Do you need your post?"

She might. Her best finery was well made but hardly *à la mode*. She'd worn no jewels at the Chalfont's ball, and genteel sources of employment for young women were few and far between.

"I could find another post eventually. The issue is that I abhor failure."

Max took the book from her—a worn copy of Mrs. Burney's *Evelina*. "Perhaps it's Kessler who has failed. Failed experiments can teach us a lot, though they are disappointing." Antonia looked tired to him, in a prim, annoyed sort of way. He wanted to kiss better whatever disquiet bothered her, and yet, he knew how out of sorts failed experiments left him.

"What sort of librarian doesn't know that new books must be shelved, Mr. Haddonfield?"

"The sort who is purposely kept in the dark about that aspect of her duties."

She took back the book. "Mr. Kessler will return tomorrow. He has given me a last chance, he says, and if these books aren't all correctly shelved by tomorrow morning, he will have no choice but to dismiss me."

"Then let's be about it," Max said. "I came here today intent on building a hinged flap on the bottom of the library's back door, so the cats can come and go without requiring you to leave a window open. I can shelve books instead."

"Haven't you a job, Mr. Haddonfield?"

"I have a vocation, and it can wait a few hours. Where does *Evelina* go?"

Antonia explained the system to him, and Max was soon arranging novels on shelves, and rearranging them as the shelves filled. The afternoon wore on with Antonia occasionally trotting down the steps to wait on a patron.

Part of Max had been hoping that last night's kiss had been a wayward impulse, a little indulgence between adults who found themselves in a private circumstance.

"No such luck," he muttered, using his folding knife to open the last box of books. These were donations, like the other two boxes, books that were far from new, but still valuable. Miss Antonia was downstairs chatting with Miss Dottie and Miss Betty as they prepared to leave—Max had been introduced when he'd fetched an afternoon tea break for the ladies.

Max enjoyed the simple sound of Antonia's voice. She was well educated, her diction that of the upper classes. She read French easily, and she worked with the steady focus of a woman with inherent self-discipline. Max had caught her staring at his mouth, though, and caught himself stealing glances at hers.

And at her hands, her hips, her *everything*.

"I've locked up," Antonia said. "I can finish the final box on my own."

"No, you cannot. The streets are already dark and I'd be no sort of gentleman if I left you here alone with all these books yet to catalog."

She settled onto her stool with a weary sigh. "You are very dear, Mr. Haddonfield, but you are also a distraction."

"I am?"

"You needn't sound so pleased. I might work more quickly if every three minutes I wasn't recalling your kisses."

Max took a book from the box. "Only every three minutes?"

"Oh, very well. Constantly. You are like a tune that won't leave my head. I have matters to consider, work to do, but there you are in my imagination, with your sweet caresses and—I am making a cake of myself."

Max kissed her on the cheek. "I am distracted as well, but I refuse to give Kessler the satisfaction of winning by cheating. Sooner begun is sooner done, Antonia, and I want very much to finish this task and move onto more interesting endeavors."

She smiled at him, seized a book, and went back to her shelving.

Max went back to being distracted.

TO SHARE a task with a man was an odd sort of waltz, one Antonia was enjoying. Mr. Haddonfield occasionally read her passages at random, sometimes silly, sometimes profound. He had an ear for lovely prose, and an ability to sink into the activity put before him.

Antonia, by contrast, resented that a lot of musty books interfered with her enjoyment of his company. She silently reveled in the faint scent of fresh baking wafting from his direction, and loved how he stopped what he was doing to greet the cat and scratch its chin.

"He left when Mr. Kessler started ranting," Antonia said. "I thought perhaps Lucifer had removed permanently to more peaceful surrounds."

"Not when the weather's turning wintry on us. He likes it here."

"For the most part, I like it here," Antonia said, diving into the final box for another armful of books, except the box was empty. "Mr. Haddonfield, we have finished."

He rose, the cat in his arms. "About damned time, pardon the emphasis. Shall we finish the lemon cake and warm up the leftover tea before facing the elements?"

Antonia really, truly ought to be getting home. She typically sent a ticket porter to fetch the coach at the end of the day, but who knew if porters were to be found after dark?

"I ought not to tarry." Though when would she have another chance to spend a quiet quarter hour with a man she thoroughly enjoyed? Why not be a bit daring? A bit independent? She'd been alone with Mr. Haddonfield for the last hour, and a pleasant hour it had been too.

Unlike the time she'd spent with Peter first thing in the day.

"You were willing to toil away all day to appease Kessler's demands, Antonia. Take ten minutes to sit with me and enjoy a snack." The cat rubbed his head against Mr. Haddonfield's chin. "With us, rather."

Lucifer's purring was audible from two yards away, and beyond the curtained windows, the street was quiet. Sometime during the afternoon, Mr. Haddonfield had dropped the *Miss* before Antonia's name, and she liked that too.

Liked it rather well. "I suppose the cake will get stale if we don't eat it."

"A terrible waste." He set the cat down gently. "Miss Dottie and Miss Betty would disapprove."

He'd charmed them into taking tea with Antonia at midafternoon, and they'd regaled her with tales of court life back in "Dear Old George's day."

Antonia picked up the cat, gave the shelves one last look, and headed for the stairs. "How do you suppose Miss Dottie and Miss Betty came to be haunting libraries when, in their youths, they were the toasts of polite society?"

"Their youths were some time ago," Mr. Haddonfield said, collecting the boxes and following Antonia down the steps. "Fortunes wane, families decline. A small competence becomes even smaller when it must last for decades."

Something in his tone caught Antonia's ear. "Has your family fallen on hard times, Mr. Haddonfield?" The Earl of Bellefonte did have the family name of Haddonfield, but that signified nothing. Mainwarings, for example, were thick on the ground in some counties.

"You and I have shared a hundred gothic adventures, Antonia. Please call me Max."

His smile reminded her that they'd also shared some lovely kisses —not that she was about to lose track of that memory.

"The boxes can go in the back hallway, *Max*."

He strode off, giving Antonia a candlelit view of his retreating form. He was stunningly well made, and he moved with the inborn grace of a man comfortable in his own skin. He'd brought a bag of tools with him to the library. Antonia could not imagine any gentleman of her acquaintance knowing how to use a bag of tools, much less carrying them about himself.

"Clearly, I do not know the right gentlemen," she muttered to the cat.

"When Lucifer replies, you'll want to keep that to yourself," Mr. Haddonfield—Max—said. "Now, about that lemon cake?"

Antonia swung the kettle over the coals glowing in the hearth and took the lemon cake down from the mantel.

"Have you blown anything up lately?" she asked, taking a slice and passing the rest over.

"Not in the sense most people use that term. Shall we sit?"

The library had one comfortable place to sit—a sofa before the hearth. The sofa occupied the warmest spot in the whole building, because it was situated under the mezzanine's overhang. With the curtains on every window closed, the effect was surprisingly cozy.

Antonia took a corner of the sofa and let the weariness of the day settle over her. "In what sense do you blow things up?"

"The baking sense. We enjoy leavened bread and use yeast to give other products lightness. The yeast gives off gas when mixed with the wet elements of bread dough—or we see bubbles form in something like malt wort—and heat expands that gas as the item bakes. This all takes time, though, and yeast can impart a characteristic flavor. It also doesn't like salt, and beyond a certain quantity, doesn't like sugar either."

"This is what you're studying? The properties of yeast?"

"I'm researching the properties of yeast and experimenting with other possible sources of leavening. The ideal agent will be cheap, have no taste, and work quickly. I'm also experimenting with different preparations of yeast, and I find that some work more quickly than others."

"Why?"

"Why do they work more quickly? I suspect because the size of the individual particle when pulverized in a dry form—"

Antonia patted the place beside her. "Why investigate this topic?" She loved bread still warm from the oven, but she'd never once—not ever—considered how bread was made.

"Because bread that requires two risings takes longer to prepare, and time is money." Mr. Haddonfield sat beside her, making the old sofa creak. "Because leavening with whipped egg white or whipped heavy cream takes effort and expense. Because the French have come across a simple means of making soda ash—sodium carbonate—from brine, which when reacted with an acid becomes sodium bicarbonate and that has potential for many uses, including in the kitchen."

"You are passionate about this."

He popped the last of his lemon cake into his mouth and dusted his hands. "My siblings find my vocation amusing. Many bright minds are intent on developing faster means of transportation for goods and people. Other bright minds are making stronger steel, cheaper copper, and the like, but every bit as much work is done in the kitchen as in the factory. Why not lighten the load in the kitchen too? We can live without enormous bridges or quick passage across the seas, as we have for generations. We cannot live without safe, affordable, nutritious food."

While Mr. Haddonfield poured two cups of tea and added a dash of sugar to each, Antonia finished her cake. "You seek to lighten the load of women with this work."

"I spent a year apprenticed to a cook that I might familiarize myself with basic food preparation," he said, resting an arm along the back of the sofa. "The effort needed to produce a palatable, safe, nutritious meal is enormous. Miss Betty and Miss Dottie are tiny, for all they seem to be in good health. Would they be more robust in their old age if preparing a decent meal was easier for them?"

"You have quite the imagination." And he was both fierce in his beliefs and confident of his priorities. What a refreshing change from men who sought only to while away their mornings at the tailor's or to be seen riding bloodstock in the park.

"You have an imagination too," he said. "What occupies your fancy when you have the time to indulge it?"

His question might have come from a particularly engaging dinner partner, but darkness had fallen, and Antonia had spent much of her day with the man seated so casually at her side. She would soon have to make a decision regarding Peter—none of her options in that situation appealed to her—and yet, she had this stolen moment with a fellow she liked and increasingly respected.

"When I have time to indulge my imagination lately," she said, taking his mug and setting it aside, "I think about you, Max Haddonfield, and about kissing you."

His smile spread like a sunrise across a bountiful land in high summer. "Do you truly?"

"In fact, I'm thinking about kissing you right now." She bussed his cheek, which took every bit of her courage, then hesitated.

He lifted her to straddle his lap—lifted her easily—and then he was kissing her back like she was the answer to all of his dreams, and a few of his wildest fantasies too.

As he was surely the answer to hers.

A LONG AFTERNOON watching Antonia reach for the highest shelves, handle books, and bend to retrieve more books from boxes had sorely tried Max's self-restraint. She was well formed, generously endowed, and she'd bumped up against Max any number of times in the cramped confines of the gothic shelves.

He would never importune a lady uninvited, but his imagination had shed every pretense of gentlemanly decorum hours ago.

He and Antonia needed to talk. She needed to understand that he was not without means, though he preferred to use those means for his vocation. He was well born, not a fact he set much store by, but it would matter to her.

Apparently, getting his neckcloth untied mattered to her more.

"Antonia, we mustn't." Not yet, maybe not ever.

She kissed the thought right out of his head and replaced it with sensation as she sank her weight over his falls. Whatever else was true, Max had to kiss her back, had to finally, finally learn the shape and softness of her breasts in his hands.

Her next project was unbuttoning his shirt and slipping her hands over his chest and around his neck.

"Did you know," she whispered right into his ear, "watching you handle books *unsettled* me?"

"The affliction is apparently contagious, for I—Antonia, what are you doing?"

She gathered her skirts and petticoats. "I am for once doing as I please, for once ignoring the strictures polite society trusses me in from the time I pour my second cup of tea until I lay my head onto my pillow. I will soon be a spinster or worse, and I have squandered so many opportunities. I refuse to squander this one."

Something in her comment wanted further investigation—what was worse than being a spinster?—but Max's deductive powers were consumed with figuring out how to undo the buttons of her bodice.

"Let me," she said, brushing his hands aside.

In moments, Max was staring at the frothy lace trim on a pair of snug chemises. "You don't wear stays?"

"I must for formal wear, but I often walk here in the morning, and one wants to breathe. A fitted chemise allows more freedom." She untied the bows holding her décolletage closed and some of the urgency seemed to leave her. "You will think me very forward."

"I think you very delectable." Max eased the linen and lace aside, and wished the English language offered more effusive terms. He stared at pale, abundant female perfection, alabaster smooth in the firelight, ever so much warmer than alabaster.

He buried his face in the cleft of her breasts, reveling in the scent of lemons. "Why me, Antonia? Why allow me this honor?"

Her head fell back as he caressed the soft undersides of her breasts, then teased her nipples. "Because you look at me and you see me. Because we deserve this. Because that feels wonderful."

She tasted wonderful, of tart fruit and sweet woman, of desire and abundance. Max was soon more aroused than he could recall being since his randy boyhood.

"We should stop, Antonia. I can satisfy you without. . ."

She had scooted back to start unbuttoning his falls.

"This is not wise, Antonia." How he loved the sight of her, half undone, determined on her objective, that lock of hair again curling against her shoulder.

"Wasting this opportunity would be unwise, Max. I envy Miss Dottie and Miss Betty. They were young and happy once, they knew themselves to be desired and envied. They turned heads and broke hearts. They didn't sit among the potted palms wondering how soon they could leave the ball without causing talk."

Max could not fathom every nuance of what drove Antonia, but he knew that to refuse her, to reject what she offered, wasn't in him. Her lively, sensible mind might grasp his reasoning, but the tender heart she guarded so well would be hurt.

"Antonia, do you understand what follows if we continue? I will exercise restraint,"—somehow, he would find that strength—"but conception is always a possibility."

She framed his face in her hands. "I understand, and I thank you for the question. My mother made sure I was not kept in ignorance, and at finishing school, I met a groom."

"Yes?" Whoever that young swain had been, he'd made Antonia smile.

"I was not always the buttoned-up, practical, plain woman you see now. Before my parents died I had more courage."

Didn't we all? "You are not plain, Antonia, and at the moment, you don't qualify as buttoned-up either." Practicality had left the premises a good twenty minutes ago.

She looked down at her breasts, expression quizzical. "I could grow to like being unbuttoned in your company." She resumed undoing Max's falls. "I like unbuttoning you too."

She liked *handling* him, exploring textures and contours with a careful curiosity that made Max's vow to exercise restraint a slender spar of clarity on a vast sea of temptation. Somewhere between measuring day-old bread loaves, befriending stray cats, and setting a good example for Dagger, Max had lost sight of the sheer pleasure of being an adult male in the company of a willing adult female.

"You will indulge my curiosity all evening if I ask it of you, won't you?" Antonia said, kissing him on the mouth. "I can't wait all evening."

There were reasons—reasons beyond rampaging desire—that

Max would not tarry in the library all evening, though at the moment, those reasons eluded him.

"On your back," he murmured. "I want you on your back." For he would need to withdraw, and that meant maintaining as much control over the situation as possible.

Antonia scrambled off his lap. "Up you go," she said. "I have need of this sofa, sir."

Then Max was over her, half-hampered by skirts and breeches, until they got their clothing arranged, the pillows arranged, and themselves *arranged*. He took his time, easing into Antonia's heat, waiting for any hitch in her breathing or tensing of her body that might signal the need for retreat.

"I like this," she whispered. "I want this."

I like you. Max couldn't get the words out, because he was too busy mentally checking his own desire, and besides, he more than *liked* Antonia. He treasured her humor and practicality, her spirit and her determination. He gloried in her desire for him, a man who spent his days measuring bread and befriending cats.

"Faster," she murmured, scooting down to get a better grip on him.

"Soon." When she couldn't speak, she was so overcome with passion. "Move with me."

"How?"

"Like dancing, Antonia, only sweeter."

She was a quick study and had a marvelously short fuse. Max tried to complete a simple calculation in his head—divide 11.5 by 3.14—while Antonia thrashed and keened beneath him, but even the charms of mathematics were barely adequate to bolster his restraint.

"Maximus Haddonfield." Antonia made his name sound like her favorite sweet. "You astound me."

He gave her a few minutes to catch her breath, and then astounded her again, though that was the limit of what he could ask of his self-discipline. When Antonia's legs had eased down to his sides, and her breathing had relaxed, he slowly withdrew.

"Must you go?" she asked.

They had not spoken of marriage, hadn't even mentioned courtship. Did she seek that from him, or was this experience a fist she raised against the approaching arrival of spinsterhood? Max would summon the focus to untangle those questions, when desire no longer clamored so urgently for satisfaction.

He extricated himself from Antonia's embrace, rose, took out his handkerchief, braced his back against the mantel, and brought himself off in a few swift strokes. When he opened his eyes, he beheld Antonia, sprawled on the sofa, skirts rucked to her thighs, eyes slumberous and frankly watching him.

"Never have I been more pleased to spend time in a library," she said, "and I do love my books."

Max had to concentrate to make sense of her words. She hadn't said she loved *him,* but then, what did he expect? He cast around for a reply—something witty, self-possessed, original—as he tidied up and buttoned his falls.

He regarded the houri on the sofa and had to look away lest he start unbuttoning again. "We should open a window."

Oh, that was witty.

Antonia wrinkled her nose, sighed, and sat up. "I'll crack the door to the back passage. We leave that window ajar for the cat."

"I'm sorry," Max said, taking the place beside her. "My store of urbane banter is at low ebb and I never commanded much to begin with. I am... I did not anticipate... Bloody hell, Antonia."

Worse and worse.

"Is that a good bloody hell or a bad bloody hell, Max?"

The unforgivably foul language spoken in those prim tones made him smile. "It's an utterly flummoxed bloody hell. You have slain my rational mind, ambushed my grasp of logic, and drowned my self-possession in pleasure. I don't know whether to thank you or apologize or. . ." *Propose?* The idea appealed much too strongly.

"Or kiss you," Antonia said, bussing his cheek and then drawing her chemises closed. "This is not at all how I envisioned my day ending, though the notion of having ambushed you pleases me. If you apologize I will be very disappointed."

Max would never, for any reason, intentionally disappoint this woman. "Then I will thank you. You amaze me."

She tied off the second chemise and started on her buttons, and by the firelight, Max saw color steal over her cheeks.

"The sentiment is mutual, Mr. Haddonfield."

He wanted her to call him by his name, but he understood that as passion receded, and reality intruded, proper address was like another set of buttons that must be fastened.

"May I walk you home, Miss Antonia?"

Her fingers stilled, then resumed their buttoning. "I don't want to go home, to be honest, but my family would panic, as would my household. You need not walk with me."

"Are you ashamed of what happened here?" Perhaps Max should be, but he could not muster a single whit of self-reproach.

Antonia stood and smoothed down her skirts. "Ashamed? Absolutely not. I am ashamed of wasting years trying to curry the favor of polite society. I am ashamed that I took my parents' love and support so much for granted. I am ashamed that I allowed Mr. Kessler to intimidate me, when as you say, he was dishonest and *mean* this morning. You may be assured he and I will have a very short discussion tomorrow."

"Good," Max said, pleased to see the lady on her mettle. "I think the Barclay sisters would like to overhear that discussion. I know I would."

Antonia smiled at him, her gaze lit not with mere determination —she'd always been determined—but something else, something quite attractive.

"I'll crack the door to the back if you'll bank the fire," she said, "and then we really must be going."

She bustled off, no invitation to tarry again some other evening, no final embrace to revisit shared pleasures. Max tended to the fire and straightened the sofa cushions, his mind a jumble of bemuse-ment, pleasure, hope, and misgiving.

Lucifer leapt down from a windowsill, twitching the curtain aside. A handsome coach sat waiting in the street, a pair of matched grays in harness.

"Has somebody sent a coach for you?" Max asked when Antonia returned.

"Possibly," she replied, passing Max his coat.

He held her cloak for her and shrugged into his jacket, the moment becoming awkward. What to say? *What did she want him to say?*

"Shall we be going?" Antonia asked, a bit too brightly.

"I need to tell you something."

"What exactly?"

"I'm not sure, but I don't want you to get the wrong idea." *This matters. You matter.*

"I won't get any ideas at all, Mr. Haddonfield. Three ambushes in one day rather defeats even my formidable resources."

Max had no idea what she meant by that, so he offered his arm and escorted her to the waiting coach. The vehicle was elegantly appointed, though the door panels displayed no crest. Max handed Antonia into the coach and then she was gone.

Light footsteps intruded into the mental morass that was Max's attempt to make sense of his day.

"Did you forget?" Dagger asked, shivering.

"You need not have waited for me, Dagger."

"Didn't wait for you. I popped 'round here when you didn't come home. You are due for dinner at Lord Somebody's in an hour. Thought maybe you'd forgot. I did all the measurements, just like you said."

Dinner. Lord Somebody. "Damnation." Max took off up the walk-way, his tool bag banging against his thigh.

"You said I was supposed to do the measurements."

"I did indeed, and I'm sure you made an excellent job of it." If

Max sent regrets to Lord Somebody—Humble? Hambugle?—he'd simply be putting off the inevitable, and it was just possible the viscount might be willing to sponsor some research.

Not that Max would be capable of thinking scientifically about anything for quite some time.

CHAPTER FIVE

Antonia's mind was sluggish though her body felt alive for the first time in ages. Max Haddonfield had done that, muted the endless prosing of her conscience and reminded her that life should include joy, spontaneity, affection, *pleasure*.

Cupid in the clouds, the pleasure had been astonishing. Antonia pulled the shades on the coach windows and dimmed the lamps, the better to let her thoughts wander where they would. Three conclusions emerged, the first of which should have been obvious.

The longer she subjected herself to polite society's company, the angrier she became. Where was it written that an earl's daughter had to marry at all, much less to "keep the fortune in the family"? The time spent with Max Haddonfield had shown her just how constant a companion ill-humor had become.

"I liked to dance, once upon a time," she murmured to the darkened coach. "Before men began staring at my settlements and my bosom with equal covetousness."

Max didn't even know she had settlements, and his regard for her breasts had been nearly reverent.

The second conclusion was a less welcome insight: Antonia's

lover had not ended the evening with any smitten declarations. No polite offer to stop by the next day for a recounting of the exchange with Mr. Kessler. No sweet, until-next-we-meet kiss goodnight. No suggestion that they share an ice at Gunter's on Tuesday next.

"I amazed him," she muttered, "but I'm not to get the wrong idea."

She'd amazed herself, truth be told, seizing from the moment and from the man exactly what she wanted. She had the sense the Barclay sisters would have understood. Perhaps not approved, but they would have understood.

The final conclusion to emerge from her musing was that she'd have to do something about Peter. Max Haddonfield might have been humoring her, indulging in an unlooked-for frolic, or something else, but he'd been respectful, tender, passionate, considerate—in every way, he'd been a delightful lover.

To tolerate Peter's intimate attentions, even in an abstract sense, was beyond Antonia. She knew that now and was grateful for the clarity her encounter with Max had given her.

"Though I'm not to get the wrong idea," she murmured as the coach slowed. "Whatever that meant."

MAX HAD BEEN PREPARED to put up with Lord Hamblin's bleating over the course of an informal, masculine supper the likes of which he often endured at his various clubs. In his experience, one could either *do* science or *talk about* doing science.

The men and women who did science could be coaxed into discussing their work, but they didn't wave it about in general conversation like some sign of royal favor. The real scientists tended to gravitate to alcoves, where those who believed in Newton's corpuscular theory of light could debate with the theory's detractors by the hour.

Hamblin, however, had assembled a dozen men, each of whom seemed determined to out-talk his neighbor on some arcane subject or other. The meal was informal, meaning conversation did not limit itself to guests immediately to one's left or right, but instead flew across the table, up and down, and from corner to corner.

The debate made up in liveliness what it lacked in academic expertise.

"But if a miasma is responsible for the spread of disease," Mr. Peter Nagle said, "then one could reduce the likelihood of contagion by affixing large fans to the rooftops of Mayfair and creating a steady wind in the direction of the river."

Nagle had apparently forgotten that people lived on both sides of the Thames, also to the east, west, south, and north of Mayfair.

"Miasmas have never been proven," another fellow snapped. "Contagion hasn't been proven. God's will controls the spread of disease, but I will be damned if man's will shan't control the spread of progress and that means steam power!"

A thumping round of hear-hear's followed, while Max took a surreptitious glance at his pocket watch.

"Away with us to the withdrawing room, friends," Lord Hamblin said, rising. "Let the footmen be about their work while we solve the pressing problems of civilization."

If consuming vast quantities of port was a pressing problem of civilization, Hamblin's guests were solving it at a great rate. Max had limited himself to one glass to be sociable, but he didn't particularly care for port.

"Haddonfield, glad you could join us," Hamblin said, falling in step beside Max. "What a lot of noise, eh?"

"Enthusiasm," Max replied. "Ideas cannot be developed into theories if somebody isn't enthusiastic about the endeavor."

"You have a few ideas, I'm told," Hamblin said. "Let's nip into the library, shall we?"

The herd of guests went arguing and debating on down the corridor, while the library was blessedly quiet. A roaring fire crackled in the hearth, and the scent of beeswax blended with the aroma of old books. The room was elegantly appointed, with oak wainscoting, gilded pier glasses, and the usual assemblage of aging portraits.

"You have a sizable collection," Max said. "You must be very proud of your library." What would Antonia make of his lordship's literary selections?

A young woman rose from a reading chair turned toward the hearth. "Uncle, good evening."

She was pretty in a pale, blond way, and her gaze said she knew she was pretty. She also very likely knew that standing immediately before the fire in a silk gown emphasized her endowments.

"My niece," Hamblin said, clearing his throat. "Miss Jessica Huntly, may I make known to you *the honorable* Mr. Maximus Haddonfield."

Max bowed, though the form of address bothered him. As an earl's son, on formal occasions he could be announced as an honorable. This occasion was far from formal.

"Mr. Haddonfield, a pleasure." Miss Huntly curtsied, tipping forward enough to display her cleavage.

"You indulging in one of them dreadful novels, Jess?" Hamblin asked.

"Poetry," she said. "Mr. Haddonfield, do you enjoy poetry?"

"I do, particularly the pastoral variety." Max did not, however, enjoy being waylaid by design. Miss Huntly looked familiar, and she brought to mind a snippet of gossip Max had heard in the men's retiring room the previous night. "What has caught your fancy this evening?"

She slanted him a glance. "I prefer French verse at this hour of the day. The French know how to be both subtle and bold, don't you agree?"

Oh, for God's sake. "I am no expert on French poetry, Miss Huntly. My interests are largely scientific."

Hamblin patted his niece's shoulder. "Be a good girl and run along, Jess. Mind you avoid the company parlor. A lot of rogues and scalawags masquerading as men of science in there."

He winked at his niece and she offered Max another curtsy, then withdrew, her book forgotten—if she'd been reading one.

"Dratted girl set her cap for Peter Nagle," Hamblin said. "Nagle is a handsome devil, and he has possibilities, but that's about all he has—and charm, of course. I could not humor Jess's fancies where he's concerned."

Max did not know Mr. Peter Nagle, though he'd heard enough of his bloviations over dinner to conclude that Nagle was no engineer.

"Perhaps we should rejoin the company in the drawing room?" Max had a sneaking suspicion this chance meeting with Miss Huntly had been anything but chance, and the sooner he returned to the other guests, the better.

"Jess is a pretty little thing."

Clearly, Susannah and Della had been matchmaking—again. "Your niece is lovely. I have no doubt she'll make some fellow very happy." *And that fellow will not be me.* Max started for the door.

"She has settlements, Haddonfield," Hamblin said, a bit too loudly. "A younger son like you—a *fourth* legitimate son—could use a wife with some means. I knew your father, and he was a good soul, but not the soundest manager of finances."

"But you know nothing about *me*," Max said, which sat ill with him for Miss Huntly's sake if not for his own. "You and I were introduced only last night, sir, and raising this topic with me now is very close to unseemly."

"I know." Hamblin looked around the library, a literary temple to wealth and comfort, his expression sheepish. "I'm afraid Jess has been a bit unseemly. I am hoping to marry her off before spring."

Before another social Season, in other words. "I will wish you the joy of that venture, my lord, but women have means of thwarting schemes they do not participate in willingly."

Hamblin led the way into the corridor. "She was willing to meet you, and contrary to your supposition, I know a great deal about you. One of your brothers is an earl, another—from the wrong side of the blanket—is some sort of nabob with a barony—most unusual that, two titles in one family. Two of your sisters married into titled families as did two of your brothers. Jess could do worse, as she well knows. I would make it worth your while, Haddonfield."

This scheme was desperate only insofar as it had been attempted without any pretense of finesse. The basic approach—connections on one side, wealth on the other—was the sine qua non of the advantageous match.

And Max, somewhat to his surprise, wanted no part of it. Not now.

"Think about it," Hamblin said, ushering Max into the guest parlor. "That's all I ask."

Max had better things to think about, such as how a librarian came to be riding around London in an elegant coach, and whether that librarian would be glad to see him when he brought Beelzebub around to join Lucifer in protecting the books from nonexistent mice.

"I saw our host drag you into the library."

The voice belonged to Peter Nagle, who was, indeed, a good-looking blond fellow of medium height.

"Dragged, Mr. Nagle?"

"Last week it was Bletchford, an earl's nephew. It's plain enough that I'm out-gunned and out-maneuvered, but a prudent man has contingencies in place."

Nagle had imbibed freely at dinner, and he held a glass of port now.

"Contingencies are always a sound idea. Tell me, how do you intend to power those rooftop fans you'd like to install in Mayfair?"

For most men with an interest in scientific matters, that question should have led to a twenty-minute discourse on failed prototypes, tangential applications of the successful design, and schedules by which the great innovation could be brought profitably to market.

Nagle grimaced at his drink. "I will power them with good old-fashioned human sacrifice."

"Perhaps you've had enough port, Mr. Nagle."

His gaze fixed on Hamblin, who was in earnest discussion with a knot of acolytes devoted to steam engines. "I will marry for money, Haddonfield. Nothing dishonorable about it. I've a second cousin barreling toward spinsterdom for all the usual reasons—poor thing is prim and plain—and she'll have me if I put a bit of effort into charming her. Women like charm."

Antonia wasn't swayed by charm. She appreciated scholarship for its own sake, as well as honesty, affection, common sense, *passion*. Gifts Max had to give in abundance.

And she was leagues away from prim and plain.

"In my experience," Max said, "which is admittedly based on a very small sample, a bride likes to feel she's valued for herself, not for her settlements. If you find her prim and plain, she'll probably sense that." Max's sisters had intuition that no sane brother, much less a husband or suitor, would ever discount, and science had nothing to say to it.

"Antonia isn't exactly attuned to subtleties," Nagle replied, tossing back a quarter of his port. "She sent an earl packing last spring. Told him to keep his title and his family seat in Dorset and she'd keep her settlements. He wasn't old, wasn't homely, wasn't lacking in manners. First overture she'd had in ages. She regrets that decision now, I'll warrant. Somebody has to save her from herself."

Max could see his Antonia doing that—telling a man to pike off, regardless of what the world thought of her decision. Perhaps the name Antonia imparted a certain fixity of purpose to the ladies fortunate enough to be so called.

"So you'll save her by getting your hands on her funds?"

Nagle wiggled his eyebrows. "She'll get her hands on me. Let's hope I can rise to the occasion, so to speak." He smiled a conspiratorial male smile, and Max felt a frisson of distaste on behalf of the prim and plain spinster facing such a mercenary union.

"Do I know this lady?"

More of the port went down Nagle's gullet. "You might, being an earl's son and all. Lady Antonia Mainwaring is long of tooth, short of temper, and no sort of dancer at all, but she's to be my wife, once I complete a period of mandatory doting. I will fortify myself with dreams of all her lovely money and somehow contrive to go manfully to my fate. Wish me luck."

"*Lady* Antonia Mainwaring?" Max's own voice sounded far away, and the hubbub of other conversations coalesced into a dull, unpleasant roar.

"You do know her, then. A long meg, has no use for fashion, deucedly independent, and approaching her last prayers with some dreadful novel in hand. If I'm lucky she'll grant me a white marriage, though she'll probably want babies of me."

Nagle made that fate sound like transportation to seven years of hard labor.

"You'll excuse me," Max said, clamping down hard on the impulse to plough his fist into Nagle's gut. "I must bid the company goodnight, though I do have a question for you, Mr. Nagle."

Nagle waved an elegant hand in a circular motion.

"When did your understanding with her ladyship arise?"

Nagle let out a slow belch. "This very morning after our usual cozy breakfast—kissing cousins and all that. I'm to do the pretty for a bit and then we'll be married. She can call the tune now, but once the vows are spoken, our household will run as I see fit. Make no mistake about that."

Max left Nagle swilling his port, offered Hamblin the barest semblance of a goodnight, and all but stumbled out into the cold night air.

"WHERE THE 'ELL 'AVE YOU BEEN?"

When Dagger dropped his haitches, he was upset. That fact penetrated Max's mental fog as the bitter night wind and half-frozen feet had not.

"I have been out." Max whipped off his scarf, tossed it at a hook, and missed. "Men of science, port and postulations, Lord Humbug's dinner."

"That lot went home more than an hour ago, and you left early."

An eddy of rational thought joined the bewilderment, hurt, and shame swirling through Max's brain.

"Spying on me, Dagger?"

"I waited for you. A bloke ought not to be out on his own, late at night. This time of year can get desperate for them as have not."

"Good word, desperate." Max trailed his scarf along the floor. A single orange paw protruded from under the sofa, but Beelzebub was apparently not in the mood to play.

Dagger picked up the scarf. "Are you foxed?"

"Not in the sense you mean. I have not over-imbibed, though I did consider indulging."

"You're talking careful, like all the words are trying to hide from you. Gin does that, makes the words shy."

Max hung his cloak on a peg. "Stupidity does it too, though anybody inebriated on gin qualifies as wanting sense."

"You have prodigious sense. Take your gloves off, sir."

Max took off his gloves and looked at his hands, hands that had worshiped a woman who apparently thought a lark on a library sofa was a fine way to celebrate her betrothal to Mr. Peter Nagle.

"My data does not support your hypothesis, Dagger."

"Boots next, sir. What hypothesis would that be?"

The hypothesis that I was special to Antonia—Lady Antonia. Max sat on the sofa and pulled off a boot. He'd worn his good pair, which Dagger took great pride in keeping shiny and spruce.

"Sorry, Dagger. These will need some attention."

"I'll have 'em cleaned up before cockcrow. Tell me about your hypothesis."

Talking over an affair of the heart with a boy made about as much sense as talking science to a lot of cats, but Max's sense had deserted him the moment he'd become *Lady Antonia Mainwaring's* lover.

"I have been a fool," Max said, pulling off the second boot.

"There's abundant data to support that conclusion. I had hoped I was through being ridiculed, humored, and condescended to."

Dagger set Max's boots beneath the window. "Did the other fellows at supper laugh at you?"

"They did not. Failed experiments befall us all. A true scientist feels no shame in proving a theorem faulty. Science advances on the strength of such proofs." How lofty that sounded, how ridiculous.

"Then what the 'ell is plaguing you?"

"My pride, I suppose." And the sense of having read a set of results all wrong, having missed clue after clue as to the true nature of the undertaking. Perfect speech and manners, a thorough knowledge of literature such as only a woman of leisure could acquire. Fine clothing, a solid command of French...

And yet, for an heiress, Lady Antonia had seemed genuinely distressed at the thought of losing her post at the library. She was honestly concerned that each patron have the books that would please them and meet their needs. She'd been sorely vexed by Paxton's idiocy but hadn't known how to manage him. She had been genuinely moved by Lucifer's situation.

No pattern emerged to explain those contradictions. "Have we any brandy?"

Dagger sneezed and sniffed. "Your head won't thank you in the morning for adding brandy to whatever's ailing you. You never did check my calculations."

"Use your handkerchief, for pity's sake."

An odd sound came from under the sofa.

"Dagger, what was that?"

Dagger abruptly busied himself banking the fire, making a particular racket with the poker and tongs. "Probably old Hannibal having a dream. Maybe he fancies some lady cat who's not having any of his—"

"Hannibal is too cerebral for such mundane pursuits." Lady Antonia was not mundane. She was fine, intelligent, lovely, and apparently free with her favors despite having plighted her troth to Peter Numbskull.

Except, Antonia was no flirt. Max knew that the same way he knew Lucifer was happy in his new home, the way he knew his sister Della was not happy and hadn't been for some time.

The odd noise came again, not a growl or a meow, much smaller than that. "Dagger, what have you done?"

A very small white paw darted from beneath the sofa and then disappeared.

"You said Beelzebub was leaving, so that meant we needed a replacement."

"We do not *need* replacements. We make room for them." An inaccurate statement. Max needed the replacements. He needed to know that even as his science went nowhere, and his family regarded him as a harmless eccentric, he could effect some positive change in the world even if only for stray felines.

The white paw appeared again, then a second paw, then a tiny pink nose followed by the head of a small white kitten. Very small.

"He were all alone," Dagger said, "curled up in the hedge, no mama, no mates. Little bloke was probably waiting to die on such a night."

Was there anything more wretched than a skinny kitten? "You gave him a very small portion of milk?"

"Lapped it up like a seaman at his grog, then I offered him a bit of haddock. He knew exactly what to do with that too."

Max gently extracted the kitten from its lair and held it up. The little beast's coat was clean—when a cat's hygiene went to pot, the animal was truly doomed—and its eyes were a beautiful, clear blue.

"He's likely deaf," Max said. "That might be why his mother turned her back on him. He'll need an indoor home or someplace with a very high walled garden." A dwelling with that luxury was a rarity in London. Lady Antonia might enjoy such an amenity, having a claim to a pile of *lovely money*.

But if the lady was wealthy, and she could afford to send an earl packing, why settle for the likes of Nagle, who neither respected her nor had much of anything to recommend him?

"You can take Beelzebub to bide with Lucifer," Dagger said, petting the kitten's tiny head. "And we'll keep Lancelot here until he's feeling more the thing, aye?"

"Aye." The kitten, against all sense, was purring. "Nay. The little wretch can stay, but Beelzebub won't be joining Lucifer." Max passed Dagger the ruddy kitten. "And Lancelot is no sort of name for a kitten."

Dagger cradled the cat against his skinny chest. "It fits him, and he likes it. He's a white knight, all on his own against the cruel world, and if he has a fancy name he's more likely to find a fancy home."

"The Lancelot of old was a naughty fellow." Caught between conflicting loyalties and demands of the heart.

"Sir Lancelot was brave, sir, and that matters more than a few mistakes."

The argument had abruptly become philosophical, and Max had no philosophy left in him. "Call him whatever you please. If he's not used to cow's milk, he'll make a right mess by morning. Make sure he sees Hannibal and Edward using the dirt box on the balcony."

"Yes, sir."

Max undressed, washed, and climbed into bed, but sleep eluded him. Antonia's behavior made no sense, unless she was a cruel and shallow woman, which every instinct told him she was not. Perhaps she'd wanted a lark before accepting the bonds of matrimony, perhaps she knew exactly the sort of man she'd be marrying and had reasons of her own for choosing him.

It all made no sense. Max eventually drifted off, determined that he'd stick to his experiments henceforth, and leave luscious librarians to their own gothic adventures.

WHEN THE WEATHER WAS FINE, Antonia drove out with

Peter, who fawned, flirted, and tried to bring up setting a date at least once an hour. Two weeks of that *courtship* and she was ready to box his ears, but nobody—not Aunt Emily, not the many domestic advice authors, not her own good sense—had explained how to refuse a man's suit when the lady had herself invited his overtures.

The library, which had been a refuge, had become a place where memories haunted Antonia. When she'd not only correctly shelved every novel in Mr. Kessler's boxes, but reprimanded him sharply for failing to explain her duties to her, he'd turned up nauseatingly obsequious. Yesterday, he'd offered her the paying post. She'd taken that offer under advisement, because having become attached to an increasingly rotund gray cat was no excuse to remain associated with the library.

An earl's daughter could donate her time to a charitable institution, but accepting employment even from the same organization would cause endless talk. Antonia hardly cared about the talk; though if an heiress was vulnerable to the machinations of the unscrupulous, an eccentric heiress was a staked goat in the wilderness.

"And where are we off to today?" Miller asked, holding Antonia's cloak for her.

"I am paying a call." A call she'd put off for days.

"Shall I have the horses put to, your ladyship?"

"Thank you, no. I have acquired the habit of walking, Miller. Bundle up, though we aren't going far."

Antonia had one friend in all of London, one person whom she felt she could rely upon for honesty and discretion. She'd never called on him in the capacity of friend before, but then, she'd never shared intimacies with one man while accepting the addresses of another before either.

A more foolish muddle, she could not imagine.

"Lady Antonia Mainwaring," she said, as Miller passed her card over to the butler, "to see the Earl of Casriel."

"Very good, my lady. I will see if his lordship is at home."

The fellow bowed deferentially, and Antonia was left trying to formulate the reason for her call in words that didn't make her look like an imbecile. Max Haddonfield hadn't dropped by the library, hadn't sent a note, hadn't brought another cat around. Lucifer looked up from his basket every time the bell in the library door jingled, and Antonia looked up as well.

Two weeks after the most passionate interlude of her life, and all she had from her lover was a loud silence. *I think you very delectable.*

"He also found me very forgettable."

"I beg your pardon?" a blond woman asked. She'd come up the corridor so quietly, Antonia hadn't noticed her approach.

"Lady Casriel." Antonia curtsied, for what else was there to do? The earl was rumored to be besotted with his countess, and of course she would be at home at such an early hour. Antonia knew the lady socially, which meant, not very well at all.

"Lady Antonia." The curtsy was returned. "Lovely to see you again. I believe we last met at a Venetian breakfast? I was just about to order a fresh pot, and now you are here to provide me good company too."

Such friendliness, such graciousness. "My lady, you need not, that is—I came to see your husband."

Such an admission raised awkwardness to dizzying heights, but Lady Casriel merely linked arms with Antonia.

"His lordship thinks the world of you, as do I. But for your common sense, he and I would never have had an opportunity to marry. We are very much in your debt."

Antonia let herself be gently towed down a corridor tastefully appointed with still lifes, a pair of sunny seascapes, and a portrait of a mastiff.

"The purpose of my call is somewhat personal, my lady."

"Good. If we're to sit about swilling tea and munching cakes, we might as well get to know each other. Casriel is off at his brother's club, discussing investments or politics or something equally dreary. I recall that you are quite well read."

Well read. Nobody called Antonia *well read*. She was a blue-stocking, bookish, an antidote. For a few hours, shelving novels with Max Haddonfield, she'd felt well read, and for a few hours after that, she'd felt well cherished.

But as Max's silence stretched from hours to days to a fortnight, the lovely glow of his regard had faded to consternation and then something else altogether.

"I love books," Antonia said, as Lady Casriel led her to a cozy parlor done up in cream and green. The wallpaper was a pattern of leafy boughs adorned with songbirds and the occasional gilded blossom. The effect was like walking into a summery bower in deepest winter, a conservatory without the dampness or scent of dirt.

"Books have been my refuge," Antonia went on, choosing an armchair upholstered in cabbage roses, "and my parents never discouraged me from reading whatever I pleased. This room is exquisite."

"My husband is homesick for Dorset," Lady Casriel replied, settling into a second armchair. "He calls this the pastoral parlor. He gave me leave to redecorate one parlor for my personal use, and this is the result."

A footman brought a tea tray bearing a porcelain service, also adorned with flowers, leaves, and twittering birds.

"You suit his lordship," Antonia said. "Casriel is fortunate in his marriage." And she was glad about that. The earl was decent to his bones and he deserved a happy match.

Lady Casriel lifted the pot, but set it down without pouring. "I haven't any money to speak of. We will live quite modestly."

A shocking admission, which Antonia's hostess made with a bashful smile, as if living modestly should be the secret ambition of all couples.

And perhaps it ought to be. "But you and his lordship are happy."

"Disgracefully so." The smile became an outright grin. "Do I take it nuptial vows now loom in your future, my lady? You've been seen driving out with Mr. Nagle, and he looks most pleased to escort you."

"He is a family connection, a second cousin." Antonia could allow that to suffice—she and Lady Casriel were only casually acquainted—but this woman had won Grey Birch Dorning's unending esteem, a comfortably settled widow who had had no need to remarry anybody. "Might I be frank?"

"Be nothing but," Lady Casriel said. "Casriel admires your forthright nature."

That the earl had spoken with his wife about Antonia, and admiringly, was encouraging. "Peter Nagle has asked leave to court me, and I have allowed it, but I cannot see that he and I will suit. He will be very unhappy that I've permitted the courtship but not the wedding."

"Unhappy," Lady Casriel said, pouring two cups of tea. "He'll have a tantrum?"

"He will be hurt. I have no other prospects in mind, I can't tell him I'm rejecting him for another. Peter is charming, but I don't esteem him. He has no use for books, he's not liked by my staff, and I don't care for the way he's treating my household as his own already."

"Gracious, and he is family, so the matter won't die quietly."

Antonia rose, because putting her dilemma into words made her feel more foolish—and more trapped—than ever.

"We have no interests in common, which would be a tolerable failing if we got on well, but I fear Peter and I have no *values* in common." She paced the width of the pretty carpet, feeling like songbird trapped in a lovely cage.

"He maunders on and on about using wind power to keep foul miasmas from the better neighborhoods," she continued, "but why should London's stink become Southwark's problem? Should foul miasmas and the sickness they bring become the lot of only those too poor to blow them away? He has no greater vision, he's like a small boy who has only one poem to recite or one joke to tell. Thirty years of living in close proximity to such as he—I cannot bring myself to do it."

"Why should you?" Lady Casriel asked, adding a small silver spoon to each saucer. "You turned down a handsome, mannerly earl because you preferred the company of your books. Why settle for an impecunious poor relation now?"

Antonia returned to the sofa. She could not voice all of her fears to Lady Casriel, but she could consider the question. "You're saying Peter is just another fortune hunter. I thought his papa left him fairly comfortably well off."

"How do you take your tea?"

"Plain will do."

"If Mr. Nagle is so comfortably well off," Lady Casriel said, "why hasn't he married elsewhere? Why haven't his sisters married? They are pretty, agreeable young ladies and they are connected to a title through your side of the family. One concludes they have either particular tastes or insufficient portions."

"Oh, dear." This scenario—Max would call it a theory—fit the available facts. "Or they had adequate portions and Peter has managed their funds poorly."

The countess peered at Antonia over her teacup. "Very bad of him, if that's so."

"And he could marry me, put all to rights, and I'd be none the wiser, but much the poorer. This explains why my great appeal as a wife has only recently occurred to Peter."

"If you must marry him, the settlements can be written to give *you* continued control of your fortune."

"That can be done?"

The countess took a sip of her tea. "The agreements and trusts must be carefully worded, but yes. Casriel was insistent that my money remain mine to do with as I please. The solicitors might have thought it odd, but they wrote the contract as his lordship required."

An idea tugged at the back of Antonia's mind, a possibility. She sipped her tea and nibbled a biscuit to be polite, while she considered that the challenge of how to be rid of Peter might have a solution. Possibly. Maybe.

She still had no idea how to go on where Max Haddonfield was concerned.

"I am so pleased you called upon me," Lady Casriel said when Antonia rose to leave. "His lordship will be sorry he missed you. May I confide your situation to him, or would you prefer the matter remain private between us?"

Casriel's discretion was utterly trustworthy. "I consider his lordship a friend, my lady, and had thought to put my situation to him directly. Peter presses me daily for a decision and I lacked the fortitude to give him the answer I must."

"And here, I thought you sought Casriel's aid negotiating settlements on your behalf. Are you free Thursday afternoon?"

"As it happens, I am."

"Would you like to join me for a tea at Lady Bellefonte's? She's keen on libraries as is her sister-by-marriage, Lady Susannah. You would get on well with them splendidly."

Antonia's hostess escorted her to the door, and as Antonia buttoned up her cloak, a snippet of conversation popped into her head. Something Max had said about Lady Bellefonte and cats.

"You are well acquainted with Lady Bellefonte?"

"Better acquainted recently. Casriel's next-youngest brother married Lady Susannah Haddonfield, and she is of a literary bent. I think you and she would disappear into raptures about Donne and Shakespeare, and leave all the tea cakes for the rest of us."

Antonia pulled on her gloves, ready to use the walk home to think through the possibilities Lady Casriel had raised. Peter needed money apparently, and Antonia needed to be free of his attentions.

"Haddonfield?" Antonia said, pausing with her bonnet in her hands. She knew Lady Susannah by sight, though they weren't even what Antonia would call acquaintances.

"I am gradually getting to know the whole tribe," Lady Casriel said. "Max, the youngest brother, keeps a distance to elude his sisters' matchmaking schemes, but Susannah claims he's the smartest of the bunch." Lady Casriel took the bonnet and settled it onto Antonia's head, tying the ribbons in an off-center bow.

"They sent Max up to Cambridge," she went on, "when he was

fourteen because he'd outstripped his tutors. He nearly blew up the stables when he was eight. The family has many Max stories, all told with the sort of awe reserved for the seafaring adventurer. I look very much forward to making his acquaintance."

Antonia had started the day in a welter of anxiety and confusion, but the notion that Max Haddonfield was an earl's errant son solved at least a few puzzles. He had the manners and education of an aristocrat, while the determination to be of use to society was uniquely his."He must be a different sort of earl's son," Antonia said. "What does this Max do now?"

"We're not sure," Lady Casriel replied, passing Antonia her scarf. "Max doesn't say much about his scientific pursuits, which also makes him a different sort of man, doesn't it?"

"Maybe he's waiting to be asked about those pursuits, my lady." Or about a certain delightful interlude behind locked library doors. "I will wish you good day and send you a note regarding Thursday's tea."

CHAPTER SIX

Galileo's proposed arrangement of the planets with the sun at the center of the universe had neatly explained the observable data. The Church's insistence that *Earth* occupied the center of the universe had, by contrast, required increasingly unsatisfactory corollaries and conjectures. The Church's theory had been wrong, of course, a fiction convenient for the popes and cardinals.

Max had no business dining with Lord Hamblin and Miss Huntly for the second time in a fortnight, another inconvenient truth. Some theory was afoot in their minds, some grand, unifying stratagem complete with corollaries and exceptions, and like Galileo, Max would soon be faced with the choice of bowing to their wrongheaded notions or supporting a falsehood.

"More tart, Mr. Haddonfield?" Miss Huntly asked from the hostess's end of the table. "Or perhaps another glass of the *Château d'Yquem?*"

The dessert was sweet, the wine was sweeter still, the lady's smile was too sweet by far. "No, thank you. The meal has been splendid. My compliments to your chef."

"Jess planned the whole menu," Hamblin said, beaming at his niece. "Very clever lady, my Jess."

Miss Huntly rose. "I am also a lady who knows when the gentlemen are ready for their port. If you will excuse me, Mr. Haddonfield." She extended a pale, slender hand, over which Max bowed, then she moved around the table to kiss Hamblin's cheek. "Don't keep Mr. Haddonfield up too late, Uncle. He has much important science to be about."

She left the room, the footman closing the door in her wake, and Max was unaccountably relieved she'd gone.

"Let's have our nightcap in the library," Hamblin said, as the footman began to clear the dishes from the sideboard. "I'm sure you are as ready as I am to be up and moving."

Max was ready to be home, to be checking the day's calculations, a cat purring at his elbow, Dagger snoring in the inglenook. He was ready to resume staring off into space, pondering the riddle of Lady Antonia, and wondering why no engagement announcement had been posted to the papers.

Perhaps the settlements were proving problematic.

Perhaps Nagle had lost his nerve.

"I'm told you enjoy libraries, Haddonfield," Hamblin said, closing the library door.

"Every man of learning should enjoy libraries," Max replied. "You have a sizable collection." The room was surprisingly warm for such a large space, suggesting both fireplaces had been kept roaring all day.

"M'wife bought the books. An estate sale here, a shop going out of business there. Said a library needed books, and she had a nose for a bargain, so the shelves are quite full and my pockets weren't emptied in the process. I miss Lady Hamblin's practical nature almost as much as I miss her hand guiding the domestics."

"I'm sorry for your loss, my lord. Has she been gone long?" And what had this to do with anything?

"Five years, and there's my darling Jess, no auntie to oversee her come out. My sisters did what they could, but Jess has been a bit lost, poor lamb."

The poor lamb had her uncle wrapped around her dainty finger. "Miss Huntly is lucky to have such devoted relations."

"Let's sit, shall we?"

They'd sat for the better part of three hours at supper, and Hamblin himself had declared a desire to move.

"In a moment," Max said. "I'd like a closer acquaintance with your collection first." He pretended to peer at the nearest shelf full of books while Hamblin poured two glasses of brandy. The collection was in no order—a volume of poetry next to an herbal, a book of sermons between two of Mrs. Radcliffe's works.

Any learned treatises were hopelessly lost in the wilderness of bound volumes, tracts, and pamphlets. Antonia would be horrified.

Hamblin brought Max a glass of spirits. "To your little experiments, Haddonfield."

If any pair of words had the power to sour Max's digestion, it was *little experiments*. He'd been hearing it from indulgent sisters, taunting brothers, jeering classmates, and sneering tutors for as long as he could remember.

"To truth, wherever that leads us," Max countered, for the aim of his science was to enlarge upon known truths for the betterment of all.

"Yes, that too, of course, and one truth I must discuss with you is that Jess needs a husband."

Max set down his drink untasted. "You have alluded to this topic before. While I wish the lady all good fortune, I cannot see that her situation is relevant to mine."

"Her situation, as you term it, has grown desperate."

The fire roared softly in the hearth, the clock on the mantel ticked quietly. "Desperate, sir?"

Hamblin collapsed onto the sofa and took a hearty swallow of his drink. "You are an intelligent sort, Haddonfield, for all you lack a certain polish. Jess was indiscreet with an unsuitable party. She needs a husband whom society will accept. You are a fourth legitimate son. The likelihood of your progeny ever inheriting your brother's title is nil, and you are in want of a wife. Somebody to see that your neck-cloths are starched and your meals regular."

Max abruptly understood the theorem under consideration. "That's your summation of a wife's value?"

"Creature comfort is no small contribution to a man's well-being, Haddonfield, not that you'd grasp that yet. Jess will do her part by you; she knows she's in a precarious position."

"May I ask who put her into this precarious position?"

"I'd rather not say, but you will deduce the guilty party easily enough. Mr. Nagle took advantage of a young woman's innocence, though Jess was by no means forced. She wanted to elope with him, thinking I would have to acknowledge the union then. Nagle refused to elope and wanted settlements in hand before he committed his future. When I offered only a modest contribution to his income, he changed his story." Hamblin took another sip of his drink, no longer the jovial lord. He looked old, weary, and more than a little disgusted. "Nagle said Jess had thrown herself at him, as if he was powerless to resist. All very sordid, but not that rare a tale, I'm sure."

Couples anticipated their vows often, if not a majority of the time. That part wasn't unusual at all.

"Why not simply settle an adequate income on Nagle? Keep the principal tied up in a trust and put him on a short leash?"

Hamblin finished his drink, pushed to his feet, and sighed. "Because I have lived my three score and ten, Haddonfield, or very nearly. When I expire, who's to stop Nagle from plundering Jess's inheritance? She's all I have, and I have failed her.

"Nagle will make my shortcomings look princely by comparison," Hamblin went on. "He has gambling debts, keeps company with the wrong sort, and has squandered his own inheritance as well as his sisters' portions. I've had a look into his situation, and the details are most unbecoming. If I'd been more careful, he and Jess would never have met, much less. . ." Hamblin waved a hand toward the cherubs cavorting on the library ceiling.

And *Nagle* was the man Antonia had chosen to marry?

"I am sorry for the burden this must be to you, my lord, but—"

"I will pay you," Hamblin said. "Handsomely. Very handsomely. You can explore the Amazon, visit the steppes of Asia, learn Mandarin and Hindi, and catalog bird species in the Antipodes. Whatever your scientific heart desires, as long as you make a credible pretense of being a husband to my niece. I am a wealthy man, and I am determined to see my Jess well cared for."

And there it was, the entire theorem, all but the *quod erat demonstrandum*. Max allowed himself a moment to consider the basic syllogism.

Max Haddonfield is passionate about science.

Well run experiments cost money.

Therefore, Max Haddonfield's entire future can be had for a large enough sum of money.

A month ago, Max himself would likely have considered the logic valid. "Miss Huntly is still in love with Nagle?"

Hamblin scrubbed a hand across his brow. "She thinks she is, and the harder I try to convince her otherwise, the more she won't hear my criticisms of him. She's young, Haddonfield, and so very stubborn. A white marriage would likely suit her, but she won't insist on it."

Max did the only thing he knew to do when his calculations wouldn't come right and his conclusions were thrown into disorder.

"I must have time to consider your offer, my lord, though I doubt I will accept."

"Haddonfield, you are accounted a decent fellow. Nobody has a word to say against your integrity, and Jess is really a very sweet girl."

"I'm sure she is, but I am not her choice." *And she is not mine.* "I bid you goodnight. You will hear from me within the fortnight."

He left his host pouring another brandy in the cozy library full of cheaply bought books, and stepped out into the cold night air. Hamblin had set a puzzle before him, one with multiple variables.

Jess wanted Nagle, Nagle wanted Antonia's fortune, and Max had no idea whatsoever regarding Antonia's wishes.

He did, however, have an increasingly firm grasp of his own.

MAX HAD TAKEN to playing the scarf game with the kitten after the day's calculations were complete. While the wee beast pounced, scooted, and leapt about, Max weighed possibilities and considered options.

He'd finished double-checking Dagger's math from the previous day—the boy seldom made errors any more—when it occurred to him that Beelzebub was nowhere in evidence. Dagger had gone out to dispose of the day-old breads—or sell them, which Max considered more likely—leaving Max to the calculations.

"Beelzebub?"

No paw appeared from under the sofa. Edward remained on Dagger's cot, snoozing in a heap with Hannibal; the other three cats were draped in their usual perches.

"Bee-elzee-buuuub!" Max called. He got down on all fours and peered under the sofa.

No cat.

Dagger had left bearing a sack, which meant. . . Max found half the day-old breads on the balcony, a flock of pigeons feasting on the lot. He was tossing the breads one by one to the cobbles on the alley below when Dagger trudged around the side of the building, his sack empty.

"Where's Beelzebub?" Max called.

The boy gazed down the alley as if contemplating flight. "With Lucifer, purring away in some old biddy's lap. She were calling him Mr. Beetles when I left. Lucifer's run to fat and they call him Lukey-pie."

"Get up here, Dagobert."

"You said Beelz was getting too stout to be pathetic."

"I will not ask you again." Max returned to the warmth of his apartment, half-amused, half-furious.

Dagger came foot-dragging up the steps five minutes later, chin jutting, mouth a sullen line.

"Why did you do it?" Max asked, taking the chair behind his desk.

"Because somebody had to, and you weren't getting on with it. She's pretty—Miss Antonia, that is. She smells good too."

"I know she's pretty, but you shouldn't have to deliver the cats to their new homes. That is for me to do."

Dagger tossed his hat in a perfect arc, the cap landing neatly on a peg near the door. "You wasn't—you *weren't* doing it. Lucifer isn't coming back. It was time. Who's next?"

The boy was avoiding Max's gaze, avoiding Edward and Hannibal on the cot. They were awake and looking about as cuddly as a pair of stone sphinxes.

"Please take off your coat."

Dagger complied, never a given with him, but instead of hanging up his jacket, he draped it over the back of the sofa and slouched over the armrest onto the cushions.

"I never seen that many books. Never saw. Miss Antonia talks fancy. I could listen to her all day. Can't understand half what she says, but she sounds all tidy and kind. She said Dagobert was an important French king."

Dagger sneezed, and for the first time in Max's memory, took out a handkerchief—a pretty white linen handkerchief with red and green embroidery about the border.

"Don't you dare," Max said, bolting across the room to snatch the cloth. "You nicked this from Lady Antonia, didn't you?"

Dagger folded his arms and looked away. "She asked about you."

"So you stole from her?"

Something about the boy's posture, the martyred set of his bony shoulders, the diffidence of his idle hands. . . A hypothesis popped into Max's head and nearly broke his heart.

"You think if you stop stealing, I will consider you ready for a post somewhere else, in a livery stable, as a porter, as a boot boy. You barely eat enough to keep a bird alive, lest I think you too healthy to bide here."

"You send them on," Dagger said, sniffing loudly. "Six of 'em so far, and no end in sight. They think this is their home and then you're tossing 'em out on their furry arses. Poor little mite can't hear, and he's dumb as a rock, and you're probably already thinking how to ditch him."

Lancelot chose then to plummet from the desk to the floor. In the next instant, he went pronking sideways across the carpet, pivoting to attack the sofa.

A tear tracked down Dagger's cheek, even as he smiled at the kitten. "Shoulda called him Dunce-a-lot."

This mutiny was not about cats, or not only about cats. Max passed Dagger his own handkerchief. "That handkerchief is yours to keep. Lancelot is yours to keep, and you are mine to keep as long as you choose to bide here. You will doubtless grow up on me all too soon, and lead some famous expedition up the Nile and become fabulously wealthy. That cannot be helped, but for the present, I would very much appreciate your continued services."

Dagger appeared fascinated with Max's handkerchief.

"Every time I walk out that door," Max went on, "I worry that I'll come home and find you've done a bunk on me. I was sure you'd bolt before winter set in, now I'm hoping you don't pike off come spring."

"Me? *Leave?*"

"Like a cat, coming and going as you please, until one day, it's all going and no coming home. You'll get bored with the experiments, tired of watching the cats find new homes, bored eating bread three times a day."

Dagger tucked the linen into a pocket. A silence built, punctuated by feline rumbling.

"I have a sister," he said, as casually as Max might announce that the sky looked like rain. "She's little. At the charity hospital. I take the bread there." He heaved a very large sigh for such a small boy. "I won't get bored, sir. Sissy is doing better since I started working for you."

Lancelot clawed his way up the sofa and into Dagger's lap, then kept right on climbing, up Dagger's shirt, until he was nose-to-chin with the boy.

Seeing the skinny boy and the deaf kitten touch noses did something unscientific to Max's insides. "What is your sister's name?"

"Nan. She's too little to 'prentice yet, but the hospital won't let the sweeps have her. I made 'em promise."

Dagger had been working for Max for months, and this was the first Max had heard of any siblings. "Have you any other family?"

Dagger shook his head and got a kitten paw across the chin. "Just me and Nan." He extricated Lancelot's claws from his shirt and cradled the kitten against his shoulder. The rumbling grew louder, a deaf cat having no sense of his own ability to make noise. Dagger wiped his cheek on the kitten's shoulder.

Long ago, another small boy had felt friendless and misunderstood. He'd wiped his tears on the *Principia,* which was incapable of purring and in no wise endearing.

"There is more to life than science." Max hadn't meant to say that aloud.

"Is that a hypothesis, sir?"

"It's an eternal verity. Be here when I come home, please. See that our cats are here too."

"Yes, sir."

SMILING, affable Peter stormed through the library door in such a taking that both cats dodged under Antonia's desk.

"Antonia, what is the meaning of this?" He brandished a folded sheet of paper, and the Barclay sisters put down their books.

"My letter means what it says, Peter. This is a public venue. We can discuss the matter at another time."

Peter's hair was untidy, his cravat off center, and his sleeve bore an odd streak of something brown. "We will discuss it now, madam."

Antonia rose from her desk. "*Your ladyship.*"

"When we are married," Peter began, yanking off his gloves. "You will not take that tone with me. Proper deference to the man of the—"

"Out." Antonia snarled the word with more menace than she'd known herself capable of. "Now. You have no lending privileges here, and you have no business here."

"I have been patient long enough," Peter retorted, twisting the buttons of his coat open. "More than patient, and now you turn your back on me, renege on an understanding that wanted but a few formalities—"

"I said *leave.*"

Both Barclay sisters had risen, each one holding a heavy tome.

Peter was attempting to loom, but Antonia was wearing heeled half boots and she'd remained behind her desk. He lacked the height to intimidate her, and more to the point, she wasn't in the mood to be intimidated.

"If I leave," Peter said, "you are coming with me."

He seized Antonia by the forearm in a painful grip, which was the outside of too much. She delivered him a stout slap with her free hand.

"Unhand me, or I will allow you to starve in the gutter."

"Let her go, Nagle, or a peaceful end in the gutter will be your dearest aspiration, one I will deny you."

If Antonia hadn't recognized that voice-of-doom tone, the whiff of fresh bread would have informed her of the speaker's identity. Max Haddonfield, hair wind-blown, cheeks ruddy with cold, *loomed* at Peter like an angel of divine wrath.

"Mr. Haddonfield," Antonia said. "Good day." He wore the same rumpled coat and the same disreputable scarf, and his expression promised death to Peter in the next three seconds.

"My lady."

Peter stepped back and jerked on his waistcoat. "You interrupt a lovers' quarrel, Haddonfield. Not the done thing."

"He's not my lover."

"One gathered as much," Max said. "Though a certain young lady of my acquaintance cannot say the same. He used her very ill indeed, because he thought he could toss her over and get his hands on a much larger fortune."

Antonia had suspected something drove Peter's scheme to "keep the fortune in the family," but hearing the details was still unsettling.

"Jessica Huntly," Miss Dottie muttered, still gripping her book. "Lost her aunt at exactly the wrong time, went a bit wild."

"We do keep up," Miss Betty added. "Poor thing is headed for ruin. We tried to tell old Humbug he needed to take the girl in hand, but he would not listen."

"Nagle," Max said, "you have behaved abominably toward not one but two women. The first will be the mother of your child, the second is your kinswoman. You will increase your chances of surviving this disgrace by apologizing to her ladyship."

A month ago, Antonia might have told Peter an apology was unnecessary, and one need not belabor a bad moment. That was then. Now, Peter's behavior put swine to shame and he did very much need to apologize.

Lucifer hopped onto the desk and sat on the blotter with his tail curled about him. Beelzebub joined him, both cats regarding Peter as if he were a particularly loutish mouse.

"Antonia, I am sorry if you misconstrued—"

Max cuffed him on the back of the head. "Try again, Nagle. If that's your idea of an apology, married life will be very uphill work for you."

Peter rubbed his arm. "Antonia, I am—"

Another cuff. "Proper address when groveling, Nagle. You have much to learn."

Miss Betty harrumphed. Miss Dottie sniffed. Lucifer hissed, showing formidable fangs.

"Your ladyship," Peter said, "I am sorry if I have given offense, or if I in any way misunderstood the nature of your sentiments. I understand that we would not suit and I will take my leave of you."

"My lady?" Max asked.

"Adequate," Antonia said, "but something must be done for Miss Huntly. She has been grievously wronged."

Peter smoothed a hand over his sleeve. "She comported herself most indecorous—"

Miss Betty drew back her arm, clearly ready to let fly with Reverend Fordyce's wisdom.

Antonia was beginning to enjoy herself. "Peter?"

"Miss Huntly will have him," Max said, "though she's an heiress, and Lord Hamblin didn't trust Nagle to handle her fortune responsibly. I found a solution for that conundrum."

Peter stopped fussing with his cuffs. "A solution?"

"For Miss Huntly," Max said. "She will marry you, but my brother has agreed to stand as trustee of her fortune. He's an earl, and not a man who tolerates ill-bred behavior toward the ladies. Stands about"—Max held a hand four inches above the top of his own head —"that tall, and is something of an amateur pugilist. My oldest brother, equally competent with his fists and sporting a minor title, will happily serve as a co-trustee should that be necessary. If you misappropriate a single farthing of Miss Huntly's money, your fate will be too unfortunate to mention in the presence of ladies."

"Mention it," Antonia said. "Please."

Max offered Antonia the sweetest smile. "Nagle will be unable to sire more children."

"Believe him," Miss Betty said. "The Earl of Bellefonte is the grandest specimen of English manhood ever to make a grown woman sigh."

"Sister does not exaggerate," Miss Dottie added.

"You went to your brother?" Antonia asked.

"I'll tell you everything," Max replied. "Soon."

Antonia waved a hand toward the door. "Peter, away with you. You have another apology to plan and it had better be more impressive than the paltry effort you put forth here. I will look after your sisters, but your fate is in your own hands. Do not call on me, do not write, do not so much as inquire after my health if we meet by chance. Take *very* good care of your wife, or I will offer her the services of my solicitors and permanent refuge in a suitably comfortable dwelling."

"And I will offer Miss Huntly the use of my fists applied to your person," Max added. Peter scuttled for the door, trying for a dignified exit and failing.

"Sister," Miss Betty said, "we must be going. Too much excitement gives me the wind." They were off to gossip, doubtless, or to pay a call on Lord Hamblin. They paused long enough to pet both cats, then bustled out the door.

Leaving Antonia alone with the man who'd haunted her dreams for the past three weeks.

"Peter and I weren't engaged," she said. "We had no understanding, but I should never have—"

Max put a finger to her lips. "If you express the slightest regret about the time you and I spent together, my heart will break. In the scientific sense, a heart does not break, but mine surely will. Perhaps we could have this conversation on the sofa?"

"It's the middle of the day, Mr. Haddonfield."

"So take a break for your nooning, my lady. We have much to resolve, and it's better discussed behind a locked door."

"A fine notion," Antonia said, scooting around the desk and going to the door. "A very fine notion indeed."

~

"THIS IS YOURS." Max passed over Antonia's handkerchief,

slightly the worse for time spent in his pocket. "I am yours, if you want me. I warn you though, I come with various attachments."

Antonia sat beside him on the couch, not touching him, alas. "You make yourself sound like a scientific instrument."

"Science is one of my attachments. I am passionate about my research and I will continue to pursue it no matter how pointless my objective might seem to others. I will not part with Dagger either, and I am about to acquire another assistant in the form of a small person named Nan. I have two cats of my own and Dagger has a personal feline as well. My means are humble so you should probably send me packing with a flea in my ear."

He had to tell her that part—he was poor, compared to her. Not destitute, but he couldn't drape her in diamonds either. "I lack ambition," he said, lest she mistake him, "in the sense most people use the word."

Antonia smoothed a hand over her skirts. "I have ambitions. I would like a life that has more to it than dancing at Almack's, driving out in Hyde Park when the weather's fine, and shopping. I hate shopping. Loathe it beyond all telling."

"Clerks," Max said, "buzzing about like flies. You wave them away and two minutes later, they're back, practically offering to count out your money for you."

"Precisely. How humble are your means?"

Max told her his annual income and named the principal sum from which it derived. "If I had more, I'd spend it on more experiments, or on helping out a fellow whose good ideas will never see the light of day unless somebody provides some funds. Expeditions are all very glamorous, but they carry with them the taint of—"

"Privateering," Antonia said, "of disguising the hope of personal gain in the glamour of exploration and adventure."

"Exactly." She understood Max's perspective, while many of his colleagues found his quibbling laughable.

"I have attachments too, Max. I like books."

And books cost money. An unfortunate truth for a poor fourth son lacking commercial ambition. "I like them too, particularly the well written ones."

"You like science, I like books." Antonia spoke slowly, as if she were inching up to a difficult point or a new theorem. "You haven't much money, I have more than I need or want. What if we used that money to make a scientific library?"

We? That had to be reason to hope. "A scientific library?"

"A library of practical science, of the treatises nobody will pay to publish, of the major works few can afford to buy. Some of the volumes would never leave the premises, some of the more important references. Others could circulate." She rose to pace between the sofa and the hearth. "I would want this library to be cozy, to be well heated and well lit, not some draughty old church made over from the last century."

"A scientific *library?*"

"Not only science, Max. Books that explain science to children, books that recount the adventures of the explorers. Books that tell of the stars and the people who charted them."

Max rose, for Antonia—who had a few cat hairs on her bodice—had never looked more beautiful to him. "I have a confession, my lady."

She came to a halt immediately before him and took his hands. "Tell me."

"The mouse droppings."

Antonia's brows twitched down. "Go on."

"They were cardamom seeds. You have no mouse problem here, but Lucifer needed a home, and Dagger once remarked that cardamom seeds bore a resemblance to evidence of mice. I perpetrated a subterfuge, not for the first time. I am sorry for it, and I am not sorry for it at all."

"Cardamom seeds."

"They are quite dear, but the alternative—"

"Money spent for a good cause," Antonia said. "Have you any

other confessions, Max? Theorems you'd like to air? Postulations? Corollaries? Hypotheses?"

As Max had walked the distance from his brother's house to Antonia's library, he'd tried to fashion a lofty, ringing declaration, something about two hearts of a sympathetic nature, minds in synchrony, and values that presaged enduring compatibility through all vicissitudes. A treasure trove of big words suitable for Dagger's collection, and far too much trouble for such an important moment.

"I love you," Max said. "I cannot see the love, touch it, measure it, weigh it, or tell you what scent it bears, though my love for you is the most important reality in my life. I have only humble means, but my love is limitless, and I promise you it always will be. When I thought you were engaged to Nagle, I didn't measure my day-olds for three straight days. Dagger despaired of me."

"Peter told you we were engaged?"

Someday when Peter bided a safe distance from Antonia, Max might tell her all Peter had said. "He lied. I didn't know that when I came here today, but I did know he'd served Miss Huntly a bad turn. You were entitled to the truth if you planned on marrying him."

Antonia slid her arms around Max's neck. "You came here thinking only to warn me?"

"I would have had a word with Nagle, but he obliged me by spouting off for all to hear. Truly, you were never engaged to him?" Max shouldn't need to ask, but then, he shouldn't be thinking so fondly of the sofa sitting three feet away either.

"Not ever. Peter pushed, he wheedled, he assumed." Antonia gave Max her weight. "I have a confession too."

"Confess quickly. I predict that in less than two minutes, I will be kissing you madly, and thanking the Almighty for the foresight that had you locking the doors."

"I love you too. I've loved you from the day you walked in here, looking half-dangerous and half-dear. I love you for your brilliant mind, your great heart, and your occasional deception in the name of homeless cats. I love how you kiss, how you—Max!"

"How I scoop you into my arms and lay you gently down on the sofa?"

"Well, that is a fine quality."

He arranged himself over her on the cushions. "We should deal with our clothing, but I must kiss you first."

She laughed and ruffled his hair. "How fortunate, for I must kiss you too."

The library was closed for a good two hours that day, and it closed again on the occasion of Max and Antonia's nuptials. The reading tables were pushed back, and the ceremony was held before the hearth, with Dagger, Nan, the Barclay sisters, a sizable crowd of Haddonfields, and five cats in attendance.

The science library came to be a surprisingly short time after the nuptials, complete with the excellent lighting and comfortable chairs Antonia had insisted on, three library cats in deference to the size of the establishment, and in the director's office, one very well upholstered sofa.

TO MY DEAR READERS

So there I was, authoring along, and referring occasionally to my Regency characters having a fresh, warm scone with breakfast or at tea... Is there ever a bad time to have a fresh, warm scone? My readers, who are quite savvy, pointed out to me that yes, Grace, there are scone recipes dating from the 1500s, but until the 1830s, the primary means of leavening any baked good was yeast. Those early unleavened scones were more like oat cakes.

Or hardtack. Even when slathered with butter.

Oops. Wouldja believe my dad was a tenured professor of food science? The things I learn from my readers...

I started digging into the history of baking soda and came across several stories. One claims that baking soda as a leavening agent was developed in the 1830s by a man of scientific bent who was married to a woman with a yeast allergy. Other sources make the whole business much more a matter of systematic experimentation, with baking soda one of many additives tested for its leavening qualities.

All quite interesting. By the time Max is on his quest, soda bicarbonate (baking soda) had been around for at least a decade in England, and I am very confident that he and Antonia will come across it just as soon as they get back from their first annual honeymoon balloon ride, and finish the first round of acquisitions for their science library, and, and, and. . .

If you'd like to read the rest of the Haddonfield tribe's stories, I've listed them below the excerpts. In terms of upcoming full-length novels, my next publication will be ***Forever and a Duke*** (excerpt below), and my next novella will be a holiday duet with Christi Caldwell, **Yuletide Wishes**, coming out Oct. 22, 2019 (excerpt below). You can stay up to date with all my various release dates, deals, and discounts by following me on **Bookbub** or signing up for my **newsletter.** I also have a **Deals** page on my website that I update every month or so.

Happy reading!

Grace Burrowes

Read on for an excerpt from ***Lady Mistletoe's Holiday Helper!***

LADY MISTLETOE'S HOLIDAY HELPER—EXCERPT

From **Lady Mistletoe's Holiday Helper** by Grace Burrowes, in the Regency novella duet, **Yuletide Wishes**

Lord Marcus Bannerfield has hired Lady Margaret Entwhistle to decorate his home for the upcoming holidays. He has little patience with Yuletide folderol, but wants the house to feel welcoming when his orphaned nieces arrive. The hour has grown late while Lady Margaret has toiled away on her plans and schedules, and Marcus's mind has become fixed on one particular aspect of Christmas tradition…

Marcus fetched a pillow and lowered himself to sit on the raised hearth behind the desk where her ladyship toiled. Very unlordly of him, but the night had reached an unlordly hour, and his day had been long.

"We never did decide where the infernal kissing bough should go, my lady."

She capped the ink and put aside her pen. "You need not have a kissing bough if you don't want one."

Marcus abruptly and quite passionately wanted at least three, all hanging in close proximity to wherever Lady Margaret tarried. The impulse took him halfway by surprise, but also halfway as confirmation of a looming suspicion.

He was attracted to his houseguest. Of all the peculiar turns to be served by masculine humors that had mostly learned to leave him in peace.

"I will hang my kissing boughs," he said, "so Aunt Penny can ambush the unsuspecting. She has a powerful sense of humor, which the footmen apparently share."

"I love that about her," Lady Margaret replied, sprinkling sand over her jottings. "I have not laughed in ages as I laughed at dinner."

And Marcus had loved seeing Lady Margaret overcome with mirth, but that had been hours ago. "Aunt Penny will assume command of the decorating tomorrow should you oversleep, and my household will never recover from the results. Won't you please allow me to light you to your room?"

Because Marcus sat on the hearth, and Lady Margaret had turned the chair behind the desk toward the flames, they were nearly at eye level. Another question came to Marcus's mind: *Won't you please share a kiss with me?*

He sat back and consulted his pocket watch. "You will never last through tomorrow's great busyness if you go short of sleep again tonight. I can have a maid wake you early, but let's to bed, shall we?"

The question should have been a brisk conclusion, not an occasion for the lady to smile—to smile mischievously—at his wording.

"Your effusions of charm have convinced me, my lord, as has my aching back. If I remain here much longer, I will fall asleep over my papers anyway. An early waking would be appreciated. You are well advised to go out tomorrow immediately after breaking your fast. You will think a thousand devils have invaded your house at first light."

A few imps had apparently invaded Marcus's imagination, for Lady Margaret was looking more kissable by the moment. He rose and offered her his hand.

"The arms of Morpheus await, as do warmed sheets, snug quilts, and soft pillows. I will call upon family tomorrow, and your invading army can plunder the peace of my home unopposed. Expect Aunt Penny to appoint herself your second-in-command."

Lady Margaret took his hand—her fingers were frigid—and rose. "I have never had a second-in-command. We will either come to blows or conquer the known world together." She leaned closer, close enough to drop her forehead against Marcu's chest. "Thank you for your many kindnesses, my lord. For the first time in ages, as the holiday season approaches, I wish somebody very specific well-earned, sincere joy."

She straightened quickly, before Marcus could turn the moment into an embrace. Where the hell had his reflexes gone, the ones that had saved him so often in battle? He inquired politely about Charlotte's knee on the way up the steps, he asked what time her ladyship would like to be awakened—*roused* had almost come out of his mouth —and he made sure the candles in her sitting room were lit before offering her a good-night bow.

"And good night to you, too, my lord. I did not think it possible, but I am enjoying the hospitality you have extended."

Marcus set aside his candle and possibly the last of his wits too. "Is that an early farewell? If so, might I ask for a farewell kiss?"

He kept his hands to himself when he made that query, for this woman had been ill-used, and the consequences to her had been grave. Still, he did not withdraw the question. Lady Margaret was no defeated wretch to be cozened into reluctant folly. She was a very self-possessed female and the first woman to attract his masculine notice since he'd sold his commission several years ago.

"I ask for only a kiss," he clarified, "one freely shared. Or I can bid you good night and make no mention of this request ever again."

Oh splendid. She was smiling at him again as if he'd bungled the words to *Good King Wenceslaus.* "You have stolen other kisses?"

"On rare occasion." Very rare. Vanishingly rare.

"You aren't much good at it, asking permission first, then offering assurances of discretion and disclaimers of honorable conduct. If you were a thief, you'd summon the watch to observe your crime before you committed it."

"I am not a thief, and a shared kiss should be the furthest thing from a crime. Sending a fellow off to mind his own business is certainly a lady's prerogative as well."

He wanted to kiss her—and more—but he also liked standing close to her and debating the philosophy of flirtation.

Lady Margaret gathered her shawls, and Marcus resigned himself to a night spent in self-recrimination—after he'd indulged in self-gratification. Instead, she opened her shawls like angel wings and stepped near enough to envelop him in their warmth.

"My holiday token," she said. "It's time I bestowed one out of joy, rather than duty. Past time."

And then she pressed upon him the sweetest, boldest, most luscious kiss imaginable.

Order your copy of **Yuletide Wishes**, and read on for an excerpt from *Forever and a Duke,* book four in the **Rogues to Riches** series...

FOREVER AND A DUKE—EXCERPT

Forever and a Duke by Grace Burrowes

Wrexham, Duke of Elsmore, has a problem—somebody very clever is stealing from his ducal coffers. He takes the extraordinary step of appealing to Eleanora Hatfield, a ferociously talented bank auditor, to help him quietly resolve his difficulties. Much to Rex's consternation, the woman he's hired to catch a thief is making off with his heart...

Mrs. Hatfield unbuttoned her cloak, and without thinking, Rex drew it from her shoulders, gave it a shake, and hung it on the drying pegs above her hearth. A small silver teapot sat in the middle of the mantel, a sketch on either side in plain wooden frames. He wanted to study those drawings—wanted to snoop about her entire abode—but not when Eleanora could see him doing it.

He braced himself for a scold as he passed her a shawl that had been draped over the back of a reading chair. "Shall I light the fire?" he asked, for want of anything else to say.

By the limited illumination of a few candles, the relentlessly businesslike Mrs. Hatfield looked weary. "I'll be going out again, just across the street, and I don't light the hearth until I'm in for the night. Thank you for your escort, Your Grace."

Eleanora Hatfield, like much of London, had no cooking facilities in her domicile. Of course, she'd go out to fetch a hot meal, and of course she'd shoo him away before she did.

Rex wasn't feeling shoo-able, for once. "I'm still dressed for the weather," he said. "I'll get us some food, while you consider a strategy for organizing our efforts over the next two weeks."

He bowed and left before she could argue. By the time he returned, she'd curled up in a chair, her shawl about her shoulders, her hearth crackling. She'd also fallen asleep.

Rex dealt with the cat first, unwrapping a morsel of fish and leaving it on its paper in a corner. For himself and his hostess, salty fried potatoes came next and slices of hot roasted beef followed. The scents were humble and tantalizing, and apparently enough to tempt Mrs. Hatfield from her slumbers.

"You bought beef and potatoes."

She looked at him as if he'd served her one of those fancy dinners Mama made such a fuss over. Six removes, three feuding chefs, footmen run ragged, the sommelier pinching the maids, and all the guests more interested in flirtation than food.

"Voltaire has started on the fish course," Rex said. The cat was, in fact, growling as she ate, and sounding quite ferocious about her meal.

"Her manners were formed in a hard school," Mrs. Hatfield said, sitting up. "Where are my—?"

Rex passed her the spectacles, though he preferred her without them.

"Have you cutlery," he asked, "or do we shun etiquette for the sake of survival?"

"In the sideboard." She took a plate from him. "I can put the kettle on if that—you brought wine."

"A humble claret, but humility is a virtue, I'm told."

The shared meal reminded Rex of something that ought to also be part of a peer's curriculum: Some people had the luxury of chatting and laughing as abundant food was put before them. Other people had such infrequent acquaintance with adequate nutrition, that the notion of focusing on anything other than appreciation for food was a sort of blasphemy.

Eleanora Hatfield ate with that degree of concentration. She did not hurry, she did not compromise her manners, but she focused on her meal with the same single-mindedness she turned on Rex's ledgers.

"You have known poverty," he said, buttering the last slice of bread and passing it to her. "Not merely hard times or lean years. You have known the bleakest of realities."

She took the bread, tore it in two, and passed half back to him. "There's no shame in poverty."

"I doubt there's much joy in it, either."

"We managed, and I am impoverished no longer." She launched into a lecture about concentric rings of responsibility, redundant documentation, and heaven knew what else. Rex poured her more wine, put an attentive expression on his face—he excelled at appearing attentive—and let his curiosity roam over the mystery of Eleanora Hatfield.

She'd known hardship, and she'd probably known embezzlers. She'd decided to wrap herself in the fiction of widowhood or wifehood, but not the reality, and she was truly passionate about setting Rex's books to rights.

The longer she talked about the many ways his estates could have been pillaged—while he'd waltzed, played piquet, and debated the Corn Laws—the more he appreciated her fierceness and the more he wondered how she'd come by it.

"When should I call upon you tomorrow?" he asked, rising and gathering up the orts and leavings of their meal.

"At the end of the day," she said, standing to take the greasy paper from him. "I'll use this for kindling, and I leave any empty bottles in the alley for the street children to sell. In cold weather, their lives grow more perilous than usual."

She drew her shawl up and looked away, as if those last words should have been kept behind her teeth.

Rex shrugged into his great coat, wrapped a cashmere scarf about his neck, and pulled on gloves lined with rabbit fur. Autumn had not only turned up nasty, winter was in the offing.

"I want you to consider something," he said. "Something in addition to the various ways my trusty staff is bilking me of a fortune."

"Not all of your staff, we haven't established that."

Not yet, though anybody seeking to steal from the Elsmore fortune was doomed to eventual discovery, now that Eleanora Hatfield was on the scent.

"Please consider a theoretical question: If instead of allowing my coffers to be pillaged by the enterprising thieves in my employ, I had donated that money to charity, where would you have had me put those funds?"

He had her attention now, and having Eleanora Hatfield's attention was not a casual state of affairs.

"You are asking about thousands of pounds, Your Grace."

"No, actually, I am asking for your trust. You will soon know all of my secrets, Eleanora. You will know where I have been lax, where I have been less than conscientious about my duties. You will know who has betrayed me. Not even my priest knows me that well, not even my siblings. I am asking much of you, and in return, all I can offer is an assurance that your secrets would be safe with me."

Her gaze was momentarily dumbstruck, then puzzled, then troubled. "Thank you, Your Grace, but in my line of work, I can afford to trust no one."

Interesting choice of verb—*afford*. "You like it that way."

"I need it that way."

How honest, and how lonely. Elsmore brushed her hair back over her ear, and when she did not protest that presumption he bent nearer. She stood still, eyes downcast, though he well knew she was capable of pinning his ears back.

"Eleanora?"

She closed her eyes, and he realized that was as much permission as he would get from her. He kissed her cheek and let himself out into the chilly corridor, pausing only long enough to make sure she locked the door after him.

As if her mind had imparted its restlessness to his own, Rex walked the distance to his home, turning over questions and ignoring the persistent freezing drizzle. Two streets from his doorway, he took off his gloves and scarf and left them in an alley.

Why had he kissed Eleanora Hatfield? Even a chaste gesture such as he'd bestowed on the lady was an intimacy, and with the least intimacy-prone female he knew. Why cross that line? Why blur those boundaries? His musings yielded no satisfactory answers, but then, a man who failed to notice his trusted staff dipping into his coffers, a man who overlooked drinking from the wrong tea cup, was probably overdue for an audit of his own sentiments and motivations.

Order your copy of **Forever and a Duke!**

HADDONFIELD READING ORDER

And about those Haddonfields.... Here's a reading order for Max's siblings, except for Lady Della, whose happily ever after yet awaits some inspiration (ahem, Ash Dorning):

Nicholas: Lord of Secrets
    Ethan: Lord of Scandals
    Beckman: Lord of Sins
    Tremaine's True Love (Lady Nita Haddonfield gets main character honors, George Haddonfield's HEA is the sub-plot)
    Daniel's True Desire (Lady Kirsten Haddonfield)
    Will's True Wish (Lady Susannah Haddonfield)

Happy reading!
    Grace

Made in the USA
Middletown, DE
21 November 2019